TERMINAL VELOCITY

LAST CHANCE DOWNRANGE - BOOK 4

LISA PHILLIPS

TWO DOGS PUBLISHING, LLC

eBook ISBN: 979-8-88552-140-6

Paperback ISBN: 979-8-88552-141-3

Large Print Hardback ISBN: 979-8-88552-142-0

Published by: Two Dogs Publishing, LLC. Idaho, USA

Cover by: Ryan Schwarz

Edited by: Christy Callahan, Professional Publishing Services

1

Joseph Russell was not his name. It was the one they had given him.

Over the years he'd had so many names he'd long quit the urge to claim the one given to him at birth.

Joseph lifted the knife and sliced down in a long, clean cut.

He'd been trained to do exactly one thing. Too bad it was frowned upon in polite society and came with a hefty prison sentence. However, in his tenure as a professional he had rid the world of so much evil most everyday people couldn't even comprehend that he found a measure of comfort in the fact he'd done good.

At one point in his life he'd considered it God's work. As if he'd been His hand of justice in the world. Another thing he had to rewire in his brain.

The idea of being reborn, or born again, was not lost on him. Joseph just didn't know who he wanted to be this time.

He tossed the chicken thigh pieces into the bowl and grabbed the next one.

The kitchen door swung open and one of the girls

walked in. There were two, and he hadn't bothered to learn their names.

Her blonde ponytail swung behind her head as she flounced in wearing the camp uniform of khaki shorts and a polo shirt. "What's for lunch, handsome?"

The girl was almost twenty years younger than him. He wanted to say something about sexual harassment in the workplace, but unfortunately this was punishment and not a career choice.

Joseph lifted his knife and pointed it at the blackboard on the wall, where he'd written the menu in chalk.

"Anyway, Brad said team meeting in ten minutes in the cafeteria."

He lifted his chin and gave her a nod.

Blondie flounced back out the same way she'd come in. At least he heard the shuffle of her tennis shoes on the floor and the swish of the door.

Then he was blessedly alone again.

The way he'd been since Genevieve's death.

He could barely think of her name without the grief welling up. Picturing her in his mind, her stomach rounded with his child. Holding her close, feeling the baby kick him…

The knife burned across his finger.

Joseph let the blade clatter to the cutting board and headed to the sink. Wash. Dress.

Since he had ten minutes, he pulled on gloves to cover the bandage and sliced the rest of the chicken double time. He poured it into the cooking pan with coconut milk and sun-dried tomatoes. Spices. Herbs. Another hand wash.

On the way out of the camp kitchen, Joseph grabbed the baseball cap from the hook by the door and settled it on his head.

Brad and Karen stood over by the door, opposite the serving hatch at the kitchen where Joseph handed out meals.

Between the door and the kitchen were rows of benches like a school cafeteria. Sometimes they were slid out of the way to clear the floor for activities. Or on talent show night.

"Good." Brad clapped his hands. Something he did a lot. "You're all here."

Karen, Brad's wife, moved to the first row of benches, sat with her back to them all, and looked at her manicure.

The two blondies glanced back at Joseph, then whispered to each other. They couldn't have sat closer to one another if they tried, side by side on the tabletop.

He sat across the aisle and didn't look at them.

"Emmalee, there's a disaster in cabin three that needs cleaning. Taylor can help you. I'd like that taken care of before the end of the day."

Both girls slumped.

From his vantage point Joseph spotted the curl of Karen's lips.

Brad continued, "Next week we have the mystery writer's conference coming in, so all the kids' camp stuff needs to be put into storage and the books and movies need to be stacked on the shelves in the common room, and the cabins. Karen?"

She stiffened but said, "Of course, darling," her voice saccharine sweet.

"The menu is planned for the conference?"

Joseph said, "Delivery is set for Thursday."

"Good." Brad didn't meet his gaze.

Not that Joseph purposely intimidated the guy, but he also hadn't set Brad straight. If he treated Joseph with respect—and a little fear—instead of the way he was with everyone else, that was just fine.

Brad had accepted him for the summer on a trial basis. As a favor.

Like this was rehab. Or a way to get Joseph somewhere he'd be less likely to kill somebody. Considering he had no phone and was only allowed to leave for errands and to attend church, he wasn't sure that was a good plan. But when Russ gave orders, they were followed. Otherwise Joseph needed a new identity and would end up spending the rest of his life on the run.

The lure of a permanent home here in Benson had been too strong. Not because of this place, but because the Accountant's Office program meant he had a shot at peace and not constant threat.

The Accountant's Office was like private witness protection. He wasn't on the run from the US government, so far as he knew. However, plenty of groups—and countries—wanted him dead.

So here he was, firmly under the radar with a best friend who was in her eighties. Edith had been grandfathered into the Accountant's Office program—not that her family knew anything about it. Joseph had been sentenced to a stint in camp nightmare as a chef because he'd done what he did best. Rid the world of a threat—a terrorist—and saved lives in the process.

Russ's answer? Cold turkey. Unfortunately this wasn't an addiction. It was the way he was wired to do what others couldn't. It was how he'd been trained for years. Trying to rewire his brain and establish all new thoughts and habits wasn't going to happen overnight.

One of the blondie twins raised a hand. "Are we doing the ghost tours for the writers?"

"Of course." Brad chuckled. "They asked for quiet writing space, but I've had several emails from registered attendees, and they'd like the full tour of where Celeste met her tragic end on the clifftop."

Blondie chuckled. "Are we using the western slope this time, or the ridge at the silver mine?"

"It was neither of those." Everyone turned to him, and

Joseph realized he'd said it aloud.

One of the girls said, "You've *been* out there?"

The other girl shoved her friend. "Taylor, you *know* he has. No one can resist the mystery."

Karen narrowed her beady gaze on him. Brad just blinked like he'd realized Joseph was still there.

"June twelfth in 1971 was a Tuesday," Joseph began. "Three days before that they had a big storm. The trail up to what's now Veteran's Lookout was totally washed out. It took half the hill with it and wasn't repaired until six years later when they had to practically rebuild the side of the mountain to make way for the highway. If Celeste jumped to her death, it wasn't from up there. She wouldn't have been able to get up to the western slope or to the silver mine."

Brad frowned. "Her body washed from the river miles downstream. Where did she jump from?"

"How should I know?" In point of fact, he didn't think she'd jumped at all.

Taylor and Emmalee burst into cackles. "He totally knows where she suicided."

Emmalee swallowed her laughter long enough to say. "He does."

Joseph folded his arms across his chest.

"If you could find the treasure for us, that would be great." Taylor's comment caused another eruption of laughter from the girls.

Karen rolled her eyes.

Brad's eyebrows rose. "Maybe I'll send the writers to the *kitchen* for the scoop on the lost treasure and Celeste's untimely death."

Please don't. "I'll be busy making pastries."

Brad shifted his stance. Karen stiffened. Like a flinch, a phenomenon Joseph had been observing since he arrived here. It wasn't fear exactly. He didn't think Brad beat her.

More like a healthy awareness of his proximity and a tendency toward anxiety. She was skittish around him, and yet with everyone else she had to have the upper hand.

By whatever means necessary.

"Hmm." Brad pressed his lips together.

Joseph didn't much care what the guy thought. They'd been down a cook before he showed up. With Karen filling in, things had been a total disaster since the woman refused to touch red meat. She barely knew how to use a stove, let alone how to cook for thirty hungry fifth and sixth graders. Meanwhile Joseph had cooked for the entire dorm at boarding school for years. But the difference between them was that he was willing to learn.

He was also interested enough to investigate the mystery that surrounded the retreat camp, high in the mountains. He'd looked into what happened in the '70s so far. When Celeste was found dead. When he was done solving that he planned to start on the murder from twenty years ago.

He doubted there was treasure buried in these hills. No matter that was what most people were interested in.

He was about to comment it was time to be working on dinner prep when an awareness entered his peripheral.

A *shuffle-stomp* gait.

The groundskeeper approached the side door from outside.

Brad said, "I'll divide up assignments for the mystery writers' group and hang it on the board in the staff lounge. I've posted online and up around Benson looking for more staff and volunteers for the summer. Until they come in, we'll—"

The side door crashed open.

"Y'all started without me." The man's voice sounded like the rumble of semi tires on the highway. A graying black lab ambled in behind the groundskeeper.

Brad bristled. "We haven't gotten too far through the list."

Washington Harper had both blondies shifting in their seats even though he got nowhere near them. Joseph had seen them more than once change direction if they saw he was coming toward them.

Washington's keys clattered on the seat as he sat and let out a long sigh. The guy was probably in his fifties but moved like he was eighty. As opposed to Joseph's friend Edith, who was the opposite. Considering he wasn't allowed to talk to her or see her while he was up here, he didn't know why she kept coming to mind.

Washington wore a grubby T-shirt, jeans, and boots. His gray hair, pulled back in a ponytail and secured with a leather tie, hung down his back. His face was as weathered as the western slope of the mountain—rutted and cracked.

The guy had lived at this retreat camp his whole life. Another mystery this place held. Too bad Joseph wasn't here to solve any of those. He was supposed to use the change of scenery and hard work to get some perspective and figure out what he wanted to do. Considering he didn't even know who he was supposed to *be* now, that was proving difficult. It had already been a month. He should've worked it out by now.

But no.

Brad droned on about repairs. Karen struggled to pretend like she cared. Taylor and Emmalee whispered to each other. Washington's chin touched his chest, and he started to breathe in a slow rhythm. Asleep.

The old lab wandered over and sniffed Joseph's knees, so he gave the dog a scratch under his chin.

As soon as the meeting ended, Joseph hopped up and headed to the kitchen before anyone could waylay him. He didn't stop there but pushed out the back door where the dumpsters were contained in a fenced area and let himself out, closing the door so wildlife couldn't investigate the trash.

On the way to his cabin he spotted four deer, one adult, and three adolescents. A family unit. Not that he would know what that was like, considering he'd never had one of his own. The past few months he'd been able to get to know Edith, but now that was done.

He refused to hate Russ just because he'd told Joseph no contact with Edith while he was up here. As if he should be surprised the moment he got close to someone, it was taken away. He shouldn't be as upset about losing a short-lived friendship as he was.

He disarmed the makeshift security system on his cabin door and shut himself inside. After the first time his things had been gone through, he'd left a tell on the door so he'd know if it happened again.

Joseph opened the closet. Taped inside were a map and every newspaper clipping he'd been able to find regarding the death of twenty-two-year-old Celeste Garland. Everyone called it a suicide. That she'd jumped off the cliff, broken-hearted, and plummeted to her death.

He'd already figured out it was murder.

2

———

D r. Sarah Carlton wasn't going to make chief medical examiner if she didn't solve this case. Lately, everything had that qualifier attached to it. In the end it turned out to be pretty good motivation for sticking to her diet and exercise routine. And remembering to put gas in her car.

She clicked her mouse and opened the new file, the fourth victim in a series of deaths related to a narcotic. The lab still hadn't figured out the breakdown of the chemical substance found in her blood. When they did, Sarah would know whether this death resulted from the same drug that killed the other three.

Still, even without answers her instincts told her this was the work of one person. Someone who had cut their supply of narcotics with something else to make it go farther. The result was an irreversible reduction of their customer base, because unfortunately they couldn't continue to sell drugs to people who were dead.

Sarah had to find the FBI enough evidence to go on that they could open these deaths as homicide cases. She needed a way to link them together and lead them to a suspect. Without anything to go on, there wasn't much the FBI could do. Soon enough whoever had created this destructive substance would alter their cocktail enough that no one else died.

After that the case would be at risk of going cold.

She grabbed a pen and tapped it on the edge of the desk. Usually her job involved hands-on work in the morgue—collecting evidence, performing autopsies, investigating—the way she felt she had been called to do. When she was stuck in her office, all she could think was how to get out of there. Either into the morgue, or outside for some sunshine. Assuming night hadn't fallen while she worked—which it often did.

There was a soft knock on her door, and it eased open. Her assistant, Patricia, stuck her head in long enough to say. "I'm heading out unless you need anything else. And the chief wants to see you in his office."

"Thanks. Have a good night."

Patricia closed the door, even though the chief had summoned Sarah. No one knew her the way that Patricia did. Still, recently Sarah often spent time with one of the FBI agents who had moved here a few months ago. Addie had a fiancé, but Sarah enjoyed catching up with her from time to time.

She smoothed down her skirt and pulled on her jacket, buttoning it. Unless she was in the field, Sarah always dressed as a professional. After all, she wouldn't make chief if she didn't present herself the best she could.

The last best friend she'd had dropped her because Sarah refused to abandon a night of studying to go out dancing and likely drink too much. Even back then she'd known she wouldn't get where she wanted to be without making some sacrifices. These days it was all she could do to navigate her relationship with her father and stepmom and get where she wanted to be in her career.

Considering there hadn't been any prospects worth anything for a family of her own, and she didn't want the responsibility of raising a child alone, she lived in a one-bedroom condo.

The last best friend, the one who'd ditched her for a fun night out, was now married and had three kids. According to Facebook she was part of two different book clubs. Sarah comforted herself with the fact she didn't have time for any of those things.

If she was going to make chief.

She knocked on his door and waited for his call out before she twisted the handle and entered.

His office was twice the size of hers, and the man behind the desk about five foot two. He never wanted to have face-to-face conversations in the hallway. Every time there was something to discuss, Albert Hawthorne scheduled a meeting in his office where he could sit behind his desk. He wore a suit, though the jacket hung on a coat tree in the corner. His tie was red today. His hair, gray and bushy, matched his eyebrows and beard.

"Sarah, come in."

She settled in the seat across from him. Hawthorne was due to retire in the next year. Then again, he had been threatening to put in his papers for at least three years. Sooner or later, he wasn't going to be able to put it off. She planned to be ready and waiting when his seat became vacant.

Her books would look very nice on the shelves in this office.

"You wanted to see me?" It was past eight in the evening

according to the clock on his mantle, but it wasn't uncommon for them both to still be here.

"How is the investigation into the four overdoses going?"

Sarah sat back in her chair. "The lab is still breaking down the components of the substance consumed by the fourth victim. As soon as I have those results back, I'll be able to confirm if all the deaths are related."

Given the manner of death and a couple of other observations she'd noted, Sarah could reasonably argue they were at this point. However, cold hard evidence was key to a court conviction. The precise breakdown of a drug's base components could lead to a type of signature that might identify whoever formulated it.

Much like bombs have signatures, drugs and their ratios often also contain a telltale sign of who might be behind it.

"Good." Hawthorne nodded, the distant expression in his eyes he got when his mind was elsewhere and busy. "Paul can check the results if they come in before you return. If there's progress to be made, it can happen when you're back and we won't be continually pestering the lab for faster results."

She wanted to get clarification on the last part, and her tendency to call the lab directly for updates. No one there seemed bothered by her.

However, the other part of what he'd said just plain didn't make sense. Sarah frowned. "Am I going somewhere?"

Perhaps there was an out-of-town assignment she wasn't aware of yet. Their office covered the whole county, which meant hundreds of square miles. They investigated any death unattended by a physician, any violent or nonnatural deaths, and the death of any minor, even with no significant medical history. The police department or FBI often called them to scenes where a death had occurred.

"For the past few weeks, you've been working inordinately hard," the chief said. "I was extremely impressed with the job you did immediately following the bombing at the club."

Sarah had just finished talking to her therapist about that and didn't wish to return there. However, she managed to nod. "Thank you."

He continued, "We all pitched in, but you carried a lot of the weight of sorting through victims to identify each person lost that night. Eighteen people have been named and laid to rest because of you. However, you also didn't take a break in all that time. Now that things have calmed down, I think it's time for you to rest for a couple of weeks."

"You don't have a job out of town?"

Being busy kept her sane most of the time. If she stopped to think, the fear always crept back in. Every victim became one she had seen a long time ago. Despite being a qualified adult, Sarah returned to the night when she'd been nothing but a terrified child.

She would rather work now to lay to rest those she could identify.

Hawthorne shook his head. "I was in a meeting this afternoon with the mayor and the police commissioner. They were discussing the retreat camp being short of volunteers."

"Because no one wants to become the next legend." All the stories were ridiculous. She would know because she'd been there and seen it firsthand.

"Nevertheless, they mentioned an upcoming conference for mystery writers. A few of the local police officers have been tasked with sharing their knowledge in afternoon semi-nars. Our office did at one point have a request for a knowl-edge share. Now that I've considered it, I think it's a great idea. As of just now, you're signed up to volunteer for the next two weeks."

"Two—"

"Call it a vacation. Call it a punishment. But, starting on Monday there will be plenty of time for you to rest in between pitching in. You get to share your expertise with a group of writers, and after that it's a kid's camp. I'm sure you'll have plenty of time to decompress from this job."

She was just about argue.

Before she could figure out what to say, he carried on. "If you're going to be chief medical examiner one day, then you need to know how to leave your job at the office and take breaks when needed." He leveled her with a steady gaze. The power of his undistracted attention made her want to squirm in her seat. "Don't do what I did and sacrifice your personal life and health for the sake of this job."

The way he spoke made it sound like it was a personal mission to get her to switch off. But she couldn't help being excited that he considered her as his replacement. As long as she wasn't in competition with anyone else.

But there was no way Paul was even being considered. She'd been here much longer and worked twice as hard as he did.

Was her work ethic going to end up being a detriment? She'd never thought it would be, but the world didn't often make sense to her.

She stood. "Thank you, Chief Hawthorne."

"You're welcome. I'm sure you'll have an excellent time."

That wasn't exactly what she'd been thanking him for, but why argue when her dream job was on the line?

She left his office and headed back down the hallway to hers. It was just two weeks. She could survive that.

All she had to do was talk to some people about her job and give them stories they could incorporate into their work. Unlike the police, mystery writers always wanted to figure out ways for the bad guy to get away with the murder.

Thankfully she was on the other side of that, aiding the cause of justice.

Making peace, instead of allowing the pain of never knowing the truth to continue.

The flipside was that she'd hardly realized it was Friday night. That meant she needed to send a lot of emails before Sunday. Come Monday morning she had to be at the retreat camp.

She'd need appropriate clothes. Footwear. Bug repellent. Her mind began a list, and she picked up her pace when it was too long to remember everything. When she was back in her office, she could use the app on her phone that kept all of her notes in one place.

She would need to go shopping as well.

The door to her office was ajar, which was strange since she had closed it before heading to the chiefs. The light inside was on as well.

The yellow glow shifted.

No. Not her light. A flashlight?

Her footsteps faltered. She should go to the security desk and get someone. Or call from another desk phone.

Old fears resurfaced. The rush of cold terror welled like the rising tide from where it usually lay dormant. It hit her. Steady. Unrelenting.

No one will believe you.

Sarah moved to the door to see for herself. She had to see, then she would know. Even if no one believed her, she would know.

She eased the door open.

A man stood in front of the desk with his back to her, going through her papers. He wiggled her mouse.

She stood her ground. "What are you doing?"

He spun around. His hood pulled up, his face in shadow. The dark figure raced at her while her heart pounded, but in her mind she saw an entirely different face—one her rational adult brain now knew was a mask.

The face of a monster.

He slammed into her.

Sarah stumbled against the door and fell back as he darted down the hall.

3

———

Joseph adjusted the pack on his shoulders. Every once in a while he would pause and take in the world around him. The trees and the terrain, harsh and unyielding. Nature did what it wanted. People thought they had dominion over it, but they ran for their lives when natural disasters occurred. Hiding from the power of nature.

Or bears.

He walked alongside the river Celeste had been discovered in fifty years ago, lying on the bank wearing that white nightgown. Dead. Whether she jumped to her death or was murdered and then pushed off the cliff. The autopsy was one thing—he'd read it, and there was little to no information on it. Reality was something quite different.

"But where did you fall from?" That was the question. One he asked himself out loud alone in the woods.

He'd never had many friends. The family he'd been given for a while was gone now. All revenge had earned him was a nasty scar by his ribs and a death threat from the brother of the man responsible for their murder.

Joseph had thought many times about ending his own

life. Yet it seemed so pointless to quit in the light of one tiny spark of hope—the flickering ember that one day things might be better than they were now. Or the fact that if he ended his life no one would be around to remember Genevieve and the son she'd been carrying.

He reached out and touched the rough trunk of the closest tree. Grief from that life threatened to swallow him. He gripped the trunk and felt the sensation of rough bark prick at his palm. This was the here and now. He needed to keep moving or the past would swallow him. He was supposed to be a new creation in the life he lived now. Born again to serve God, according to the pastor. Something he understood, as he understood what Jesus had done for him. But Joseph had yet to see the accompanying change in his life.

It hadn't rid him of the pain.

Joseph pushed off the tree and didn't look at the indentation in his palm. He sprinted up the trail until his lungs burned and his legs threatened to give out, hardly worrying about which direction he was going. Or what might be at the end of this path.

The forest around the camp was thick and often shrouded in mist, particularly early. It was barely eight in the morning, and he'd been out for nearly two hours now, trying to figure out where upriver Celeste had jumped. Or—more likely—been pushed.

He stopped, long enough to catch his breath. The river forked here. Or it had, at one point in history. Erosion had carved a new path. But previously, the river had snaked to the right. He frowned and climbed the hill above the camp to the west. If he got high enough, he would be able to see where the sun had risen over the mountains.

The hill curved to the left, and he rounded the bend to a

sharp drop-off. Below him was a dilapidated structure hidden in a small clearing in the trees.

He'd never been this way in the weeks since he'd arrived at the camp. There was nothing there for him beyond getting back into Russ's good graces—something he thought he'd done when he became a Christian recently. While that should have been enough to give him some peace here, his mind wanted to occupy itself with this mystery instead.

It wasn't like he could sit idle between meals. Even cleaning the kitchen as thoroughly as he did wasn't an activity that took all afternoon. Or night. But he'd already been out long enough. He would need to come again and make his way to this spot more quickly if he wanted to look around this cabin. Which meant he'd have to wait until Monday when he had a day off before the busyness of the arriving guests.

By the time he got back to his cabin, he'd figured out what desserts he would make for the mystery writers on which night. Karen had suggested homicide-themed dishes, but there was no way he was going to do something so ridiculous. She could label everything whatever she wanted. He wasn't making pastries in the shape of murder weapons, or victims.

One of the girls passed him as he entered the camp, walking the trail to his cabin. He thought he might get by her without being drawn into small talk but at the last second, she said, "Mail is on your doorstep."

"Thanks." His tone didn't leave room for an invitation to continue the conversation.

Joseph grabbed the letter and filled a cup with water at the sink before he slid a finger in the envelope and tore it open.

My dearest Joseph.

He nearly snorted. She was in fine form this time, but he

dragged over the pad and used the first three words as the code to unlock the cipher contained in the rest of Edith's ramblings. Most of it read like they were long lost pen friends sharing news of their lives with each other.

He decoded as he read, uncovering her message behind the words.

My visit to the library provided me with a wealth of information. Celeste was engaged at nineteen to a local man, a business owner who had several properties around town, including the land the retreat camp was on. Although, he had nothing to do with the running of it. Incidentally my research indicates it was some kind of facility in the '40s and '50s before it was closed. It became a camp late in the '60s when they tried to revamp its image. Her betrothed's father owned it before him. She died in the early '70s. Two months after the engagement, three days after it was announced in the papers that they were getting married in a matter of weeks.

He knew that in some places it was customary to announce a marriage in the local paper, and maybe that was done in this area in the seventies.

The message continued.

I'm going to talk to his daughter, the only surviving family member, to find out what kind of man he was. Maybe he's the one who pushed Celeste off that ledge.

A fissure of worry moved through him. Researching at the library was one thing, but going to speak to someone? Joseph didn't know for sure that the daughter presented a threat, especially to a former trained agent like Edith. She should still take backup, even if it wasn't him because he was stuck here.

He'd written to Edith soon after he discovered the mystery of the camp. He needed something to occupy himself with. She'd cracked the code he used fast and replied in three days. She was fully on board to help keep him busy. Something Russ didn't understand.

The Accountant's Office might have given him a new life, but that life involved changing everything about himself.

Joseph didn't know what he wanted to keep and what could be discarded, at least not yet. Maybe it was better to have time to figure it out. However, solving a mystery that had been floating around this place for fifty years was also a worthy use of his time.

The fact there had been an additional murder more recently, thirty years ago, and the tale of the missing treasure, meant a whole lot less time musing about himself and why it seemed like he didn't know how to be the kind of person everyone—including God—expected him to be. Time he would likely spend staring at the photo he'd hidden under the floorboard.

He wrote Edith a return letter, cautioning her to be careful. By the time she received it, she might already have visited the woman. Given that, he was inclined to pray. Russ thought it was a valuable endeavor.

Everyone with the Accountant's Office was expected to attend church. He'd done that as a child and it hadn't saved him. Maybe it would make sense this time, but he couldn't figure out how. He knew God could take care of Edith while Joseph wasn't there. Whether He used Edith's grandson the police officer to do it, or not.

He walked his reply letter down to the front office and tossed it in the mail bin.

As he emerged from the office and off the porch, his hiking boots crunched the gravel and he realized he hadn't switched them back for tennis shoes. No one needed to know he'd been wandering around outside camp.

As he turned for the lane back to his cabin, a vehicle pulled in. A silver Mercedes that had no business on these mountain roads. Whoever it was should have rented an SUV before they traversed the pitted, muddy back roads that snaked up from the highway.

Dirt coated both sides of the car. The woman who climbed out looked at the door and shook her head.

Sarah Carlton, the medical examiner, opened her back door and grabbed a small rolling suitcase from the seat. She raised the handle and tugged on it, beeping the locks for her car.

The tiny wheels of the suitcase bounced on the gravel and got stuck. She tugged it loose and continued. She shoved her hair back with her free hand. She moved like she was stiff, as though she had been injured.

Joseph changed directions and strode toward her like he hadn't just hiked for two hours. "What happened to you?"

Sarah lifted her brows and looked down her nose at him in that way she had. "Excuse me?"

"Just answer the question, Sarah." He folded his arms across his chest. Since they met, she'd used her job and intelligence to keep him at a distance.

That was fine by him considering he wasn't looking to get close to her. Problem was, all that did was make him want to break through her shell and find out what was underneath. Which was a terrible idea.

"Nothing happened," she said. "And I'm fine, thank you for asking."

He narrowed his gaze. "Are you here for a visit?"

"Sure. The only reason I'd be here is voluntarily and not because I've been ordered to take a vacation and"—she raised that stiff arm and made air quotes—"'help.'"

He didn't like the way she moved. She had definitely been injured somehow. "Did you hurt yourself?"

"Someone broke into my office the other night. It's not related to me being here, but of course the chief used it as another reason why I should lay low for a couple of weeks."

"Sounds familiar."

She frowned. "Why are you here?"

Because I killed a terrorist. "Russ ordered me to work here for a while."

Still frowning, she said, "Why does Russ get to tell you what to do?"

Oops. For once telling the truth had not been the right thing, and now he had to figure out what to say. The interim police commissioner also ran the Accountant's Office, so yeah he got to tell Joseph what to do. However, he said, "It's complicated. Who broke into your office?"

"It's complicated." She raised her chin. "So I guess I'll see you around?" She strode toward the office where Karen stood on the porch.

Sarah would be here? Things might be looking up for once in his life. If he was interested in yet another distraction. Except that he was supposed to be lying low and figuring out this faith thing, not spending time with a woman who interested him.

A few weeks back, a local bad guy had set off a bomb that killed eighteen people—and nearly killed Joseph. He'd been in the club when it exploded. Sarah had responded to the scene in her role as a medical examiner but provided medical care as well. As a doctor she'd been able to save several people.

According to Stella and Eric, she'd also bandaged his head while he babbled in an English accent. They'd told him about it after and expected him to explain. He'd simply told them he was good at accents, and he'd been confused.

Not the truth—that he'd been taken from boarding school in England and trained as a spy. Or that he'd ever worked as an assassin for hire. A few months ago he'd run into the guys from Chevalier Protection Specialists. They had pointed him toward the Accountant's Office, which provided him with a new life.

A fresh start.

One he wouldn't mind featuring more of Sarah, and less of death and murder. Not that she'd give him the time of day. She kept him at arm's length, the way he should do with her. Even Edith thought it was a bad idea, though only because she disliked inviting someone that far into her life.

He'd had that complete connection with someone once. Before it all ended in bloodshed. It was for the best to stay away from her. He couldn't go back to the place where he was vulnerable. It hurt too much. He wasn't looking for a relationship. Just a friend.

One who was going to find out who had hurt her.

4

"I can have a word with him," the woman said, "if he was bothering you." She leaned on the porch rail, arms crossed.

"Oh, no." Sarah shook her head. "We know each other."

The woman's eyes widened. "Are you exes?" It seemed as though she thought that was a juicy development.

Sarah didn't know why it was any of this woman's business. "It's nothing like that."

After the night she'd had and being shoved against the wall in her office the day before, she didn't have the patience left for whatever this woman was about.

"I'm Doctor Sarah Carlton." She stuck out her hand.

"Karen Deverly." The woman gave her a perfunctory smile and headed inside.

Sarah followed behind her, thinking about what had happened at her office.

The intruder was nowhere to be found. The police and even the FBI had shown up to investigate. They'd looked at the surveillance tapes from the office. Well, not tapes exactly. It was all digital and had been for years, but that didn't keep the images from being grainy. Not that a high-quality picture would have helped anyway.

The man had his hood up and never looked at any of the cameras. Almost like he knew where they were.

She had a couple of bruises, and it didn't look like anything had been taken from her office. But Addie, who was a local FBI agent and her friend, insisted she come up here as ordered. Not just so Sarah could do what her boss asked of her. Also to give Addie time to investigate and hopefully find the person who'd intruded in her office while Sarah was out.

It didn't make sense why someone would break in. Or why her boss would send her here. However, Sarah had never understood people much. Even her dad, Robert Carlton, the man she was closest to, didn't make much sense to her.

In fact, since she'd been exiled up here for two weeks, she hadn't returned her dad's most recent calls. Eventually she would have to explain to him what was happening. Hopefully he wouldn't throw too much of a fit. For a lawyer, she'd have thought he would be independent. Or find an assistant to do the tasks he seemed to believe Sarah should do for him. Maybe she could hire him one while she was gone.

She finished the paperwork Karen gave her and pulled out her phone to make a note of her idea.

"Come on, I'll show you to your cabin."

"Thank you." Sarah lifted her suitcase clear off the gravel so it didn't get stuck again. Thankfully they didn't see Joseph on the way either. She wondered which cabin was his, but then chided herself for worrying about that.

"It really is great that you're here, with you being a doctor and everything." Karen glanced over her shoulder and flashed a Hollywood smile. "The nurse can't make the children's camp so that's perfect, really."

"The teens camp that's happening after the mystery writers?" Sarah had always thought young people didn't want to be called children.

Karen shrugged. "They're all kids to me. Even the two girls who work here. Babes really."

Sarah frowned because the woman wasn't looking at her. She didn't know what to make of her.

Kind of like she didn't know what to make of Joseph. After the bombing it seemed like he was interested in her. But then all of a sudden it was like a switch flipped. It seemed he realized he'd been using a British accent at first—making her wonder about his history. He'd gone back to a smooth American accent around the time he decided to start ignoring her. It was fine really, considering she didn't have time for games. Not if she was going to be the chief medical examiner.

Karen used a key to let herself into the cabin, then handed it to Sarah. "This is your quiet space for the next couple of weeks. There are towels in the bathroom, and the coffee pot is over there." She pointed at a small desk with a lamp.

There was also an armchair and a twin bed. In the corner was a freestanding wardrobe. The curtains were white with blue stripes and didn't quite cover the window. She would need to secure them with a couple of safety pins or clothespins.

"This whole place looks great. Thank you so much for accommodating me at the last minute." Sarah smiled.

"We're happy for all the help we can get." Karen looked at the slender gold watch on her wrist. "Dinner is in a couple of hours. It's either inside or behind the main building where there's a patio. You can meet all the other employees and get to know everyone."

"Sounds good." Sarah nodded, ready to be alone in this

quiet space. The cabin was quaint, but nice. This might not be a terrible couple of weeks, even if she didn't see why she had to take a vacation at all.

Karen trailed out, leaving the door open, and trotted down the porch steps.

Sarah let out the breath it seemed she'd been holding while pretending she wanted to be here, or that any of this was her choice. Even if she might be able to make the most of her time off, this still wasn't what she wanted to be doing.

Since she talked to Addie, she'd warred between being annoyed and deciding to make the best of it. All the back and forth was getting exhausting. Maybe she wouldn't be so grudging if it was her choice to be here. Instead, she'd been ordered to relax, which was pretty much the perfect way to ensure a person did *not* relax.

At least she would be able to talk shop with mystery writers. That would be interesting. And providing medical coverage for young people on a summer adventure surely wouldn't be boring.

She squared her shoulders. "I can do this. No problem."

She'd like to say she had succeeded at everything she'd ever tried. The truth was that after her disastrous attempt at volleyball, she'd concluded she in fact *couldn't* do anything she put her mind to. The things that counted, the stuff that really mattered, she applied herself until she got the result she wanted.

Which was why her computer and all of her files from the investigation were tucked in her suitcase. Why sit around doing nothing when she could be reading through the case details and potentially coming up with a breakthrough?

"It'll be fine."

Just like walking through the main street of the camp had been fine. Being here so far hadn't brought back any memories whatsoever of the last time. Then again, she barely remembered the camp itself or anything she'd done before the third night when everything changed. Sarah had followed a barn cat down the trail and gone too far away from the cabins.

When she'd seen a man out walking, she'd been too curious. She'd come face-to-face with that man, stumbled, and landed in a deep hole.

Sarah had screamed for dear life at what was at the bottom.

He'd pulled her out and grabbed her face. Told her to shut her mouth. After that, everything went black.

When she'd woken up, Sarah had been in her bed.

Everyone she'd told her story to was certain she'd had a nightmare.

Sarah knew better, but some nightmares were real. It was why she'd chosen to use her knowledge and aptitude to become a doctor and a forensic pathologist. Now as a medical examiner she could reveal those things the killer wanted to hide in the dark. Give the truth to people living in a nightmare of their own.

There was a soft tap on the door. She glanced over and saw Joseph through the window. Another place she would need to secure the blinds so no one could see in after dark.

She opened the door with no intention of letting him in. "Did you need something, Joseph?"

His expression softened. "I want to apologize. I didn't mean to come on so strongly when I asked what'd happened to you."

"Oh." She wasn't sure a man had ever apologized to her before. "Do you want to come in?"

She took half a step back and he entered. Not much farther than just across the threshold. Hands in his pockets. Elbows tight to his sides. "I didn't mean to scare you."

She shook her head. "I don't think you'd ever scare me."

He blinked. "You might be surprised."

She wasn't sure what to make of that. The first time she met him he'd been concussed and stumbling around outside that nightclub after the bombing. "There was an intruder in my office, and he shoved me against the wall. I banged my elbow, so no heavy lifting for a few days. Other than that, I'm okay."

His expression tightened, but only a minuscule amount. "Do you know what he wanted?"

"Information on something." Sarah shrugged. "I don't know which of my cases it would've been."

She often dealt with irate family members. People unsatisfied by the only answer she could give them, the truth. They wanted her to confirm what they suspected or tell them something other than what they knew to be true.

Mostly they were just people in pain. Full of fear, the way she had been her entire life.

Now that she'd come back to the camp she realized it was so different, and this place didn't feel very familiar. Too many years had passed.

Her nightmare had nothing to do with the camp. It all happened in the woods, where she definitely wasn't going to go.

Despite wanting her entire life to feel like she was strong, the fear was just something she lived with. Her therapist had told her that it didn't matter what other people believed. It only mattered what she knew was true.

These days the truth was what she could measure. A hypothesis she could test in her lab. Results. Proof. Evidence that could stand up against the scrutiny of the law.

Fear didn't go away just because she was presented with cold hard facts.

Her dreams persisted in tormenting her. Life seemed to

never quite give her what she wanted. Even if she made the best of it, she couldn't help feeling dissatisfied.

Like how Joseph seemed interested, then gave her the brush-off.

"It shouldn't have happened." He shot her a look.

"It wasn't the first time something like that has occurred. But I do hope it was the last."

Given his expression, he didn't seem to be comforted by that. "What about security at the ME's office?" he asked.

"The chief and the FBI are dealing with that." All she was going to worry about was her case and being able to tie those deaths together. Of course, there was a chance she was wrong, and they were unrelated. Whatever the evidence indicated is what she would report.

"I'm glad you're okay." He took a step toward the door. He was going to leave, and then would probably go back to ignoring her.

"It was nice to see you," she said, genuinely meaning it. If she was willing to admit the truth for herself, she was sad to let him go.

Two weeks with him might have been…not fun, but at least enjoyable. Getting to know each other and becoming friends. He probably had as much to do as she did and didn't need to see the longing that was probably on her face.

She turned away to the wardrobe and decided to look inside just to see if they had any hangers. Not to blink away the burn of tears in her eyes. She pulled the doors both wide. Inside the wardrobe was the same mask she had seen in that nightmare.

Black eyes. White face. Red slashes cut diagonally across the cheeks.

Sarah screamed.

5

—————

J oseph spun around and raced back into the cabin. Sarah stumbled back. He caught and shifted her out of the way of the offending wardrobe. Inside, a costume mask hung from the center hanger. Not something that would frighten the average adult. But for some reason, this one scared Sarah into screaming and reeling back.

He tore the mask from the hanger and turned back to her but kept the mask out of sight. "What is it about this thing that scared you?"

So far she had brushed off an intruder's attack in her office as being no big deal. Added to this, it could indicate she was being targeted.

She shook her head.

He moved closer to her, "Don't tell me this is nothing. Who other than the people you work for and your friends knew you were coming here? Someone put this in here, right?" He tucked it in the back of his belt.

She would potentially dispose of it, and then he would never see it again. Joseph needed to know if there was anything he could learn from it. However, he also figured she knew what it meant and could answer many of his questions. Maybe even who had put it here.

"I don't know who'd do this," she said. "Or how they knew I'd be here in this cabin."

"It definitely narrows the pool of suspects." He folded his arms.

She blinked. "Were you a cop or something?"

"I've never in my life been in law enforcement, or the military. I worked for the government." *Just not America's.* "Then I was with a private organization. They didn't try to do good in the world. I also had no choice whether I stayed with them or not."

She might as well know why he was going to help her but also stay away from her. Just because he was here didn't mean he would get close to her. Or that God intended for anything to happen between them.

"I'm sure it being here doesn't mean anything." She lifted her chin. "It's probably just a coincidence."

He wanted to ask her if she actually believed that was true. He figured she would only argue her point rather than admit she'd been called out.

"Thanks for turning around so quickly when I screamed. I appreciate it, but it was nothing."

He wanted to fold his arms but didn't. "I guess we'll see if that's true or not."

Since he wasn't going to get anywhere further with her, Joseph left the cabin taking the mask with him.

He heard her call out, "Hey, why are you—"

Joseph trotted down the steps and headed for the kitchen. Something was going on. He couldn't help thinking about that lone cabin in the woods he'd never seen before. Definitely worth checking out, even if it likely didn't have anything to do with Celeste's death or anything else that'd happened here in the last few decades. Sarah clearly had her own deal going on. If he was going to get her to open up, he'd do better waiting her out than putting the pressure on.

In the meantime, he could look into the mask and what it might mean to her.

He couldn't believe she'd said she would never be scared of him. He'd given her a little snippet into what his life was before the Accountant's Office, but the truth was she would never fully know him. Telling her everything would be an effective way of proving he wasn't someone she should have in her life. However, it also meant being vulnerable enough to share the worst parts of himself.

He should probably just focus on his own stuff and not worry about Sarah. She had friends who were FBI agents. She probably didn't even need him.

He headed back into the kitchen and got everything prepped for dinner. Since it would just be burgers, there wasn't much to do except chop toppings and make sure there were enough potatoes to cut into wedges. He was just about done when Brad strode in.

Joseph looked up from the counter, a hot washcloth in one hand. "Help you?" The smell of cleaning products lingered in the air along with paprika. He should figure out what he was going to do the rest of the afternoon. Maybe make a couple of pies for dessert.

"This isn't going to be easy," Brad said. "But I'm just going to come out and say it."

"Okay." Joseph dropped the cleaning rag on the counter.

"You need to stay away from my wife. You've been making passes at her since you showed up here, trying to get her attention. Now you're catching her in quiet corners. Touching her? I did a favor for Russ letting you stay here." He crossed the distance between them and poked a finger in Joseph's chest. "But this is a warning. You're on a short leash."

"And if I have no idea what you're talking about?"

Brad scoffed. "It figures you'd deny it. Karen told me everything. So I'm telling you now, you need to stay away from her or you're out of here."

He wanted to fire back a comment about how hard it would be for Brad to find a replacement cook at short notice. Or the terrible job Karen would do while he found someone.

"Since I never go near her, staying away from her won't be a problem."

"I should install security cameras and catch you in the act." Brad puffed up his chest and blew out a breath.

"Do it." Joseph shrugged. Cameras would only prove the accusations were baseless, but Brad wasn't interested in the truth. He wanted to be the bigger man, defending his wife. "I hardly ever even talk to her. And she never comes in the kitchen." Joseph shrugged. "It's not too hard to stay away from her."

Assuming she managed to stay away from him. Something he wasn't going to comment to Brad. The guy would only get more irate thinking Joseph turned the responsibility back on Karen.

Brad spun around toward the door. "Whatever." He moved to where Joseph had hung the mask on the hooks by the door. "Where did you get this?" He snatched the mask down.

Joseph told him where it had been. "What's the significance of that mask?" There had to be some kind of story for everyone to react to it the way they were.

Brad said, "Don't worry about it." He rushed out the door, taking the mask with him.

Joseph gritted his teeth. Now he'd lost his chance to look more closely at it. Clearly Brad thought there was some significance to it. Or he knew exactly where it had come from and who put it in Sarah's closet. The question was whether it was purposely to scare her.

Now there was something to consider.

Maybe he should write to Edith and have her look into Sarah and her background. Get him some answers as to why the mask freaked her out.

Now he had Karen to worry about as well? He had to wonder what else she would come up with next. He should call Russ and tell him what was happening. Maybe get pulled from this detail…or whatever it was called. Punishment. Purgatory. Or a stint in summer camp torment.

The truth was, he'd been in worse places and managed to survive. But considering this was supposed to straighten out his thought processes and ingrained tendency to solve problems exactly one way, he might have to stick it out. No matter what.

Complete the mission.

They always called it that. A way of appealing to his sense of honor—once they knew he had one. After that it had been all about ending evil people so they couldn't hurt anyone, usually terrible monsters. People they could prove to him shouldn't remain alive.

Being free of that group felt like waking up from a long nightmare. Realizing how his life stacked up to what most people's formative years had been turned out to be a revelation.

He'd been aware that he wasn't the same as most people. He hadn't minded until he met Genevieve. Now he was alone and different again. Russ intended to either fix him or create situations where he fixed himself. Except now that he'd met Sarah he actually wanted to be different. Even though he knew he never would be. This whole "faith" thing hadn't worked.

Edith was one of the few people in the world who actually understood him. Meanwhile people like Brad and Karen couldn't comprehend who he was.

Since he had a couple of hours until dinner, Joseph put on his workout gear and went for a run. The quiet. The rhythmic pounding of his shoes on the trail, and the steady breaths in his ears—that would remain steady unless he came across a bear again—meant he could let go of his frustration for a while.

He ended up back at that ridge, following a deer trail down to the cabin.

He slowed as he approached it, keeping out of sight while he took long breaths and let his heart rate decrease. It seemed like Russ thought everything about him needed to be reprogrammed. Joseph already knew he wasn't okay, and he would never be like good people in the community.

He couldn't just be who he was. Not when the way he'd been trained dictated everything.

"And where does that leave me?"

No one answered him.

The cabin looked rundown on the outside, with peeling wood planks and even a hole or two that had been patched up from the interior. The windows were cloudy yellow glass, and what looked like aluminum foil had been taped up inside. Someone didn't want anyone to see what was happening in here.

Joseph doubted it had anything to do with Celeste or the other murders that had occurred, the ones no one talked about because it was bad for PR. Or Sarah, and whatever was going on with her, for that matter. But why stop now when he was so close to solving at least one mystery? Even if this one was just what was happening in this cabin on the camp's land.

The cabin had a door in front and at the back. He

decided on the back door, so it wouldn't be as obvious someone had entered. If anyone even cared.

He was only going to check it out for the sake of getting the truth about at least one thing in his life.

Joseph pushed away the frustration of everything he couldn't change and jimmied the lock on the back door.

It took a second for his eyes to adjust from the sunlight to the dark interior of the cabin. Two tables had been set up, along with a whole lot of chemistry equipment. A ventilation shaft in the ceiling that must connect to the chimney. No generator ran outside, so they weren't currently circulating the air. If this was a working meth lab, it was going unused but didn't look abandoned.

He didn't touch anything but walked through the whole place and looked at every square inch of it. He'd be able to recall it all later when he told Russ. Or Edith. Or Brad, for that matter. The guy probably needed to know there was a meth lab on his land, if he wasn't already aware.

He was circling back to the rear door when he heard the sound of tires on gravel out front.

Multiple doors slammed. He heard the chatter of voices, muted through the walls. At least three, it not more people, and he had no weapon to defend himself with.

He strode to the back door and stepped out. Closed it softly behind him just as he heard the front door slam against the wall inside. Joseph raced for the trees so he could hide.

He ducked behind a thicket of bushes and pulled out his flip phone.

But he didn't know who to call.

6

Sarah zoomed in on the photo and looked again at the abrasion on the fourth victim's arm. All three other victims had a similar patch of red skin. Raised. Almost a square, like they'd worn a patch of some kind. Initially she'd figured it was a rash. On later victims she wondered if it wasn't intentional.

She didn't necessarily have proof that was the method of delivery. It would be strange, but not impossible.

"Unless…" The word echoed up to the rafters of her cabin.

If the drug had been ingested orally, there would be indications in the stomach contents. Unless it had completely metabolized before their deaths. If it was a patch, they could've used some kind of transdermal method of delivering the drug.

She slid over her phone, the only device she had internet on right now. She needed Wi-Fi for her computer, but that also opened her up to vulnerabilities in cybersecurity if she connected to the camp network. If she used the ME's office VPN to access the office network directly, it was far more secure but would also let them know that she was logging on to do work.

The chief didn't know she'd brought everything with her, and he needed not to find out.

Sarah called Addie from her phone. It took a few rings, and the FBI agent answered, "Franklin."

Sarah smiled. "That's going to be Wilson soon."

"Yes, it is." Addie chuckled. The FBI agent was due to get married in a few weeks. "How is camp?"

"Oh, um…fine?"

"You don't sound convinced."

"I only just got here." Sarah tried not to write things off before she'd given them a shot. She considered telling Addie about the mask, but why hear the disbelief in her friend's voice that it was anything to be concerned about? Instead, she said, "I was looking at my files for the four deaths. Can you tell me if there was anything in the patient's backgrounds that indicated they'd each received medical treatment prior to their deaths?" She then told Addie about the matching abrasions. Each one on the victim's chest, just below their collar bone.

"Huh." Addie shuffled some things, and Sarah heard the clicking of a keyboard. "We didn't come up with any medical treatment. At least not on the first pass. I'll take a deeper look, though."

"Thanks." If they'd all been to the same clinic or hospital, it meant a connection between them aside from the drug that had killed them.

"You still think they're connected?"

That question meant Addie didn't believe there was enough evidence to draw that conclusion. "Right now, they just…match. Nothing else ties them together." And they didn't have the results on the drug breakdown.

"Maybe that's the point."

"What do you mean?" Sarah frowned.

"Well, if you want to kill people then you make sure no one can tie it back to you. If you want to kill a few people, you either do it all in one go and hopefully make it look like an accident. Or you make sure they can't be tied together."

"You're a very scary woman."

Addie laughed. "I'll send you an email if I find a correlation. After all, you'll be busy helping campers."

Sarah groaned.

"Bye." Addie hung up, still laughing.

Sarah flopped back on the bed for a second before she got the motivation to get up. Mostly because she was hungry.

She secured all her files and slid the laptop onto the shelf in the bathroom, in the middle of the stack of towels. Just in case the person who'd broken into her office came here looking for the information she'd brought with her.

She locked up the cabin, a rumble of hunger in her stomach. It was almost dinnertime and she had to face Joseph at some point. It might as well be when she had food in her mouth because he would have to hold off asking her more questions.

The last thing she needed was him digging around in her past. He would discover her nightmares and then be convinced, as everyone else had, that she made the whole thing up. He would probably even believe she'd planted that mask in the wardrobe just to scare herself.

So that he would swoop in and try to save her? It was a plausible theory.

If she wanted to be saved.

Right now Sarah had no idea who could have planted it in the closet. Or if it'd even been intentional. Maybe it was a practical joke, or part of a Halloween costume left behind. Surely there was some simple explanation.

Not the alternate theory—that whatever she'd seen in her waking nightmare had come back.

She shook off the shudder of fear that came over her and looked at the sun. It warmed her face, and she caught the scent of grilling hamburger on the breeze.

Brad stood at the grill behind the dining hall, beside the patio area where two blonde girls assisted Karen with a checkered tablecloth.

"Ladies, this is Sarah." Karen waved at the two women. "This is Taylor and Emmalee."

Sarah had no idea which girl was which.

She looked around. "Do you need any help?"

After all, it was why she was here. Not to just hide in her cabin and use the quiet time to get work done.

Karen waved at the door. "Grab some paper goods and plasticware from the pantry, enough for all of us."

She wanted to ask where Joseph was but nodded and headed inside. He was probably in the kitchen trying to figure out the solution to her problems. Like the kind of guy who jumped in when a woman was in trouble, and yet at the same time he kept his distance from her. Unless he was bombarding her with questions.

She really didn't understand the guy at all. He wasn't the kind of guy she'd ever met before. Especially not considering her ex-fiancé didn't care one whit about her job. Let alone if somebody was hassling her. All he cared about was whatever case he had going to trial at the time.

The kitchen was empty, but she found the storage room where paper goods were located. Who cared where Joseph was? Her track record of relationships meant she should steer clear of him, for his sake. Sarah pulled down a stack of paper plates and located the little boxes of plasticware.

"Hey, I don't think we've met."

She glanced back over her shoulder. The younger man

who stood there looked a lot like Brad. His son, maybe? "You're right. We haven't."

She held the plates in front of her, not just because it gave her a buffer between the two of them. His eyes were dark and assessing. But he was just a young man in the same place as her. There wasn't a threat.

"Austin." He stuck out his hand.

She would have to shake it, or she would seem rude. Sarah shifted the plates so she had one arm free.

He clasped her hand with both of his and held on even when she tried to pull away. She smiled and tugged on her hand. "It's nice to meet you."

"It is nice." He stroked the back of her hand with his fingers. "You're a very beautiful woman. I bet you hear that all the time." He chuckled, probably thinking his smile was disarming.

It would likely work with Taylor and Emmalee. But Sarah was at least fifteen years older than all of them.

She shifted the things in her arms. "I should get this stuff outside."

"I'll help you out." He took the plates from her and put them on the counter. When he turned back, he moved far too close into her space.

"Can you give me a little room?" She waved him back, but he didn't move. "I need to get the rest of the stuff down."

"That's why I'm here, to help."

"Fine, then you get the plasticware and I'll take the plates outside." She tried to move around him. He slid his arm in front of her stomach, his finger sliding over her hip. Sarah took a step back. "Excuse me. I didn't invite you to touch me."

"Sor-ry." He dragged the word out with a sarcastic tone. "I didn't know you'd be so touchy about it. I was just trying to welcome you, since you're new here."

Sarah's jaw clenched. "That's not the kind of welcome I'm interested in."

"Maybe if you loosened up a little bit." He took a half step toward her. "Have a couple of drinks with me later. See what happens."

"No, thank you."

He huffed. "Whatever, prude."

As if she would rise to respond to that. She'd been called worse. Sarah found her teacher tone. "Bring the plasticware outside, Austin."

She grabbed the plates and pushed through the swinging doors out of the kitchen. Maybe she didn't mind so much that Joseph seemed intent on jumping into every situation involving her. But where was he? Nowhere to be found when she could've used some back up.

She let out a sigh and pushed the door open.

Austin followed her out, close behind. Karen turned as they emerged outside onto the patio. "Oh, good. You've met my stepson, Austin."

"I guess a meeting is one way you could describe it." She dumped the plates in their bag on the table.

Karen chuckled. "He is a friendly one, our Austin."

The young man sauntered to the girls and handed over the stack of boxes. "Ladies." The two young women giggled. He said, "I'll go get the cups, since Sarah forgot all about them."

Sarah glanced at Karen and saw a frown on her face.

Karen said, "We need cups to drink out of."

"Austin was being so welcoming I got distracted." Both young women hissed, shooting her glances. Sarah rolled her eyes. "Trying to avoid throwing up in my mouth."

She wanted to get into the intricacies of Karen needing to explain to him what inappropriate behavior with people who worked at the camp was. Maybe no one had ever complained about him before, or his parents were used to dealing with his improprieties. Before she could start, the groundskeeper stumbled around the corner.

"Washington!" Karen shot the guy a look. He didn't respond to her call. "Probably drunk."

Sarah concentrated on getting the plates out, unwilling to deal with another man right now. Not that the women here were any better. No wonder they were struggling for volunteers. This place was supposed to be peaceful. It seemed more like nothing really happened, which wasn't the same thing.

Not even close to it.

She needed to keep her head down for the next two weeks and then get out of here. Back to her life, where she could prove to the chief that she didn't need a vacation.

Taylor and Emmalee circled around Austin, following him back into the dining hall. Giggles erupted before the door closed.

Washington, the groundskeeper, stumbled onto a bench seat.

"Had a few already, huh?" Brad laughed.

Sarah watched the guy shake his head. Washington listed to one side. He barely managed to catch himself, pitched forward and took a header onto the dirt.

"So dramatic." Karen rolled her eyes and wandered over to Brad.

Sarah headed for the man lying in the dirt. She called out to the camp directors, "Is this normal?"

Karen said nothing. Brad shrugged.

She crouched beside the big man in his rumpled clothes and rolled him to his back. He was out cold, his T-shirt damp with sweat. A square abrasion on the inside of his elbow.

She reached two fingers to his throat.

As she felt for his pulse he began to convulse. Foam

bubbles coated his lips, and his whole body bent and contorted off the ground.

"What on earth..." Brad started to walk over but stopped, the spatula raised.

Sarah rolled him to his side and pulled out her phone, dialing 9-1-1 as quickly as she could.

Before she explained what had happened to the dispatcher, his heart stopped beating.

7

J oseph raced to the trees and ducked down. One man walked around the cabin to use the back door. There was more than one vehicle, and he could see the grill of a red pickup in view by the front corner of the cabin.

Gray clouds obscured the sun and cast shadows across the clearing. He spotted at least three Caucasian men and one African American. This wasn't a group brought together based on some kind of fringe ideology, like one race would ever be better than the other. He'd have been impressed by the diversity if they weren't working together to make money creating a substance designed to suck people into addiction and despair.

He used his phone to take photos of the front of the truck, the cabin, and every person he saw. Four unique people, one of whom was clearly the boss. The guy was slightly older than the others and grizzled. His face worn by years of hard living.

"Bring that stuff in." The grizzled man waved at the truck and spurred each man into action.

One said, "Someone was definitely here."

"Why should I care about that? They ain't here now."

The underling said, "Whoever they are, they know we're here. That could mean trouble."

The grizzled man drew a .45 from his belt. "I'm ready for trouble. You know that." He pointed the gun at the underling and chuckled.

The man stood frozen the whole time.

"Go help the others bring the supplies."

Joseph figured they had recently been using the cabin as an active lab, but now they were back to ramp up production.

This was no fly-by-night operation. Or something brand-new. They were pros who had a system down. Probably with multiple labs. Joseph gritted his teeth and watched them, wondering just how far this operation spread.

Was the grizzled man the boss of it all?

He took a few more photos of the guy. He could send them to Edith, but the likelihood she knew a local meth dealer was slim. These days she was only interested in things that threatened people she cared about.

He could text a picture to Russ, but it would be immediately obvious he wasn't laying low at the retreat camp.

Joseph wished he could send them straight to Addie at the FBI office. Doing so would require far too much explaining and answering questions and would reveal too much about him. Addie would get curious about Joseph as well as the crime.

For all the complaining he did at Russ's demands to go straight, at least in his own mind, he did want this fresh start. If only for the chance to see what life was like when he lived it as everyone else did. He'd like the opportunity to feel good about the work he was doing. Not just justifying it in his own mind, but truly living an honorable life.

He wasn't normally the kind of person who hid in bushes

and tried to figure out how to anonymously give information to the FBI.

"Come on." The grizzled man clapped. "I want the next batch ready for testing ASAP."

"Did we get the subjects yet?" One of the men walked past with a cardboard box.

"You think it'll be like last time?" The grizzled man cuffed him on the back of the head. "You do sloppy work like that again and we're going to have a problem."

Joseph pulled open the notes app on his phone and typed up as much of the conversation as he could.

The underling emerged from the cabin, no longer holding the box. "I can help round them up?" He shifted as if nervous, like he knew he needed to prove himself. "Nothing will go wrong."

The grizzled man said, "No one can guarantee that. It's my job to minimize the risk. We didn't get this far by conducting a sloppy operation."

The guy nodded.

His grizzled boss lifted his chin. "When I get their information, I'll decide who goes in."

The nervous guy nodded. Joseph figured he wanted to offer to take the job, but also didn't want to push it. He had something to prove. And a sweet gig he wasn't willing to risk.

Business was going well.

Joseph didn't know what having a formula and test subjects meant, but his mind could come up with several things. None of them boded well. And there was little he could do about it from a retreat camp, anyway. Even if he was the kind of guy to get involved just because it was the right thing to do. He wasn't a cop, or any other kind of law enforcement. The FBI didn't need a shady confidential informant with limited information.

In the past, he'd have simply destroyed this place and

everyone here. Problem solved. After all, they intended to do the same thing to other people's lives. Their victims would take the drug and get addicted, or they would spiral farther down into the darkness of that life.

He'd seen the destruction it wrought. Men like this had no conscience when it came to the people whose lives they ruined.

So why let them live?

But dealing with it in the old way wasn't how he was supposed to live this new life of his. Russ would reject him from the Accountant's Office program if he discovered that Joseph had killed multiple people. Even if they were drug dealers, they were still human beings. Every life had to have value—or none of them did. Joseph didn't get to decide who lived or died.

Russ had explained that very clearly to him.

The grizzly man's cell phone rang. He unclipped it from his belt. "Yeah?" He listened for several seconds, then said, "Good. What about the doc?"

Joseph noted the conversation in his app.

"Well, I want that ME off the trail, so start scaring her big time."

A female, a medical examiner? A doctor. They had to be talking about Sarah.

Joseph called 911 from the phone and tucked it beside a tree. Then he turned and ran back toward the camp, not even caring if he was seen. There was a threat against Sarah.

A shout rang out. Then a gunshot.

The bullet clipped a tree far too close beside him. He changed directions and picked up his pace. He would have to slow down before he reached the camp or he'd collapse, but he could get out of sight if he kept pounding the dirt at this speed.

If they tried to catch up to him, it didn't work. Twenty

minutes later, he hit the boundary of the cabins. An ambulance was parked in the center street, lights flashing.

Joseph slowed slightly and jogged over, as if drawn by curiosity. He wasn't convinced it would work but prayed anyway that Sarah hadn't been hurt while he wasn't here.

No one was inside the ambulance. A second later they rounded the dining hall, two paramedics pushing a stretcher. Sarah was on her knees on top of the bed, giving chest compressions to what looked like the groundskeeper.

"What happened?"

One of the EMTs glanced over, an attractive African American woman. "Heart attack, probably. But we won't know until the doctors make a determination."

Sarah frowned at him. "It wasn't a heart attack."

Joseph figured the doctor had *already* made a determination.

However, the EMT didn't seem to agree. "We need to take him in. Try and keep him alive until we get to the hospital."

Sarah glanced at Joseph again and shook her head. He was just glad it wasn't her lying on that bed.

They reached the back of the ambulance and the EMT took over. Sarah swung her knee around and jumped from the stretcher. They all pushed it into the back of the ambulance.

The male EMT said, "Thanks." He closed the doors on the female, still doing chest compressions.

Seconds later, the ambulance turned on the street and headed out quickly.

"What happened?" He studied Sarah's face.

She brushed her hair back, flushed from the exertion of trying to save the groundskeeper's life. "He had an abrasion on the outside of his arm. I don't think it was a heart attack, but I have no idea what happened. His heart stopped beating."

"What do you want to do now?"

She glanced toward the back of the dining hall where she'd come from. "I don't know what everyone else is doing, but they were all back there. The girls and Karen, Brad and his son Austin."

Joseph had heard about Karen and Brad's son but hadn't met the guy. "How did they seem?" He didn't know why he asked that question, but she didn't appear confused by it.

Sarah said, "They thought he was drunk or something. Then when he collapsed, they all just stood there watching. Maybe they were in shock, and I have medical training, so I knew what to do."

"Not everyone is comfortable in an emergency situation. Some people just freeze." He squeezed her shoulder even though doing that was a slippery slope to hugs.

"Let's go look at his cabin. Maybe there's something in there that will give us a clue as to what happened." She set off toward it.

"Are the police going to show up?"

Sarah said, "I have no idea. All we got was an ambulance, but I figure if Washington doesn't make it, then someone will arrive to ask everyone questions. Hopefully it's Addie."

"You think this should be an FBI investigation?" He walked alongside her.

"Maybe. But given how the police are perceived right now, it's probably just me assuming the FBI would do a better job. And that's not fair, because the police department has more than earned my respect even before Detective Maxwell was exposed as a serial murderer."

"I heard about that." He hadn't shown up in Benson until after it happened, when the Accountant's Office brought Edith onto the floor of the downtown high rise where they all now lived.

Edith had been here for years, but that didn't mean she needed any less support than the rest of them. Apparently, Russ had been unofficially watching out for her for years.

Sarah sighed. "I have no idea what's going on at this camp, but all this is really freaking me out."

Joseph nodded. "I thought it was just an eeriness because of the stories about suicide, murder, and buried treasure. But there's definitely something a lot more recent going on." He told her about the meth lab and the men he'd seen not too far from here.

He didn't tell her about the phone call. After all, he couldn't be sure that guy had been talking about Sarah. No one had pursued him, or so he could figure out. They'd shot a couple of times, and yelled, but no one could outrun him. And if they were targeting him, then it didn't matter because he'd be here to protect her either way. Threat or no, she wasn't going to get hurt.

Sarah climbed the steps to the cabin. He touched her arm and had her wait while he went inside first.

"You think there's a killer still lurking in there?"

"I think you do good work, and you're an asset to this community. One who is worth protecting."

She frowned, but he didn't want to get into a conversation. They needed to know what had happened to Washington considering it could've been murder.

The door was unlocked. He pushed his way inside where a high-pitched whine drew his attention.

Joseph rounded the twin bed that looked a lot like his, except the blanket was plaid and the whole cabin smelled like cigar smoke. "It's his dog." He crouched beside the lab. "Looks like he's been hurt."

Joseph ran his hand down the animal's side. The dog shifted and let out a wine.

"Kicked, maybe?"

Joseph said, "If someone tried to hurt Washington, then his dog would definitely have protected him. Maybe that's what happened."

"And if Washington dies?" Sarah's voice had a worried tone. "What happens to the animal then?"

"We find a home for him." Joseph didn't figure anyone who lived at the camp would want to adopt the dog. None of them seemed like the type to take in a homeless animal. Joseph on the other hand wouldn't mind having some company in his quiet cabin.

"Okay, good." Sarah blew out a breath. "What on earth is going on here?"

Joseph glanced over at the door, where a shadow crossed the threshold. "That's a really good question."

Everything in him said to gather up the animal, head for his truck, and get them all out of here.

Before something worse happened.

8

———

Thoughts spun in Sarah's mind. She looked from the dog to Joseph, and then at the room in general.

There had definitely been an altercation in here. Even someone with messy tendencies would right a fallen chair, rather than continue to work around it. Especially when it blocked the side of the bed Washington would get in and out of. But she didn't need to worry about his sleeping habits, or the disarray that was his cabin.

Sarah bit her lip. "I really hope Washington isn't dead."

Not just because that would mean he couldn't tell them who tried to end his life. It just seemed so sad and pointless to kill the old groundskeeper.

"I know what you mean." Joseph lifted the dog onto the bed. He seemed to bear the weight easily, laying the animal on the covers.

"Do we need to take him to the vet?" She looked at her watch. Town seemed so far away, as though they were stranded up in the mountains. But the truth was it would only take twenty or so minutes to get there.

Right now she would rather be anywhere but here. There was something not right at all about this place.

"You want to come with me?" Joseph glanced at her.

She nodded.

"I'll make sure they're good for dinner and then we can go." He glanced at the door, a blank expression on his face. That lack of a look said more than if it had given her a clue what he was thinking because it was so unlike his normal expression. There was something dark about it she couldn't put her finger on.

If there was something wrong, then she needed to know. "What is it?"

If they were going to town, even for a short trip, she'd take her laptop, files, and personal stuff with her. There was no point leaving it here where it could be gone through by the wrong person.

The only one she trusted was Joseph, though she couldn't have said why.

He shook his head. "Do you have any guesses as to what happened to Washington?"

She had been wondering about that ever since she saw the abrasion on the outside of his arm. It was hard to say if symptoms matched the other deaths, but with the red rash there was a definite correlation.

"There were four overdose deaths recently. All of them had the same red mark as Washington, but I can only theorize they are connected at this point."

Joseph nodded. "Okay." He squeezed the bridge of his nose. "Add that to the fact I found a meth lab in the woods on retreat camp land and the phone call I overheard? We're taking the dog and going into town."

He hadn't mentioned a phone call. She frowned. "I need to get a few things from my cabin."

He said, "And I need to fetch my keys. I'll pull the truck close and then grab the dog."

They both turned for the door.

Brad moved to block their way out.

"Let's have a team meeting." Brad waved them out of the cabin. "Real quick, before you guys head out. We just need to figure out what happened."

"As long as it is quick." Sarah decided to use her official tone, making her sound a lot like a teacher with high expectations. "We need to get this dog medical treatment. In case he was hurt badly."

"Speaking of…" Brad crossed the porch ahead of them. "Are you thinking someone tried to kill Washington?"

"The police will have to make that determination. I'm just the medical examiner." Even if she played a pivotal role in death investigations, she had nothing to do with bringing charges. All she could do was report on what she found during an autopsy.

"So you don't think it was murder?"

Sarah shrugged. "Since I won't officially be working the case, I can't say either way. Right now we don't even know if he's dead, right?"

She realized at the bottom of the steps Taylor and Emmalee stood in a huddle with Austin. Karen was several feet away, facing them. With Brad as well, it looked like they were being surrounded.

A shiver of worry moved through her, and she felt Joseph move closer to her back. She wasn't in this alone. "What's going on?"

There certainly weren't enough answers for all their questions—or hers. She figured Washington's death could be related to the overdoses, but how on earth was she supposed to be able to figure that out from here? Now there was a meth lab involved as well, and Joseph seemed to think she needed to stick with him. That was fine by her.

She'd received death threats before as part of her job. It wasn't unheard off.

Karen spoke first, leveling a dark gaze at Joseph. "Why don't you tell us where you were when Washington was stumbling around about die?"

Joseph said, "Nowhere near here."

Sarah shivered.

"You're going to have to come up with a better alibi than that." Karen folded her arms.

"She's right," Brett said. "We all need to know where you were."

"Joseph didn't kill Washington." Sarah scoffed. "That's ridiculous."

He had no motive to do it as far as she could see. Then again, she didn't exactly know him that well. Maybe it wasn't completely out of the question. *No.* She'd already realized he was the *only* person she trusted here. No way were these people and their outlandish doubts going to sway her.

He was the only one it seemed like was on her side.

And the only one completely silent.

Wasn't he going to tell them that he didn't do anything to Washington? Maybe he didn't want them to know that he'd found that meth lab in the woods.

Because he thought they were in on it?

She glanced over at him, her mind spinning anew with questions. She needed information or she was going to spiral.

Karen said, "Why don't you just confirm what we all know."

Sarah glanced around. Austin should have stood in front of the two young women, protecting them from whatever threat he thought was imminent. If he was the kind of guy who defended a woman against danger.

Instead, he was beside them. That left them wide open to face what might be coming. It told Sarah everything she needed to know about the guy. And with what had happened in the pantry, it didn't add up to him being anything but a terrible human being.

Brad and Karen's son scoffed. "I guess Joseph isn't man enough to admit to what he did. As if anyone cares about Washington." Austin's expression slipped a bit, but he rallied.

The two young girls half smiled, as though trying to find something amusing about what he'd said.

Had Austin put that mask in her closet? For all she knew it could've been Washington.

Sarah said, "We don't even know he's dead. That's a pronouncement the doctor at the hospital needs to make."

"I guess that means it's a conspiracy, since you're only defending Joseph and he isn't speaking up for himself." Karen reached to the back of her waistband and pulled out a gun, which she pointed at Sarah and Joseph. "Both of you are in on it together. Of course Joseph disappears conveniently. Then you're the one who 'takes care' of Washington, pretending to treat him while you finish him off."

Brad moved off the porch to stand closer to Karen. Out of the line of fire. "I'll bet that's what it is. They only came here to rip us off."

Sarah felt her eyebrows rise. "Karen, will you put that gun down, please. I don't appreciate having a weapon pointed at me."

"If Joseph admits what he did, I'll put it down." Karen lifted her chin.

Sarah said, "And then you're going to call the police?"

The girls erupted into chuckles.

Austin grinned. "As if."

Brad shrugged. "We don't call the police here. People like us solve our own problems."

"Like taking care of murderers." Karen whipped the gun at Joseph.

Like he and Sarah were the threat here? It was ridiculous, considering they were the ones staring down the barrel of Karen's gun and facing off everyone else. It would have been interesting that they'd all seemingly lost their animosity toward each other, if there wasn't also the threat of death staring Sarah in the face.

"Karen," she started, hardly knowing what to say.

Joseph laid a hand on her arm and tugged her behind him. "I don't know what's going on here, but Sarah is going to get in her car and leave. She has nothing to do with it."

She wasn't sure how to respond to that. On the one hand he was saving her life. On the other, it seemed he thought she needed to be protected. Not that she wanted to face a gun unarmed, but she also didn't want to be shoved aside and managed. Until the gun was fired. Then he could protect her all he wanted.

Things were a lot simpler in her office when she was working. Here in the field, it appeared things had gotten dicey.

She didn't think this was the kind of vacation her boss had imagined for her.

"We're *both* leaving," Sarah said. "We need to take the dog to the vet." And get away from these people, one of which was likely the murderer. If Washington was dead. "So put the gun down, Karen. And all of you need to step aside."

Karen chuckled. "That's not how this works."

The old lab ambled out of the cabin and came to lean against Joseph's leg with a groan. She still figured he needed to see a vet. The dog could have internal injuries given how long it took him to get up. He was still hurt.

"Taylor," Karen said, "it's your turn, isn't it?"

Taylor didn't look too excited, but she also didn't hesitate. "Yeah, it is."

The younger woman took the gun from Karen. Brad slung his arm around Karen's shoulders and turned her away.

"Tell us when it's done," he called back.

The two of them walked off, talking low to each other.

Sarah glanced at Austin, who might not have a gun but was still the biggest threat as far as she was concerned. Especially stacked up against two young women. But then, she didn't know for sure did she? Taylor and Emmalee could have all kinds of murderous tendencies.

Taylor lifted the gun with a shaky hand.

Emmalee looked like she was about to be sick. She stumbled away a couple of steps. "I'll see you guys later."

That left Taylor and Austin.

Joseph muttered under his breath, "Much better odds." He strode down the porch steps, leaving her standing with the dog.

She patted the dog's head and hoped she didn't have to use some kind of command to get the animal to go with her. Sarah moved to the left side of the porch. There was no railing, so it was just open. A single post at the front corner held up the roof that shaded it from the sun.

"We should go in the woods, shouldn't we?" Taylor asked Austin.

"Unless you want to clean blood off the porch." Austin rolled his eyes. "I thought you'd done this before."

Those rolled eyes met hers while Sarah inched away. Ready to run if necessary. The last thing she wanted was to leave Joseph at the mercy of a gun, but if she had to make a run for it then she needed quick access. A direction she could go where Taylor wouldn't be able to shoot her in the back as she tried to flee.

Austin tracked her movements. Sarah shivered under the intensity of his gaze, not wanting to think about what he was looking for from her.

Joseph's body was tight, like a coiled snake ready to strike. He shifted his weight. With one swipe of his arm he grabbed the gun from Taylor. He kicked Austin in the stomach, twisted Taylor's arm behind her back and shoved her away, taking control of the gun.

Austin straightened, fury in his gaze. Joseph slammed the gun down on his head. Austin crumpled to the ground.

Emmalee shouted.

Joseph spun to her. "Run!"

9

———

Despite his order, Sarah didn't move from her spot. She just stood there frozen. But Joseph couldn't worry about her. No one was within arm's reach of her right now, and he was the one with the gun. That meant he could focus on Taylor and Austin and get back to protecting Sarah when that threat was neutralized.

Joseph had to get him and Sarah away from the camp.

The situation had quickly turned deadly—too quickly. There was no weight to the accusation that he was the one who'd killed Washington. Thankfully Sarah had been certain he didn't do it. That meant something to him. Still, Joseph quickly figured out the likelihood that everyone at camp was involved to at least an extent with the meth lab and whatever was going on. Sarah, and all the information she had with her, had walked right into their trap.

By accident, or because somebody had planned it this way? He wasn't sure.

Taylor spun around screeching. The woman was like some kind of mythical banshee who headed for Sarah, her nails bared as she screamed.

Joseph grabbed her around the waist and lifted her off her feet. She scratched at his arm hard enough to draw blood.

He gritted his teeth and flung her to the ground several feet away. She jumped up again and grabbed for the gun, trying to snatch it away from him. If he killed her then Russ would kick him out of the Accountant's Office, no matter if it was self-defense or any other reason. He wasn't allowed to take a life.

He kicked her away. She came back at him, scratched his face, and tried to bite his shoulder. It would be unbelievable enough to give him pause if he wasn't busy trying to fend her off. She had to be hopped up on something. Added to the adrenaline it was like a switch had been flipped.

He pushed her away again. She stumbled back and landed on her butt in the dirt. Which of them would tire first?

Joseph glanced to where Sarah still stood on the porch with the dog. She needed to get her stuff, but he didn't want her going without him at this point.

He took one step, and two hands grasped his ankle. Joseph turned back, planted his foot, and kicked out. His shoe slammed Austin's shoulder.

Not wanting to get into a hitting and kicking match with him as well, Joseph pointed the gun right beside Austin's head and squeezed the trigger. The bullet embedded in the dirt just past him, missing his body. The deafening crack of the gunshot did the job he needed it to do. It worked like a flash-bang, exploding right beside Austin's head.

Joseph didn't want the temptation of shooting anyone else, so he used his thumb to eject the magazine and threw the gun as hard as he could to the side. It landed several feet away. One bullet in the chamber, but still less of a risk.

He kicked the stunned Austin in the head, and the kid fell

back onto the dirt. Taylor had rallied, so he squeezed the side of her neck and cut off the blood supply. After a few seconds her eyes rolled back in her head, and she collapsed.

"Sarah." He called to her as he raced for the porch, holding out his hand.

She stumbled down, took his hand, and said, "Come on," to the dog.

He clasped her hand tight as they ran to the other cabins. "I need my keys. You need your stuff."

"My place is closer."

He nodded, focused on running and ensuring no one tried to kill them. Keys, her things, the car. Then they were out of here. Assuming the dog cooperated.

The animal ran ahead of them stiffly, but it was old and injured. He didn't know which of those things contributed to the uneven gait, or if it was both. He couldn't worry about it, but he could pick up the animal if necessary.

Joseph dragged Sarah's hand for a second, so she got the idea and hung back behind him. He jumped up first onto her porch and headed for the door. Inside, both Brad and Karen rummaged through all of her things. Karen was in the bathroom, where she dragged towels from the shelf. She'd already dumped the contents of the cupboard onto the floor by the look of it.

Behind him, Sarah gasped.

A laptop clattered to the floor in the bathroom.

Brad shoved the mattress off the bed, then shook the pillow as though something was hidden inside. Both had angry looks on their faces while they destroyed all of Sarah's things.

Joseph started to back up. She grasped the back of his T-shirt and held on tight.

In the bathroom, Karen lifted the laptop and slammed it down on the edge of the counter. Plastic and electronics cracked. Karen hit the thing over and over again, until the laptop broke into several pieces.

Joseph frowned. Not how he would have chosen to destroy someone's information. Did Karen not realize it was probably saved to the cloud? Both appeared fired up with intensity. Soon they would realize they were done here and turn on Joseph and Sarah.

He turned to her and whispered, "Come on."

There wasn't much they could do here now.

Given her expression she didn't like it, but she held on to his hand as they hopped off the porch and headed for his cabin, where he grabbed his keys from beside the door. Apparently no one thought he had anything of value in his place. He wouldn't have been surprised to find evidence planted that indicated he'd murdered Washington. He had no doubts that was the tactic these people would use as soon as the police came around asking questions about what'd happened to their groundskeeper.

"Come on." Joseph knew he was repeating himself, but it was better to keep things simple. To keep them both focused on the goal of getting to the parking lot. Taylor had tried to kill them. Ordered to do it by Karen. If they stayed here, their lives were in danger.

Regardless of the fact Joseph could probably take out all five staff members that remained, he didn't want to then have to face down everyone who'd been at that meth lab cabin. That was even more people he would have to neutralize in order to save Sarah's life. Given this was potentially a conspiracy that reached farther and wider than just the retreat camp, he didn't want to lock himself into one plan of action.

"What on earth is going on here?" Sarah's words were breathy, her tone frantic. She did a good job keeping pace with him.

"It doesn't matter. We aren't sticking around to find out." He glanced around. Hopefully no one came out from behind anywhere and took a shot at them.

She stumbled on a pothole in the dirt road. Joseph reached for her, but she caught herself and carried on. "I'm okay."

He glanced behind. Austin strode toward them with a determined stride. Too far away for Joseph to see the expression on his face, but there was a definite intention in his gait.

And he had a bat in one hand.

Joseph didn't want to find out what the guy intended doing with that. He planned on being away from here before that happened.

This whole situation was eerily similar to an experience he'd had in Indonesia once. The whole mission was to take out a cult leader using a medicinal herb to brainwash everyone who lived in his compound. That entire place had been freaky, and Joseph didn't like the fact it reminded him way too much of this.

He didn't think Taylor, Emmalee, Austin, or his parents were on anything other than conventional narcotics. However, they all seemed to have been swept up in a frenzy of trying to keep their illegal activities to themselves. For some reason they needed to lock down Sarah and her things to do that.

Which meant she represented a threat to them.

He was only a convenient scapegoat—because they had no idea who he'd been before this life, or what he was capable of. Unfortunately, Joseph needed Russ's permission if he was going to show these people what he could *really* do.

It was the cleanest way to get this finished. But not the legal one.

The parking lot came into view. Sarah let out a whimper. "I can't believe they were destroying all my stuff."

"Everything on the overdose deaths was in the cloud, right?"

"Yes, but that was city property. And all my personal belongings." She huffed out a breath. "You wouldn't understand the responsibility I have to safeguard it. I wasn't even supposed to bring it with me."

Her words cut through him. As though he wasn't enough of a professional to understand needing to take care of a laptop, or the need to secure intellectual property belonging to the city? Apparently, she thought he was way too much of a blue-collar guy to know about that.

He couldn't help the hurt feelings. It didn't make him any less driven to keep her safe. She just didn't know the first thing about him, and he wondered how she'd react when she found out.

Joseph said, "When your boss hears what happened, I'm sure he'll understand. No one could have anticipated things would turn out like this."

He could hardly even believe it himself. Things had changed so fast.

He squeezed her hand. "Everything's going to be okay."

Washington's dog raced ahead to where Joseph spotted Emmalee in the parking lot. He saw the glint of something in her hand and felt his muscles tighten. But it wasn't a gun. The dog leaned forward and let out two barks at the woman. Apparently understanding in his dog way that she represented the threat.

Emmalee slashed out at the dog with a knife. He realized then that was what she had in her hand. Joseph hissed, but the dog only backed up, circled around, and barked at her again.

Defense, or a warning. Either way Joseph was glad for it.

The dog was coming with them.

Emmalee slashed at the tire of Sarah's car, and Joseph

realized it was the last one that still had air in it. The front wheel he could see was low to the ground, the tire flat. Given the angle of the roof, Emmalee wasn't quite done damaging the tires so they couldn't leave—but she'd rendered the vehicle useless.

He tugged on Sarah's hand and headed for his truck. By the time he got close enough he realized Emmalee had finished with her destruction. Sarah's car had been the last option for their escape. Unless they stole one of the retreat camp cars.

Emmalee blocked their way. She held that knife up and swiped at the dog, then yelled in their direction, "You aren't going anywhere!"

Sarah's steps faltered.

Joseph slowed his pace. He glanced behind them and saw Austin still coming. Now Taylor was with him, blood streaming down the side of her face.

The cuts she had made on his arms stung.

Brad and Karen hopped off the porch of Sarah's cabin and headed this way as well.

They were surrounded with no way to escape.

Sarah whimpered. "What are we going to do?"

"Get out of here." Just not on four wheels. They would have to make a run for it on foot to get to the highway. Find some way to call for help, or a rescue.

Emmalee swiped again at the dog. She must have caught him with the edge of her blade. The animal whimpered, backed off, and then ran for the trees behind the parking lot where the terrain rose steeply.

If they could get beyond that bridge, they could head for the highway on foot.

"Come on. The dog has the right idea." Joseph tugged on her hand and swung her so she went first.

The second Sarah raced for the trees on the hill,

Emmalee did the same thing. Joseph slammed into the young woman. She stumbled and he grabbed the knife from her with a shove of his off hand. He pointed the blade at her face for a second as she slowed, then he raced after Sarah.

At least one of these people knew what would happen if they gave chase.

10

———

S arah raced for the trees. She patted her pockets, searching for her phone. It wasn't in her back pocket. After calling 911 for the ambulance to help Washington, she lost her cell phone.

No way to call for help.

She heard a yell behind her but didn't look back. If it wasn't Joseph and he didn't need her help, then she wasn't going to look. Too much had happened that she'd seen with her own eyes.

She couldn't bear to see anything else. She was over-loaded with images. Fighting, scratching, and bleeding. Karen and Brad going through her things. Washington not breathing.

In a clinical way she could tell she was in shock, but that didn't exactly help her talk herself through it. Not when she was currently scrambling up a hillside following a dog that seemed to know where he was going. At least, she hoped he did.

Sarah's foot hit a loose bit of dirt and slid back. Her knee slammed into the ground, and she cried out.

Joseph was there right away to scoop her up. "Come on. You can do it. Just to the top of the hill."

She nodded, not wanting to waste a breath on responding. She gulped air and put all her energy into moving her legs as fast as she could.

It seemed like forever that they ran. Or just farther than she'd ever gone in her life while pushing that hard.

"Sarah."

She glanced over. Joseph had his hand out. It would be a reflex to reach for it like she had before. To clasp their hands together and walk that way.

Sarah deliberately slowed her pace and took his hand but made herself think it through first. Yes, she wanted to hold his hand. There was solidarity in it that she needed.

He said, "I think we've gone far enough for now if you want to stop and rest for a minute." Out the corner of her eye she could tell he was looking at her while he spoke.

Sarah didn't glance over. She did want to see whatever expression was on his face. "I feel like if I stop walking I won't be able to start again."

"Okay." He squeezed her hand and slowed. "The cabin where I was earlier is closer to us than the highway from here. If we make our way there, we'll be able to meet the cops. Hopefully they're there by now."

"You called the police?"

"That's where I left my phone," he said. "I called 911 and left it tucked in a hiding spot. If the officers can find it they'll have all the photos I took of the men in and around the cabin. Including the one talking about you."

Sarah frowned. "You didn't mention that part."

"I'm sorry. I didn't want to alarm you. But given everything that's happened since then you probably could use all the information here."

Given his tone, maybe she didn't want to know. "Does it

have to do with Brad and Karen being in my cabin trashing all my things?"

He shrugged. "When I was at the cabin, I overheard the one who seemed to be in charge talking on the phone about a woman, a medical examiner. He told whoever was on the other end of the line to get on with scaring you."

"Well, it worked." She had no idea if that was the intention of everything that'd happened at the camp. But what else could it be?

He kept that measured, steady pace to his stride. "We don't even know if whoever he was on the phone with is someone at the retreat camp."

Sarah drew comfort from his presence beside her. "I hope it is. Otherwise, we have even more people to contend with." Yes, she was putting some of the responsibility on him by saying "we." But given he was here with her, and still holding her hand, she figured she didn't need to face this alone. Whatever it was.

She shook her head. "Whoever these people are, they're probably the ones who made the substance that caused those overdoses."

He said, "When he was talking to one of the others, he mentioned test subjects."

"That makes sense." She ran over the case details in her mind. One of the deaths had occurred after the woman was sexually assaulted. But the others hadn't been touched in that way. They had all died similarly.

Up ahead of them, Washington's dog trundled up a path.

"He seems to be doing better."

Joseph glanced over. "That's what you want to talk about?"

"It's also a nice day for a walk." If there weren't crazy people stalking them.

She didn't see any close by now and hadn't for a while.

Maybe they were in the clear. But that didn't mean she managed to relax.

He squeezed her hand. "Yes, it is nice. Assuming we don't run into anyone else trying to kill us."

"I was out here once, a long time ago. Under not too dissimilar circumstances." She couldn't believe she'd said that out loud. But there it was, the fear below the surface that was a constant in her life. Reality inevitably broke through.

"Do you want to tell me about it?" he asked.

"In a way, yes. But also no." What else could she be at this point but honest?

The fact was she didn't know this man very well. They seemed to have been thrown together into a high stress situation, and he clearly had training. Given how he'd successfully disarmed and subdued two people. Actually, three since Emmalee had tried to kill him while Sarah raced up the hill.

She'd been absolutely no help whatsoever.

"I should get some fighting training. Something more than basic self-defense." She sighed. "Otherwise, I'm never going to be able to effectively defend myself."

She'd managed to fend off Austin in the pantry. Kind of. If it came down to an actual fight, how would she stay safe?

This whole situation was way over her head.

And then there was Joseph, who seemed to take it all in stride. He kept a cool head and knew exactly what to do.

"I can teach you, if you want?" There was a hopeful tone to his voice, as if he genuinely wanted to do that. Maybe even wanted nothing more.

"If we get out of this in one piece."

The idea of walking any farther made her want to lie down on the grass and start crying. Her thigh muscles burned, and her whole body flushed with the stress of exertion and sweat.

She pushed away all awareness of her own physical body

and thought about the trees. The sky, and the dog in front of them. Life found a way to survive, even when the odds were completely stacked against it.

"If I train you how to fend off an attacker, will you tell me what happened to you out here?"

She squeezed his hand this time. More a reflexive wince than a gesture. Sarah had to explain. "No one ever believed me."

She wasn't sure she could handle it if Joseph didn't believe her. She needed to be able to trust him, which also meant trusting how he would react. Given how everyone else in her life had disbelieved her, and how both of her parents changed their minds and behavior on a whim, she knew she needed someone steady in her life. The same way she needed the day in and day out of her job. The reliability of seeing her friends at work. Her routine.

"I can guarantee you," Joseph said, "that whatever you tell me, I will believe you."

Sarah wanted to hope in that. But it almost seemed too good to be true.

"Why on earth would I ever *not* believe you? You've never given me a reason to think you'd lie."

"Because I wouldn't." Sarah had never liked people who lied any more than she liked herself when she did it. But she also knew no one was perfect.

"Well, there you go."

As if that settled it. After decades of people not believing her, one guy came along and threw it all for a loop because he just automatically trusted her.

And there she was, still struggling to believe in him. Though, only about this.

Did she need some safe guy who knew nothing about fighting and would never get in a situation like this? That wouldn't have helped today. Maybe she'd met Joseph right at the exact moment she needed him. Never mind what she thought she was looking for. He would never be the kind of man who would fit into her life, but she couldn't help being intrigued by him even if he scared her as much as he interested her.

The dog slowed up ahead and sniffed the air.

Sarah and Joseph both stopped. She glanced over at him and frowned. "What do you think he smells? Are there bears or anything out here?"

"You don't need to worry about four-legged animals. It's the two-legged predators we need to be wary of."

"How reassuring." She grinned.

He squeezed her hand, and they set off again, catching up to the dog.

"Do you really think he knows where he's going?"

"He's headed in the direction of the cabin I found. Maybe he went there before with Washington. It could be they walked this path frequently, and he's learned where to go so it's automatic to take this path and go this way."

Sarah shook her head. "I've never had a dog. So I have no idea what they do."

"No?"

She shrugged. "How about you? Any pets as a kid?"

He seemed to struggle with what to say. "Since I know you'll always tell me the truth, I'd like to do the same with you. But that means, until I get the okay, there's a lot I can't tell you."

Sarah didn't know what that meant, but he seemed pretty earnest. "How about you tell me something you know you *can* say."

"I never had a pet. I have no siblings, and I didn't have a conventional childhood." He scanned the trees around them as they walked. "In fact, I'm not even sure how to live like a normal person."

Sarah chuckled. "Good, because neither do I."

He smiled in reply to her, then swiveled his head to look in front of them again. "That smells like fire." He picked up his pace, which forced her to do the same.

"I can smell it, too." The tang of smoke laced the air. She hoped in vain there wasn't a blaze anywhere near here. Getting stuck on the run in the middle of a wildfire wasn't anywhere she wanted to be.

"The cabin." Joseph groaned.

The dog kept going, walking close to the burning structure. Flames licked out the windows, and the roof looked like it was about to collapse.

"The fire department needs to put this out before it spreads to any of these trees." She didn't like the look of the flames or black smoke coming out the windows. In fact, the smell of it made her head pound.

Joseph said, "It looks like there's enough clearance between the house and the trees. It's unlikely the fire will jump, but there's always a possibility. Especially if a breeze kicks up."

"I don't think we need to get any closer. Whatever's in there is burning up and putting out gasses my head doesn't like."

"Let's see if the phone is still here since the cops aren't." Joseph let go of her hand for the first time in an hour. He jogged to a downed tree and looked around. "Someone must have taken it."

She looked at the cabin.

He continued, "They probably want to keep their operation quiet because they haven't perfected the formula. Since it's clear someone found this cabin, they needed to get rid of everything to cover their tracks."

She winced. "It has to slow them down if they need to

find somewhere new. And you called the police, so they had to have dealt with that."

He looked around. "They had to have intercepted it somehow."

She didn't want to think that these people had someone in their pocket at the dispatcher's office or within the police department.

"I'm wondering if they have other places already set up. For all we know this could be barely an inconvenience." He frowned. "Then again, considering they're breaking into your office and purposely trying to scare you, it might turn out that you're more of a problem than me."

She wasn't sure how she felt about that. Whoever put the mask in the closet had to have known about her past. This wasn't a spur of the moment thing, it seemed more planned. Maybe even sophisticated.

Someone didn't want her putting together the clues of who was behind those overdose deaths.

What was it Joseph had said? That they had test subjects. This wasn't so they could kill someone with their perfect formula, at least not yet. It was more like they needed to fix it. They had to make a better drug, unless the plan really was to end the lives of whoever took it.

The roar of ATV engines interrupted her train of thought.

Sarah spun around but didn't see them. "We need to start running again."

11

____

Joseph hadn't let his guard down yet, but the period of reprieve left his adrenaline lower than it had been. For good or ill, he and Sarah were both drained and running out of energy. If it came down to another chase, they wouldn't last long.

He gauged the distance of the ATVs. "We need to hide somewhere. It's better than making a run for it when they'll only catch up to us."

She spun around, fear plain on her face.

"Come on." He needed to at least keep them both moving considering who knew how many ATVs were headed this way.

Joseph figured it was the guys from the cabin he'd found. Though where they'd gotten the ATVs from, he didn't know. Maybe they kept them close by.

Or it was everyone from the retreat camp hot on their trail. They could've jumped on the machines and caught up easily enough.

Regardless, they had to get out of sight.

Washington's dog angled toward a tree and sniffed around it.

"Come on."

Instead of peeing, the dog put two paws high on the trunk and barked. Joseph didn't want to get distracted by nothing, but the tree was wider than his arms could stretch. Looking closer at it revealed footholds and handholds he never would've noticed if they ran by. "Hang on a second."

"Do we have time for this?"

He frowned. "I think it's a hunting blind."

The tree branches hid the center trunk about halfway up, which meant they'd be out of sight if they climbed. He got the feeling there was more to this tree than that.

"Thank You," he mumbled, not quite realizing he was praying.

As a kid religion had been drummed into him by rote. Observance was something he was forced into obedience to, though only because it was how life at boarding school operated. The idea of divine intervention in a person's real life was something Russ talked about—not anything Joseph had ever actually experienced. However, his recent experience at church left him at least hopeful, even if it seemed like not much had changed.

"Let's try and climb this." He held out a hand to her so she could go first. That way he could cover her, and she wouldn't be the one on the ground left to defend herself. "Can you see what's up there?"

Given her expression, she didn't like the idea. Sarah shot one look in the direction of the ATVs, still not in view. She did as he asked and clambered up the tree trunk using the same footholds and handholds he had seen. They both had to get out of sight before their pursuers showed up.

Ten or so feet up the tree, she disappeared. "Oh, you

should get up here. It's a whole platform. And there's a hatch in the floor."

Not wanting Washington's dog to give away their position, Joseph lifted the animal onto his shoulders and climbed up before the dog could squirm too much.

He'd been right, it was a hunting blind. Hopefully whoever was hunting *them* didn't know it was here.

Joseph pushed the dog onto the platform. "Lay down, dog."

The old animal groaned and slumped onto his belly.

"Good boy." He tried to sound a whole lot more appreciative than he was.

Sarah bent her knees and hugged them with her arms. She looked younger than she was, but he would never discount her capabilities. She would survive this—he was going to make sure of it.

Joseph hauled himself onto the platform and let out a breath. "Show me that hatch."

She pointed at the square in the wood at the center of the platform. Up here they were completely obscured from the ground by the thick branches. He'd seen a couple of other trees like this one while they'd traversed the woods but hadn't thought much past how thick they were. It was unusual in this part of the country, though not unheard of.

Joseph hauled it open. He kept his attention half on the sound of approaching ATVs. Maybe they would simply pass by and never spot him and Sarah hiding here with a dead man's dog. If Washington *was* dead.

He hauled the hatch up. "Huh."

Sarah peered over the edge of the opening. "Is that a ladder?"

"Looks like it goes below ground." But what on earth would be down there?

The air coming out was cooler, and there was no light

below. Neither of them had a flashlight. If they did go down, they would be feeling around in the pitch-black with no sight to guide them.

But in a pinch, it could do as a hiding place.

He reached over and ruffled the fur on the dog's head. "Good boy."

Washington had to have known about these hunting blinds. The area wasn't supposed to be used for hunting, since kids often made their way through this area during camps. Now that he knew what the retreat camp was hiding, he shuddered at the thought of innocent children being taken care of here. That was a terrifying thought.

"Are we going down there?"

He glanced at Sarah, not liking the pale look on her face. "If they get close and they're about to find us, we might have to."

She bit her lip.

Joseph wished she had told him at least something earlier. Whatever happened to her in these woods years ago might have to do with what was happening now. Surely if it related to tunnels and trees, she would've known this was here—or had an idea what it was. He doubted she was lying to him, but the truth was he didn't know for sure. She could be excellent at withholding information when she didn't want him to know she had knowledge of something.

Joseph was trying to protect her, which meant he needed her to be completely truthful with him. After all, both of their lives depended on it.

That was why it was better for him to take his emotions out of it and not even consider getting into a relationship with her.

She tested that resolve, with the look in her eyes and the way she relied on him. How she held his hand far longer than he'd intended to hold hers. Not that he complained about it. The whole thing reminded him far too much of Genevieve. Until he figured he needed to back off a little from Sarah. He'd do that as soon as he could.

Joseph had already lost someone who meant everything to him. The last thing he needed was to get in deep with a woman who needed protection and wind up destroyed all over again.

"I don't like the dark."

Joseph's heart squeezed. "If I had a flashlight, I would give it to you."

"I know." Her voice was almost a whisper.

Down below, the roar of those ATVs got louder. The dog shifted and lifted his head.

Joseph peered out between the branches and spotted at least three vehicles. "It's the guy from the cabin. They must be out here looking for me, or both of us."

Joseph didn't bother whispering. With the noise of those engines whoever was down there wouldn't be able to hear them. They also couldn't see Sarah and Joseph up here. So long as they didn't draw attention to themselves, they would be safe. He hoped.

At least it was better than running their energy levels into the ground being chased down by a stronger force that was faster moving, with weapons. Those weren't odds he was interested in.

She grasped his elbow but said nothing. Her touch seemed like it was just for the sake of holding on to him. So she could draw strength from his presence here with her. Joseph was glad he could do that.

Sarah didn't need to be alone in a situation like this. Even if he didn't like the fact his heart was in danger along with both of their lives.

She leaned over and whispered in his ear. "Should we go down there?"

Given her fear, he was surprised she suggested they venture into the dark. He figured he was the one who'd have to coax her into the tree if necessary.

Was there really a tunnel underneath them? It could just be a tiny room. Or a trap. They had no way of knowing without venturing down there and possibly putting themselves more in danger. Given there was a wooden ladder on the inside of the trunk it seemed as though someone had gone up and down this way before. He didn't like boxing them in any more than he already had by having her climb this tree and hiding up here.

He looked at the ATVs again and saw the guy who'd been on the phone drive beneath them. The one who seemed like he was in charge. He slowed his ATV. As Joseph watched he pulled a phone from his belt and held down the home button. "Copy that."

Some kind of walkie-talkie app, he'd guess. Was this guy in communication with Brad and all of his people?

If Joseph and Sarah hid below the tree, how would they know when it was safe to come out?

They wouldn't be climbing down inside the trunk. He didn't know what these people knew about this area.

"Just hang tight up here." He squeezed her hand. "Let's wait in the spot as long as we can, okay?"

She searched his gaze with hers, then nodded. She held on to his hand. The roar of engines increased, so that he didn't hear what she said. He only saw her mouth the words, "Thank you."

Joseph nodded. If anyone was going to be out here with her when her life was in danger, he was glad it was him. Even if she tested his heart's resolve to stay separate from her despite the attraction between them.

They waited in complete stillness while the ATVs passed by. Every nerve ending in his body tingled. He sat frozen, the way he had during those high-pressure sniper operations. He was supposed to be so cool under stress. With Sarah here as well, all that training was being put to the test in a way he'd never thought possible.

Those ATVs were passing by, and no one had stopped.

They were almost home free. Seconds from being safe out here, or at least remaining unseen. They'd be able to rest before they climbed down from this hunting blind and set off for safety again.

Within minutes, the sound of engines died down. He didn't want to let out a breath, but his lungs screamed for it. No way would he relax fully, though.

Joseph moved to the edge of the platform and looked down, as much as he could see between the branches. They would wait a few minutes longer before he trusted no one would see them descend the tree again.

As he turned back, a heavy shadow shifted out of the open hatch. Austin launched out and slammed into Sarah.

She screamed, and both of them sailed over the edge.

12

Wind rushed at Sarah's hair. Austin's hold on her was much too hard, and she pushed without effect. They fell long enough for everything and nothing to fly through her mind, coalescing into one thought.

Her back slammed into the ground, and Austin landed on top of her.

Joseph! She tried to scream his name, uncaring that anyone nearby would hear her. But no sound emerged from her mouth. She couldn't breathe.

With the noise of the ATVs, she hadn't heard anyone coming up through the tunnel. Wherever it originated, Austin had snuck through and emerged. She hadn't even realized he was there.

Sarah shoved and pushed at him. His weight was far too heavy, and she struggled to breathe.

Austin grabbed for her. "You found the camp tunnels." He sneered.

Her mind clicked the thoughts together like puzzle pieces. She was winded from hitting the ground. Everything hurt, but she had the will to try to stop him.

Austin grasped her neck with one hand. "No one gets away from us."

Sarah knew then that she would *always* have the will to fight. This wasn't her nightmare. It wasn't dark. It was daytime. She wasn't alone and so young. She was an adult, and she knew how to do this.

If she could just catch her breath.

Austin produced a knife. All she could do was blink at it as he swung down. She shoved at him with both hands and pushed it out of the way. The tip caught her arm, and fire burned her skin. She cried out.

All she could think of was Joseph and how he had already protected her so many times. She couldn't let all that effort be in vain. That thought wrapped itself in her will to live and see justice for those overdose victims.

He swung again, but the knife never came down. It fell to the ground, and an arm snaked around Austin's neck. She watched his eyes widen, then heard the sickening crack.

Austin fell to the side, tumbled to the ground with a thud, and lay there with his eyes open, staring at her.

Joseph stood over her, shadowing her from the sunset. It would have been a formidable sight if she hadn't just seen him kill a man.

He held out his hand and she clasped his wrist. Joseph helped her to her feet. "Take a breath."

She was trying.

"Push air out. Or try. Then suck in."

It took a second, but her lungs remembered how to breathe. Sparks pricked at the edges of her vision. Sarah managed to take a breath before she passed out, saving herself from that embarrassment. Instead, Joseph held her elbows and she took in long breaths, getting oxygen back in her brain.

As soon as she could speak, words tumbled from her mouth. "You killed him."

He let go of her, a shuttered expression on his face. "It's what I was trained to do. It's who I—"

He was about to say more. Sarah didn't need to hear any of it. All she needed was to show him how she felt. She slammed into him and wrapped her arms around him in a hug. "You saved my life."

His arms shifted and he held her awkwardly for a second.

"What are we going to do now?" She put him out of his misery and took a step back. "Should we keep moving?"

The last thing she wanted was to look at Austin, even though she'd seen hundreds of dead bodies at work. There was something so much more visceral about watching the exact moment of death that she'd never experienced right in front of her.

During the recent bombing, she had seen a couple of people lose their lives while she tried to treat their injuries. Sometimes there was simply nothing anyone could do to stop what was inevitable.

Austin had been a strong young man. Now he was dead.

She didn't want to contemplate how glad she was that Joseph had ended a life to save hers.

He squeezed her elbow. "Don't go just yet." She started to ask why when he turned away. He climbed up the tree and returned, awkwardly holding the dog with one arm. Washington's dog jumped down and landed on the ground, shaking his body from nose to tail.

"Oh. Good thinking," she said. They wouldn't have wanted to leave the dog in the hunting blind.

Joseph nodded. "I secured the tunnel door as well. No one will be able to get through it, but it won't hold forever."

Why was he so good at this? He had procured the skills from somewhere. She wanted to ask him about it but got the feeling he would want her to talk about her nightmare in response. Sharing stories was a good thing. They'd learn each other's histories doing that. But the idea she would have to speak her fears aloud wasn't something she could confront right now.

Joseph crouched by Austin's body and started to go through his pockets. She didn't want to look too closely but stood near and took in everything around them, not wanting to be caught unaware again as he relieved the dead man of a cell phone and wallet. He handed the phone to her and put the cash in his pocket. Keys, too—whatever they were for.

She checked the phone screen. "This needs his thumbprint."

Joseph retrieved the knife from where Austin had dropped it. In the young man's back pocket, he found a tiny baggie of drugs.

"You're keeping those, too?"

He shrugged. "We may need the evidence to hand over to the police."

She was starting to wonder if they would ever see help or get to safety.

"If we end up out here all night, will you wish you'd taken his jacket?"

Sarah processed his question. She realized she would want it if they were out here after dark, and the temperature dropped. "Probably."

Joseph stripped the jacket from Austin's body. She tied it around her waist, and Joseph used Austen's thumb to unlock the phone. He handed it back to her. "Okay, let's head out."

She was completely turned around, but Austin had GPS on his phone. She figured she'd check their location and which direction they should be heading. But first, she had an important phone call to make.

Sarah dialed Addie's number, grateful she'd made a point

to remember it so she could call from her office phone directly to Addie's cell. So many numbers were just in her contacts, and she had no idea what they even were.

She reigned in her thoughts as Addie answered the phone. "Please tell me this is Sarah, not a spam call."

"It's me."

"Oh, thank goodness. What on earth is going on up there at the camp?" Addie asked.

"Everyone's gone crazy. That's what's happening."

Joseph glanced at her, the edge of a smile on his face as they walked in whichever direction he thought they should go.

She continued, "We're trying to get to the highway, but we need someone to come and pick us up."

"Who is *we?*" Addie asked, in full FBI interrogation mode. "Who's with you?"

"Joseph." Sarah tried to figure out how to explain who he was. "The cook at the camp."

"How do you know you can trust him? When a patrol car showed up there, the owner told the officers everyone left after Washington Harper was taken away by that ambulance." Addie blew out a breath. "They were barred from the entrance like they were intruding, when all they wanted were answers as to why a man nearly died up there."

"So do I. He had the same abrasion on his arm as the overdoses I've been looking into."

Addie said, "I thought you were on vacation."

"Yeah, so did I." Sarah pushed out a breath. "Now I'm lost in the woods with a man I hardly know and everyone except him seems to be trying to kill me."

Addie was silent for second. "I'm tracking your phone. Whose phone is this, anyway?"

"One of those camp people. Austin Deverly. He had a knife, and Joseph snapped his neck which was pretty much the most amazing thing I've ever seen." Not that it had sounded nice at the time. Thinking about that cracking noise made her nauseous.

"Tell me who this Joseph guy is."

Sarah glanced over at him then. "Do you know who Addie Franklin is?"

He held out his hand. "Can I have that for a second?" When she gave him the phone, he put it to his ear. "Special Agent Franklin?" He paused. "Yeah, Russ. And the Accountant's Office." He paused again. "Then ask Edith."

He handed the phone back to her.

The *Accountant's Office*? Sarah had no idea what that was. Why not name the company, if he worked for them? Joseph didn't seem like a cooped-up numbers guy. But then with everything that had happened lately she wondered if she knew anything at all.

She'd gone from being on vacation and volunteering, to this.

"Okay, I have your location," Addie said. "You're about a mile southwest of the highway. I'll meet you there, but you're going to have to hang out on the shoulder for about thirty minutes."

Sarah didn't like the idea of waiting. "We can walk down the highway toward the nearest exit. I'll call when you should be getting close."

"Okay. How much battery do you have on that phone?" Addie sounded like she was shifting around.

Sarah looked at the screen. "It's almost full, so we're good as long as I don't lose signal anywhere."

"Okay, I'm getting in my car." A door slammed. "Keep in touch."

"You, too." Sarah let out an exhale that felt like the first real relief since Washington keeled over in front of her.

"She's coming?" Joseph asked.

Sarah explained the plan. "Now we just have to stay safe until she makes it here." Her own statement caused her to shudder. She looked around and saw the dog keeping pace with them.

"You okay?"

Sarah shrugged.

"I'm sorry I had to kill that guy in front of you."

"I'm not," she said.

"Well, then."

She didn't know how she was supposed to respond to that. "I'm just glad it seems like we're close to the end of whatever this is."

Even if she didn't want to invite trouble by saying that aloud, it did need to be said. She wanted to have hope, but things in her life hadn't ever gone that way.

Now Joseph was here it was different. He represented something she'd never had before. She wouldn't have ever expected this, or described him as what she wanted, he still seemed to fit so easily with her. In a way that made her want to lean on him, draw from his strength and the cool way he handled himself.

"We'll probably be at the police precinct for hours explaining what happened." Joseph shook his head. "I hardly even know all the ins and outs of it myself."

"I know what you mean." She blew out a breath. "Hopefully they'll give us food and water."

"Or coffee. And hopefully the biggest sandwich I've ever seen."

Sarah grinned. "Any food in the world, and you ask for a giant sandwich?"

He shrugged. "I don't really eat out. I'd rather prepare what I eat myself, and I'm not bragging or anything, but I'm pretty good at awesome sandwiches."

"I'm afraid, as a doctor, I'll have to judge that for myself."

He chuckled. "We can have a sandwich making competition. The judges would have to be impartial."

"You think I'm going to make a sandwich as well?" She tried to sound affronted. "I thought that was your job."

Relief washed over his face along with the humor. Joseph swung his arm around her shoulders and hugged her to his side as they walked. As he let go, he said, "I really hope this is the end of all the terror. But I won't relax until we're sitting in front of the cops making a statement."

She nodded, letting out another long exhale. "What are we going to do about that dog?"

"If Washington didn't survive, I guess I'll take him to the shelter. Or someone we know can adopt him."

"Addie said he nearly died." Sarah paused. "So maybe he's alive? Maybe my boss will realize me taking vacations is a bad idea and let me come back to work."

He chuckled. "I don't want to know what Russ dreams up for me to finish out my probation."

"At your job. With the Accountant's Office?" She tried to nudge him into explaining.

"You know Russ Franklin, the police commissioner?" When she nodded, he continued, "It doesn't relate to his job, but he gets to tell me what I should do next. And when I talk to him, I'll ask him what I'm allowed to tell you."

"I would like to know more about you." Sarah realized they'd reached the highway while she was distracted with conversation. And him.

The sight of cars streaming past in both directions made her want to jump out onto the shoulder and wave her arms. Try to catch a ride from someone just so she could get out of here as quickly as possible.

She turned to Joseph with a grin. "We actually made—" Then she whipped back around.

Up the highway, in the direction Addie would be coming, four ATVs raced out of the trees onto the shoulder.

The riders lifted guns and headed right for them.

13

Joseph's heart sank as the four occupied ATVs headed for them. So close to being home free. Traffic on both sides of the highway was sparse, with a concrete median between.

A gunshot cracked off. His body jerked, and fire burned across the outside of his arm.

"Go. Run." He dragged Sarah across the two lanes and headed east, to the middle. He glanced back. "Dog!"

She clambered over the concrete. He did the same and tugged her down, so they crouched out of sight. The dog hopped the median, and Joseph grabbed his collar. The concrete, barely two feet tall, was the only barrier between them and traffic streaming past at seventy miles an hour on the ATV side.

He wanted to tell her to crawl, but under them was gravel and broken glass blown out of the traffic lane.

"Keep going but stay low."

He might have heard her whimper, but the sound was swallowed up by a pickup truck passing. The horn blared long and loud.

She started to move, still in her crouch. Wet blood on her forearm.

Their heads were exposed above the center median, but that would have to be satisfactory for now. They would be too exposed if they ran across the westbound lanes. On the far side was a steep hill they would have to climb. The entire time targets would be on their backs.

He ignored the blinding pain on the outside of his arm, kept his wrist tucked against his body, and stuck two fingers in his belt so he didn't have to hold up the weight of his arm. It was better, but not by much.

A semitruck on the eastbound side slammed on his brakes. The tires juddered against the asphalt, and the smell of burning rubber filled the air. Wherever the ATVs were, they didn't have much time to get away.

The last thing he wanted was for an innocent bystander to be caught in the middle.

More gunshots rang out, but they didn't land around him and he didn't get hit again. Joseph turned long enough to see what was going on over the median.

One of the guys from the ATV had his gun up, pointed at the cab of the semitruck. The vehicle had stopped across the eastbound lanes, completely blocking traffic. Smoke poured from the engine.

The ATV driver hopped off, climbed up, and pulled open the door to the semi.

He was blasted back by a shot and fell to the asphalt.

The driver jumped out, holding a shotgun.

One of the ATVs headed for Joseph and Sarah on the wrong side of the median they'd hopped over. The semitruck driver took a shot at him and hit the ATV. It crashed into the concrete.

Joseph needed to get her out of here. He glanced over his

other shoulder and kept his head down. She did the same in front of him.

A silver Mercedes headed towards them. Jacob jumped up and flagged it down. The driver was a blonde woman, and it looked like she had kids in the car. He waved her on. Next up was a gray van. He had no idea if there were occupants in the back, and he had to take the chance everything would be fine. That innocence would somehow be protected.

That he wouldn't get shot.

He figured if God really was interested in people's lives then Joseph could use His help right now.

The van braked fast and squealed to a halt in front of him.

"Sarah!" He yelled to her first, then went to the driver's door. He slammed his hand on the window to get the driver's attention. She looked at him wide eyed.

The dog barked.

"This woman needs to get out of here." Joseph pointed at Sarah. "Can you help her?"

The woman's foot must have slipped off the pedal because the car started to move. He slammed on the window again. "She needs your help."

Sarah ran around to the passenger side, where the seat was unoccupied. She leaned down and said, "Please, we need to go to the police."

Keeping her head out of sight was a good idea, but he didn't know if she tried the door handle.

"Please let her in."

The woman pressed the button under her window and the locks disengaged. Sarah climbed in. "Joseph, let's go."

He opened the back door and the dog climbed in. Joseph shut the door without getting in.

He tapped on the window to get the driver's attention. "Go."

She hit the gas. Sarah squealed and he heard the door shut as they sped away. A gunshot pinged off the back quarter panel.

Joseph hissed and ducked.

Whatever she thought—whatever she was currently saying about him—didn't matter. He needed to resolve this situation before anyone else got hurt.

Gunfire was still going off behind him. Horns honked, and tires squealed. Thankfully it didn't seem like anyone except the ATV guys had been hurt so far. That wasn't likely to last very long if this continued.

He had to end it.

Joseph moved to the median and crouched to look at what was happening. As he watched, the semitruck driver ratcheted his shotgun again. Joseph winced, but the truth was this guy's intervention had probably saved his life.

Still, the collateral damage from the retreat camp and their escape was going to be bigger than he'd planned for. He had killed Austin, which also ended everything Russ tried to achieve by helping him.

Joseph had done the exact opposite of everything Russ asked. That meant he would be kicked out of the Accountant's Office program and left to fend for himself in the world. He wasn't going to begrudge them the consequences. After all, he was the one who'd broken the rules.

Spending time with Sarah, even running through the woods and facing danger, had been like a dream. However, like anything else good in his life, it wasn't going to last.

In fact, when he put her in that van and sent her to safety it hadn't occurred to him that it might be the last time he ever saw her.

That might be for the best considering what happened to the people he cared about. Especially if he fixed this whole situation before he left town. Sure, he would have to disappear from Benson at some point. But he was going to end the drug operation and murder business first.

Joseph jumped the median. He ran at an ATV speeding toward the semitruck driver. Praying he didn't get shot by whatever the semitruck driver had in that shotgun, he jumped and tackled the ATV rider.

The guy slammed to the ground and Joseph punched him to unconsciousness. He grabbed the guy's gun and held up his free hand toward the semitruck driver. Palm out. The last thing he needed was for this guy to think Joseph was a threat.

That left one more ATV, currently on the westbound lane. The driver had to have gone down to the next exit and come back on the highway on the other side. All to try and get to Sarah and Joseph.

He sprinted to the median, hopped over, waited until the guy closed in, and then shot at the front end. The ATV exploded, flipped over, and the guy flew through the air.

A car swerved around the ATV and narrowly missed crashing into a tree.

The driver got the car under control and headed off up the highway. Someone else honked their horn. Joseph didn't know where the sound came from, and he couldn't worry about random people driving by.

He turned to find the semitruck driver maneuvering his vehicle back into a lane. As he drove away, he bumped over one of the men he had shot.

Joseph turned away. Even with all the violence in his life, the sight of a person with so little disregard for another life still bothered him.

Two pickup trucks headed up the highway side by side, coming toward him. As he became aware of them, men leaned out the passenger side on both trucks and lifted weapons. There was nowhere for Joseph to go.

He turned and started to run anyway.

A gunshot cracked the asphalt in front of him. Joseph changed directions, but the movement caused pain to lance through his arm. Another shot hit the highway on his other side.

He stopped and held out both hands. They would probably just shoot him right here. At least he figured as much until they stopped their vehicles. The driver leaned out. "Don't move."

The two men with the guns sprinted to him and dragged Joseph over the median, to their trucks.

Sirens wailed in the distance.

"Move it." One of the men yanked on his injured arm.

Joseph bit back the cry he wanted to let out and went with them because he had no other choice. Life was always better than death, even when life wasn't worth living. That was what he'd been taught, along with the philosophy that death meant oblivion—and nothing more, just ceasing to exist.

He would rather have believed he was sending people to judgment, or their eternal rest. That might have given him more comfort over what he had to do.

So much of his life had been lived where he had zero choice in where he went, or what he did. Joining the Accountant's Office meant the chance to make a life for himself. In the end, it just turned out to be more rules. Ones that were supposed to make him an honorable person.

Considering he had killed Austin, Joseph figured it hadn't worked. The skills were ingrained in him.

But as long as Sarah stayed alive and safe to finish her work, what did it matter what happened to him?

They shoved him in the back of the pickup, and men got in on either side. The doors were barely shut before the driver hit the gas and sped away from the scene.

Joseph kept his attention straight ahead. "Does someone want to tell me where we're going?"

"Shut up." The man in the front passenger seat lifted his chin to the guy beside Joseph.

As if he wouldn't know what that meant. Even before the guy's elbow lifted and came at his face, Joseph forced himself not to brace or attack the guy in response.

He could kill both men beside him before the guy in the front passenger seat got his gun up and shot Joseph just for that. But he wouldn't be able to take down this entire drug operation if he got himself killed before they arrived wherever they were going.

Joseph put his throbbing face between his knees and breathed out as though fighting to keep a hold of himself. Like he'd never been in a situation like this.

Everyone stayed quiet while the pickup truck followed the other vehicle. They pulled off a couple of miles along the highway toward Benson, but nowhere near it. The exit had no rest stops or signs.

A few weeks back, Joseph had gone undercover at a camp of guys who didn't want to live under government rules or pay taxes. Since their leader had set off a couple of bombs and killed people a lot of the residents had split from that group. He wondered if any of them now worked with the drug operation here.

If they were, they'd probably recognize him as having been at the camp. He would have to navigate that if it happened. Until then, he should probably worry about what they planned to do with him. Assuming there was another option than finding an isolated place and shooting him in the head.

He still had Austin's knife, and none of them had checked him for weapons.

They drove up a lane off the highway for nearly thirty

minutes. The ranch house they arrived at had boarded up windows and no animals in sight.

Pretty good place to hide a dead body long enough no one would find it easily.

The driver parked with the front end of the truck almost touching the dilapidated porch. He pushed out his door and turned back long enough to say, "Put him in the basement."

He took the keys with him, or Joseph would have climbed in the front and stolen their vehicle. After he fought the guys still in the truck.

One of the men beside him got out and held his gun on Joseph. The other opened his door and grabbed Joseph's elbow. "Let's go."

The second Joseph's feet hit the ground, a gun slammed into his shoulder.

His knees gave out and he fell to the dirt.

14

"Where is he?" Sarah lowered the cup of coffee with a shaky hand, unable to drink much without her stomach flipping over.

She'd been back at the police precinct, tucked in the FBI office for an hour or two. After the woman in the van let Sarah use her phone, she'd been able to get Addie to meet her on the way. Thankfully, the van driver had been headed to pick up her kids but hadn't done it yet. Sarah was so grateful the woman had no kids in her car during the highway scene that she wanted to curl up and cry just out of thankfulness.

Addie walked over with the tablet. She turned the screen so Sarah could see it. "Is this him?"

The picture wasn't a recent one of Joseph.

Sarah frowned. "Yeah, that's him. He was working as a cook at the camp, but I met him during the bombing a few weeks ago. The guy who got a concussion and was talking with a British accent."

Russ, currently the interim police commissioner, frowned. "You heard him do that?"

Sarah shrugged. "What does it matter?"

Joseph was missing and they needed to find him. That was what counted here, not whatever his mind had done when it was injured.

"Please tell me you have some idea where he might be." She respected the police department and their need to understand the ins and outs of everything that'd happened, but on this side of the desk, it seemed a whole lot like they were moving far too slowly.

Addie leaned against one of the other desks and sat on the edge. She hugged the tablet to her front. "The police officers who got to the scene after I would have, if I hadn't detoured to pick you up, reported no one there except a couple of dead guys who it looked like had been driving ATVs on the highway."

"That's because they were," Sarah said. "And they had guns, right? Ones they were using to kill Joseph and I…or trying to."

"And you didn't see what happened to him?" Russ shifted and grabbed his coffee mug.

She wanted them to be moving much faster than this. "I looked out the back window. I saw him jump the median again but not what happened after. If he wasn't there when the cops showed up, then they must have taken him."

And she was the one who had Austin's phone on her. That meant there was no way for them to track Joseph's location.

"So there were more guys there than just the ones who were killed on the highway?" Russ said. "Because there were reports from a couple of witnesses that a semi driver was shooting people with a shotgun. But we don't know if it was related."

"I saw a semitruck stop, and the driver had a shotgun."

Addie said, "The semi wasn't there when the police showed up either."

Sarah squeezed the bridge of her nose. Where was Joseph?

"Since you've ID'd him," Russ began, "I can tell you some things. Firstly, that man? He knows how to take care of himself."

Addie nodded. "He's helped the FBI on an investigation before."

It was on the tip of Sarah's tongue to ask them who he was. But why would she need to know? She'd spent enough time with Joseph to get a glimpse of the kind of man he was. What else did she need to hear that he couldn't tell her himself?

Sarah shifted and the shallow knife wound that had been dressed sent an ache through her arm. "And now you're going to sit around instead of going to look for him? Because he knows how to take care of himself?"

Addie laid her hand on Sarah's arm. "We're as worried as you are about him."

Sarah wasn't so sure about that. They seemed kind of calm. She could only think about the odds of him surviving against armed men who had already killed several people.

Before she could argue her point, Addie continued, "I need to know if you recognized any of the men on those ATVs."

Sarah shook her head. "Joseph got a better look at them. He even got pictures on a phone that he used to call 911 when he wanted the police to come to the cabin. But when we got there, it was on fire and the phone was gone."

Addie made a bunch of notes on the tablet while Russ did the same on his phone. Sarah figured they'd follow up about the emergency call. Yet another thing they would be doing instead of getting out on the streets and finding Joseph.

Addie glanced at Russ. "If we can get that phone, then we have evidentiary proof of who they are."

"We also need to find that cabin," he said. "Could be something useful there. I'll have to check with the dispatch chief and get all the information. Try and get a location."

Sarah frowned. "Was Joseph working some kind of undercover mission?"

Russ frowned. "What makes you say that?"

"Why don't you find him, then I'll answer your question?" Sarah shifted on the seat. She'd lost her appetite for coffee, even though Joseph had specifically mentioned it. She would rather get coffee with him once he was found.

Assuming he was still alive.

"They probably want him dead." She closed her eyes for a second. "The same way they wanted me. As soon as Joseph showed up after Washington keeled over, one of them accused him of the murder. They'll probably try to make it look like he did it. Maybe they'll pin all of the deaths on him."

Addie's expression didn't change. "You think there's a connection between the deaths you've been investigating, and what happened today with the camp?"

"Why would there not be a connection? There's no way those drug manufacturers could be operating on camp land and no one who works there knew about it. Not given the way they all suddenly turned on us." She wanted to shiver just thinking about it. "But there's no way Joseph had anything to do with it. He's the one who killed Austin when Austin was trying to kill me."

Russ glanced up from his phone. "Joseph killed someone?"

"He saved my life. So when you hear that all the evidence

points to him as being behind this, which I'm pretty convinced they're going to try and do, you need to give him the benefit of the doubt. Don't take things at face value. Dig for the truth and look at the reason behind what Joseph does."

The door to the FBI office opened, and Edith rushed in wearing a visitor badge. "Where is he?"

Sarah didn't know much about the eighty-something-year-old woman, except that her grandson was a police officer. That and the fact the rest of the Hummet extended family had either been arrested or killed recently. Edith and Eric were the only good ones.

She remembered then that Joseph had mentioned Edith while he was on the phone with Addie.

The older woman didn't seem at all relaxed that Joseph could "take care of himself."

Sarah said, "If Edith is worried about him as well, then I'm thinking we should probably go look for him instead of sitting around here."

Edith glanced at her. "Huh."

Sarah frowned. "What is that supposed to mean?"

"Don't worry, dear." Edith glanced at Russ. "Give me everything you have on these people, and I'll find Joseph for you."

The police commissioner shook his head. "I'm not giving you official files. You're a civilian."

"You know I'm a lot more than that."

"We all do." Addie folded her arms. "The FBI more than anyone."

Edith glanced around, a smile widening her lips. "Where is Stella today?"

"She has a court hearing in Seattle all week." Addie shook her head. "That isn't the point." Before she could say more, the desk phone rang.

Addie picked it up. "Special Agent Franklin." She listened for a second. "Thank you, yes I will be there." She replaced the handset. "Sarah, if you would come with me. Washington Harper is awake, and we can ask him what he knows about these people."

Edith said, "So you have nothing."

Addie shot her a look.

"I could get Washington to talk."

Russ said to Edith, "You're the reason Joseph got in this mess in the first place."

Sarah had no idea what they were even talking about. She stood up. "Let's go."

If they could get information from Washington, then he might be able to tell them where Joseph had been taken. If he'd even been kidnapped earlier, which she still didn't know for sure. She had no idea where he was, or if he was alive—whether he was in danger or free. It all tore her up. She didn't want to do anything else or go anywhere else unless she could find the answers to her questions.

It was an all-consuming need to find out the truth.

Addie had Sarah return her visitors badge, and they headed for Addie's car. The quicker they got there, the quicker they could talk to Washington.

"Do you really think these people are going to blame everything on Joseph?" Addie glanced over as she drove.

"I think they'll want to, but it's a question of how organized they are as to whether they manage to plant evidence. But I wouldn't be surprised if what was used to try and kill Washington isn't in Joseph's cabin whenever you get there to look around."

"I am going to find him."

Sarah said, "I just pray he's still alive when you do."

Addie said nothing else until they arrived at the hospital. They made their way to the room where Washington had been admitted. Sarah hung back, because Washington might know who she was from the one occasion they'd met—when he was dying. Also Addie was the FBI agent trained to interrogate someone. Or interview victims.

The older man looked considerably frailer than the last time she had seen him, which wasn't surprising since he'd recently fought for his life. He had probably used up all the strength it seemed was gone now doing that.

Addie stood beside his bed. Sarah remained over by the door, keeping out of the way while Addie asked questions about working at the camp.

After a few minutes of answering, he shook his head. "If you're gearing up to ask who did this to me, you can forget it. I don't want anything to do with a police investigation."

"People are dead, Mr. Harper. I think you have information that will tell me who these people are. After all, they seem to think it was necessary to try and murder you. Why is that?"

"How am I supposed to know?" He gave Addie a belligerent look.

Addie pressed. "No idea why they tried to kill you?"

He started to deny it.

Sarah let out a breath. "What about the cabin in the woods? They set fire to it, but Joseph said it was being used as a drug lab. You check out the land regularly, you didn't know that was happening?"

"If I tell you anything about that and go on record as a witness, they'll kill me."

"We can make it all confidential," Addie said. "And we can put you under protection."

"As if that ever works." Washington shook his head. "They nearly killed me once. If they find out I talked, they'll do worse next time."

Sarah tried to think what he might care about that could

sway his mind. She could only come up with one thing. "What about your dog?"

She had asked the driver to hold on to the animal or call Sarah if she didn't want to.

"What about Charlie?" Washington frowned. "Where is he?"

"He came with Joseph and I through the woods." Technically, the dog had given them a hiding spot that might've saved their lives. Hers, anyway. "If you want to know where your dog is now, then maybe you should give this FBI agent the information she needs so I can find my friend."

Addie glanced over. Sarah wasn't quite sure what that expression meant. She was interested in finding Joseph and not much else.

"Doesn't matter." Washington made a face. "Wherever he is, your friend will be dead by now."

15

The two men dragged Joseph from the trough of ice-cold water by his head.

He coughed and sputtered, even though he'd tried not to breathe when he was submerged with his chest pushed against the edge of the metal. No way out. No way to get free.

"I'll ask you again."

It took Joseph a second to focus on the voice. To find the man's face in the dark of the basement where the floor was mud against his bare knees and the rest of his body shivered against the chill. They had stripped him down to his underwear, as if that was some kind of indignity. After commenting about his lack of tattoos in this day and age, but the number of scars he had, they'd begun their interrogation.

At least, he figured that was what they intended it to be.

He focused his attention on the guy in charge—the man from the cabin who had seemed to be the leader back then.

"So ask me a question." His voice sounded like someone else's, low and graveled.

The guy gritted his teeth. One of the men holding on to Joseph's arms—not caring that he had a gunshot wound on the left side—squeezed harder and pulled on his shoulder joint.

Joseph bit down on his molars. He would likely need a dentist after this, but if that was the worst that happened, he could deal with it.

"Who sent you to the retreat camp? Why were you there?"

Joseph said, "I'm the cook." It was on the tip of his tongue to tack on, *That's it.*

However, the minute he said that they would disagree. He couldn't give them even one single thing to argue with in order to find a lie in anything he said.

He was the cook. Whatever else he happened to be wasn't up for discussion.

"Why were you sent there?"

"To cook."

"And all the snooping in the woods?"

Joseph said, "Exercise."

"You know we found your phone. All the pictures you took." Even though they'd been over this already.

The phone he'd left at the cabin currently lay at the bottom of the trough, where he could see it if he kept his eyes open while they were attempting to drown him.

The guy continued, "Cops aren't going to save you, so you can forget about getting rescued. They don't even know where to look."

He wondered if they had a man inside the police department, or a related office. Somewhere they could control the flow of intel. After all, things had gone unnoticed for this long. Now someone had slipped up and drawn attention to them, lives were in danger. Things had gotten serious. Everyone in the operation seemed to be freaked out over the idea that the police were investigating them.

Sarah was on their radar. They didn't know who else at the PD had them on radar.

The man motioned to the water.

Joseph's body was forced forward and his head shoved underwater. He held his breath, fighting a little so they would believe they were making him panic. Causing him to choke a little and sink under the fear as well as the surface of the ice-cold liquid.

After a few seconds he started to slow the jerky movements. As though he was giving up the fight. He had to make it look good, but also make them think they were in danger of killing him.

That caused them to drag him back out again. Water flew back with his hair as he was returned to his knees and Joseph coughed out the mouthful of water.

"You're a real tough guy, aren't you?" The guy scoffed. "You expect us to think you're just a cook and nothing else? Maybe, if I'd never done this to anyone else, I might believe it."

How was Joseph supposed to know the average time anyone this guy had tortured lasted? He was playing a guessing game at best. Maybe they would give up—but likely not before he was supposed to die or break.

"Who sent you to the camp?"

"You want to know who told me to go there?" Joseph spoke through gritted teeth.

He couldn't tell them it was Russ because the guy was currently the interim police commissioner. That would cause these guys to believe he was an undercover cop. A second after they heard that, he would be dead on the floor.

Joseph decided to go with the juvenile answer. "Your mom."

His head was shoved back in the water.

Thoughts about Russ remained. He wondered if Russ had actually sent him to the camp on purpose. Now there was an idea. Maybe he *was* a kind of unofficial undercover agent.

Russ hadn't mentioned anything about there being something going on at the camp. *Huh.*

Apparently, Joseph needed a little cognitive recalibration in order to have a creative thought. And go half an hour without thinking about Sarah.

The thinking about not thinking about her only made him think about her. Okay, maybe he wasn't doing so well. He wasn't sure that thought had made sense. Maybe he was about to pass out.

Only the cold remained as he descended into dreams and memories. He didn't know which it was, or how they intersected.

He strode down a street in Paris, his collar turned up against the January breeze. An unusually chilly day. But no snow, not here.

He passed a café with no patrons at the tables outside.

A bell jingled and a woman who smelled of lilacs strode out, holding a paper cup of coffee.

He was so taken with her that he stood still as she slammed into him.

"Oh, *excusez-moi.*" She smiled politely. Then her blue gaze tracked over his face. "I didn't see you there, *monsieur.* I am sorry."

He shook his head. "I'm just glad you didn't spill your coffee."

"I should not be in such a hurry." The delightful lilt to her French made him think of fields of wildflowers he'd seen once in a picture. Given where he'd just come from, that image shouldn't have been so easily recalled. There was something about her that brought lightness and peace.

And made him want to stay.

"Join me for dinner tonight." He named a tiny corner restaurant a few streets over that he had walked past yesterday. "You can tell me about your business."

He had absolutely no idea what he would share with her in return. In eighteen hours he would leave the city and never return.

This might be his one chance to get to know her.

To share her light for a little while before he went back to the darkness.

"If you are going to take me to dinner"—she lifted her chin and studied him, a mischievous expression on her face —"then you should tell me what your name is."

He held out his hand. "I'm Casper."

She took his hand, lifting the coffee cup with the other until it was close to her mouth. "Genevieve." She smiled behind the lid of the cup.

The world swam around him.

He'd since walked away from that name and left that life behind. Now all he had was darkness because that light was gone.

Fire burned across his skin. Joseph's spine contorted. All his muscles seized, and his hands and feet cramped. Heat washed over him, and with it the scent of the ocean. Salt mixed with Genevieve's lilacs.

He shifted on the bed as he awoke, feeling the cool sheets. He pushed them back and got up. The sunrise cast an orange glow across the floor, and the breeze of the morning billowed the curtains back from the balcony.

He knew she was out there. And she knew how he felt about her being exposed like that.

She reentered the room as he approached the curtains, an indulgent smile on her face. "I had to see the sunrise. That family was out there again, walking together in the morning light. The little boy went in the water all the way up to his knees."

He kissed her smile. Reached down and traced his palm over the swell of her belly, the place where his child rested for now.

He looked down at the gold band on his left hand. She put her palm over his, the simple band he had slid on her finger there for anyone to see.

Casper leaned down in the dream and kissed her ring. Then he kissed the baby. Then he kissed her.

He forced his mind from the memories…all the way back to reality.

Joseph blinked, alone in his underwear on that basement floor. His arm burned, the rest of him numb from the cold.

In his head he could still see those images. Even if he didn't want to think about what had happened when he returned from the market with dinner. The way the wine had trickled across the floor to mix with her blood.

"Then you find Washington, and you kill him." The voice was muffled beyond the door. "And if you get that ME as well, I'll pay you double."

Sarah.

Meeting her had been so different than the day he first saw Genevieve. Not just because he'd had a concussion at the time.

His wife had been pure light. Now that light was gone, along with the son she had been carrying. The future he'd thought he would get to live was as dead as his family.

In the here and now, he was Joseph. Sarah needed protecting because it was the right thing to do and not because of his developing feelings. After all, it wasn't the same as how he'd been with Genevieve. He didn't even know what to do with the quiet way his heart seemed to have opened to Sarah now. They'd been on the run, with no time for him to figure out what was happening.

Joseph wasn't the kind of man who would let an innocent woman die. No matter his history, or how he felt about her, it was simply the right thing to do.

The door opened.

He lay still on the muddy floor, eyes halfway open.

What sounded like a single person entered. That was good. A man, given the sound of his gait.

The guy bent and reached down, probably to haul Joseph off the floor. When the guy got close enough, he sprang into action.

The sudden movement shot pain through his freezing joints and the numb muscles that barely responded to him, but all he needed were a finger and thumb. He squeezed the pressure point on the man's neck, waited long enough, and let the guy fall to the side.

Joseph stripped the man of his clothes. He had no weapons, which was smart—sending the guy in like that. Otherwise, Joseph would be in possession of a weapon at this point.

The clothes didn't fit great, but he was hardly going to complain. He left the guy in the state they had left him and headed for the door.

The hallway was dark and quiet.

He crept to the end and up the stairs. Two men waited in the kitchen of the ranch house—probably the one they had driven up to earlier. They'd knocked him out before they dragged him downstairs. He felt every single one of those blows in his aching muscles, and figured they'd even cracked a rib with a steel toe boot.

His breathing sounded like a rattle, but he took out the

first man before he got a knife from the table and used it on the second. One had a phone, which clattered to the floor and the screen shattered.

Joseph called 911 and walked away from the house.

16

———

The police officer stood waiting while she unlocked her front door. Sarah moved to the alarm pad and typed in her code. "Nothing was disturbed, and the alarm was still set. Thank you for escorting me home."

Officer Eric Hummet, Edith's grandson, nodded. "I'll be around. Don't hesitate to call if you see or hear anything you don't like."

She nodded. "Thanks again."

Exhaustion weighed heavy on her, along with the need to know where Joseph was right now. Washington had given Addie a lead regarding a shipping company the retreat camp used to order bulk goods.

The FBI figured he was moving drugs in and out, and laundering money. All wrapped up in their activities. But it would take time for that to lead Addie to wherever Joseph was.

Sarah trailed through her house to her bedroom, where she showered and changed. By the time she dressed, her stomach was growling.

She made tea with a hefty dose of milk and sugar, which

she drank while she made herself eggs and toast. She thought about a sandwich, but after what Joseph had said couldn't bring herself to put one together.

She ate standing up in her kitchen and managed to get four bites in before her phone rang.

The police department had retrieved her things, including her cell phone, from the camp. They hadn't recovered her laptop, just her clothes and toiletries. She would rather have lost her phone in the mix.

Especially considering it was her father's number on the screen.

As soon as she answered, she put it on speakerphone. Leaving the phone on the kitchen table while she took another bite.

"What's going on? You haven't been answering my calls all day."

Sarah winced. "Things have been really busy. I landed in some hot water with a case, and things were intense. I lost my phone for a while."

"And when you got it back you didn't call me immediately?"

"Like I said"—Sarah took another bite—"it's been a long day."

"Well, your mother is driving me bananas. She's decided she wants another living room off the side of the house, one with French doors out to another patio."

The woman he called Sarah's mother was in fact the stepmother she'd met when she was fourteen. Nice enough, but Misty had a tendency to try too hard in her attempts to win Sarah to her side on every single argument between Misty and Sarah's father. As if she was the deciding vote about every part of their lives. In between fights, Misty acted like Sarah didn't exist.

"Sounds nice."

Her dad made a choking sound. "I'll show you the estimate. Then you'll see how nice it will be for the builder who's going to make a pretty penny off all this. Money I worked hard for."

Sarah closed her eyes. This was normal life.

Usually she could deal with it. But after the couple of days she'd had, the need to be alone so she could rest won out. "I should go, because it's probably going to be a long day tomorrow as well."

"Right, right. Of course. You'll come for Sunday dinner?"

Sarah hadn't attended Sunday dinner in years. Though, she usually made an appearance for birthday lunches and holiday meals.

She didn't blame Misty. It wasn't her stepmother's fault that no one in Sarah's life had believed the story she told from camp. Her mother lived in San Francisco and was an oncologist. A noble fight Sarah couldn't begrudge her. Benson wasn't exactly the cutting edge of cancer research.

"Bye, Dad." She ended the call and turned to put her plate in the sink.

Joseph stood at her back door. He lifted a hand to wave. It was covered with blood and dirt.

Sarah managed to not drop the plate, but it clattered into the sink in a way that made her wonder if it was lying there in shards now. But she didn't look.

Sarah dragged the patio door open. Joseph lifted a foot over the door track and listed to the side. She caught him, dragging one heavy arm over her shoulders. "Chair...or couch?"

"Couch."

She walked him through the archway to her living room where he collapsed onto the dark gray fabric and groaned.

He was hurt, probably worse than he looked. "I'll get the first aid kit."

She ran back from the bathroom moments later, flicking on the light for the living room, wondering if he would be passed out by the tie she returned. That might be easier in terms of treating him. But it was unlikely she would get any answers if he was unconscious.

She pushed the coffee table out of the way and knelt. "Are you still with me?"

"Depends on what you're going to ask me to do."

"How about lay still while I take a look at you?"

He grabbed the edge of the T-shirt he wore and stripped it off.

"You got shot." Sarah gasped. She pulled on some gloves from the medical supplies and felt around the wound on the outside of his arm. "It doesn't look like more than a deep graze, but it needs to be cleaned and bandaged."

He said nothing, just gritted his teeth while sweat beaded on his temples.

"You also probably need an X-ray on your ribs." There was a nasty purple bruise on his side. Not to mention all the other contusions and abrasions.

"Just do what you can. I can wrap my ribs."

"You can also apparently talk." She grabbed a towel and solution for his arm that would enable her to rinse out the dirt. At some point he needed to take a shower. "So tell me what happened."

She didn't want to be mad that he'd put her in that van. It was more like tricking her into it, and then leaving her there while he played the hero and tried to fix the problem. Then again, there was plenty about that to be mad over. So why not?

"The guy from the cabin grabbed me from the highway. They had a couple of pickup trucks and took me to an abandoned ranch. They wanted to know why I was at the retreat camp, and who sent me. I think they figured I was an undercover cop."

"Are you?" That might make sense why Russ and Addie knew so much about him.

"I'm nobody now. Maybe I was always nobody." His eyes drifted shut.

Sarah doused his arm with solution, using the bottle to spray the wound a little. It shouldn't hurt, but it also was unlikely to feel good.

He sucked in a breath and opened his eyes. "Do you have a phone I can borrow? I need to send a text."

She finished cleaning his gunshot wound and then went to grab her phone. "The police brought me my things." She frowned. "You probably need to go to the hospital." She also figured he had no intention of doing that given he'd come here instead of heading to the emergency department at Benson General.

He handed her back the phone. On screen he had sent a series of numbers to a contact she didn't have.

Before she even laid the phone on the coffee table, she got a response. Another similar series of numbers. She showed him the screen. "Is that good?"

He nodded. "I'll be staying here tonight, and for the foreseeable future. As long as it takes the police to take these people down. Your life is in danger, Sarah."

"Maybe it was." She needed to figure out how to say this. He'd probably been through so much it was causing him to believe the threat continued, even when it was over. "I'm fine now. I'm home, safe. I'll be going back to work tomorrow, and they've beefed up security, so I'll be fine. Between that and the police presence outside."

"These people don't care about police presence. They

don't want you to do your job because you'll figure out who they are. If you don't already know."

"And you're going to stop them?" He could barely stand. He was here because he needed medical attention and she was a doctor.

"I have to stop them." His dark gaze pinned her where she crouched beside him. "I was married. Six years ago now." He swallowed. "Genevieve was pregnant with our son when she was murdered. Assassinated."

Sarah touched a hand to her front and sucked in a breath. "That's horrible. I'm so sorry."

"It happened when I wasn't there. And it isn't going to happen again."

She wasn't entirely sure what that meant, but she caught the gist that he was determined to not lose someone else he cared about. She would never hold a candle to his wife, carrying his son. But she understood trauma and the need to do what she could to make sure she never went through anything like that again.

"I was staying at camp in the fourth grade," she began. "I wandered away late at night, even though they told us not to. I was following an animal. I saw a man wearing that mask from the closet. A killer. He chased me and I fell into a hole, a grave where he was burying a woman." She managed to swallow. "None of the rumors are rumors. But after I passed out, he must have put me back in my bed." Maybe even using tunnels like the one connected to that tree. "No one ever believed me when I told them what I saw."

"There was no one to tell what happened to Genevieve. We were alone in the world, and when I found her I realized I was alone again."

"And the monster who killed them?" Sarah said.

"That's who I am. The one in the dark you should be

scared of. The man with the mask on. That's why I know I can protect you."

"You're nothing like someone who would kill a mother and her child."

He shook his head. "You don't know anything about me."

She wanted to argue, but he would only tell her she was wrong and he was right. "Did the killer go to prison?"

"I did what was right. I got them justice." He lifted his thumb and swiped it across her cheek. "I'm not going to lose anyone else. I'll stay to protect you. But as soon as the feds or the police find these people, I'll be leaving. You'll never see me again."

Sarah sat back on her heels. "But why?"

"Because I can't stay, or I'll fall in love with you." He shifted and tugged a phone from his back pocket, which he handed to her. "It got pretty waterlogged. I don't know how this brand does with being submerged for a prolonged amount of time, but maybe the FBI can get evidence from it."

She reached for the phone. It was like he hadn't even said he could love her moments ago. Now a switch had flipped in him. He was back to business, and it was like those emotions didn't even exist.

Was that how he buried his trauma and continued to live his life? Because he had become the thing from his worst nightmare and knew he was no different. She wanted to unpack that because she could hardly believe he would be the same when he had lost so much.

But would she even get the chance to talk to him more about it? Not if he really planned to hang around only to protect her, and then leave.

"The FBI or the police can't know I'm here." He closed

his eyes. "They have to think I'm still missing, or my life will be over."

"Why take the risk that they'll see you?" She wanted to hear him say again that he cared for her.

He didn't open his eyes. "Protecting you is the right thing to do, and this threat is real."

Sarah bit her lip.

She was nothing but an obligation to him?

17

———

Joseph filled a glass of water at the kitchen sink. The clock on the microwave said 3:17 a.m. Sarah had gone to sleep hours ago, completely exhausted from doctoring his injuries. Now he had cream on every scratch and bandages on his ribs. He'd washed up in the sink with a cloth, and she'd found an oversized T-shirt in her closet she'd never worn or thrown away.

He ached from where she'd insisted on probing everything the way doctors did. Double checking his mobility and making sure one of the cracked ribs hadn't done more damage than he could heal from on his own.

He was glad she understood how things had to be between them. He'd told her about Genevieve and what'd happened, so she'd know why he wasn't going to get close to her even if he was here to keep her safe. Sarah knew why he couldn't open himself up to a relationship like that again.

She hadn't said much after he shared the story. She'd told him about her nightmare. Not long after that she had gone to bed, clearly exhausted.

He'd tossed and turned for a while, but now sleep was

eluding him. Everything from the last two days and all his buried nightmares were there every time he closed his eyes. Along with that mask from the closet and elements of Sarah's own trauma. He couldn't even imagine having seen something like that as a little kid. And then having no one believe her?

It wasn't a mystery why she did what she did, but he couldn't say the same about himself. Joseph didn't have a noble mission to accomplish. He'd taken an eye for an eye as it were, managed to catch the attention of someone who ran a group of assassins—along with the brother of the man who killed his wife.

After a career as a spy and that short retirement, Joseph hadn't had anything else to drive him. He hadn't known then what he knew now about how that life would try to suck him under.

He lowered the glass to the counter. It hit far too hard, but thankfully didn't break. Out the window he spotted someone creeping through the yard.

Of course she would pick now to visit him.

Joseph wondered what she was planning on doing about the security system that allowed him to move around the house inside. He couldn't open any windows or doors. Which she would need to do if she wanted to come inside.

The light above the oven flickered for a second. Joseph almost chuckled aloud. What he didn't do was reach for Sarah's gun—the one she'd removed from her safe and given to him. Fully loaded.

She'd gone to bed expecting him to protect her because he'd said he would. It was why he was here, and why she was currently fast asleep. Safe.

What he was going to do when she was inside her office tomorrow, he didn't know. There was no way to sneak in and keep watch on her, so he would have to rely on building security. When they'd done such a good job last time?

They'd better be on their game tomorrow.

He waited while his intruder/guest picked the lock on the back door and crept inside. As soon as she padded down the hallway to the kitchen, he said, "Coffee…or tea?"

Edith rounded the doorway to the kitchen and pushed back the hood of her sweater. "Tea, obviously."

Joseph took the electric kettle from its base and filled it at the sink. "Obviously."

Thankfully, Sarah had a box of the good stuff. He'd lived far too many years of his life in the United Kingdom to ever drink anything that didn't come in a pyramid-shaped tea bag or have "Yorkshire" on the label.

"So you're staying here?" Edith asked.

The woman knew practically everything about him, given she pinned him with one look the first time they met and completely nailed exactly who he was. It had been more than a little scary. However, the fact they had openly shared so much of their lives in the ensuing dinners and spending time getting to know each other as unlikely friends meant Joseph managed not to lose his mind being in Benson. Trying to start a new life.

It was over now, all he had to do was finish the mission.

"Yes, I'm staying here." Joseph figured that was pretty obvious, even if she was making a point…about whatever she was trying to make a point about. "You're going to have to spell it out if there's a problem."

He'd been near death a day or so ago. He could protect Sarah, no matter what came at them. That was the way he'd been trained. Deciphering subtext was something quite different.

Edith said, "And you're not risking everything for her?"

"Because you wouldn't?"

She shrugged one shoulder. "It doesn't matter what I would do. What matters is that you understand the cost of your choices."

He would stick to his decision to be here. No matter whether his heart wanted to argue a different course of action.

That was the cost in front of him, that he would lose what was left of his heart to Sarah before the mission was done. He would still leave, but she would keep all the heart he had left in him with her when he did.

He leaned back against the counter and folded his arms.

"All because she's in danger?" Edith said, "There are cops and feds here for that. And a private company of investigators, which I know because I farm out assignments on occasion. They're pretty good." She was probably talking about Vanguard, but who even knew?

Joseph said, "I'm not leaving Sarah's safety to the cop at the curb when I can be in here protecting her. Where *apparently* anyone can break in."

Edith chuckled. "I guess if anyone can keep her alive it's you. But this woman isn't the one who will turn your life around, set you free. Heal you. That's something you have to do by yourself."

He wondered for a second if it wasn't more that she might give him back his life. If he gave her a shot to do it.

Which he'd already decided he would not.

He'd been trying to get that life back—or start a new one—using the Accountant's Office, and becoming a Christian, and everything Russ told him he should be doing. Before Genevieve, he'd had a whole lot of nothing. Why would it be any different now?

It was over. The whole thing had been a waste of time.

"Sarah knows the score," Joseph said. "But these people

are serious about eliminating her before she can figure out who they are."

Edith her said nothing to that.

"She's going to drop the phone I got from these guys at the lab tomorrow so the police department technicians can try and get something from it."

"That's what you want to do?"

He glanced over from pouring the tea and studied Edith. "What did you have in mind?"

"The two girls who were at the camp? I can spoof their phones. Make it look like one texted the other and get them to meet. If we capture them and turn them in to the police" —Edith rolled her eyes, as though forced to acquiesce to a method she didn't like—"they can find out more than what Washington told Addie."

"Does that mean you've already been to the ranch house where they took me?"

She shrugged, all nonchalant. "You're the one who called the police before you left. They found your handiwork and all the evidence there. It will only be a matter of time before they put together that it's all related."

"And you want to hand over the two girls as well?"

Edith shrugged. "Maybe I'm admitting I'm too old for interrogation."

He didn't think she meant just sitting at a table and asking someone questions.

"So we get the girls to meet and swoop them up. Bam." Edith brushed her hands off.

"If you were just a few years younger…"

Edith laughed. "Maybe fifty years younger."

She'd lived a life not so dissimilar to his. Sure, she hadn't been picked up by a group of assassins when she was supposed to be a retired spy. She'd conducted enough missions even his eyebrows rose at reading through them.

That wasn't the half of what he could've uncovered about her, but he already knew enough, and it wasn't necessary. And yet, here she was in Benson, Washington, where her grandson lived.

Edith had taken out several of her own family members—with his help. She'd done what was necessary, the same way Joseph had. Maybe it shouldn't sit right that he had taken care of business. But how else was he supposed to feel about it?

It wasn't revenge, it was justice.

"How do you do it?" he said. "Walk away from who you were and what you had to do to survive?"

Edith wandered over and took her small mug of tea. "I left that life behind when I quit the CIA. My family doesn't know what I did, or the details of how I have to live now, and it will stay that way. But God led me down this path because he knew who I needed to be—for them. The same way he did for you. Because you're the man Sarah needed in her life."

Joseph wondered if she was referring to right now, or if she had some romantic notion of forever being in the cards for him and Sarah.

"We're the kind of people who are called to protect those around us, no matter what. No matter how."

Joseph said, "I figured that was about protecting them from the lives we led."

Edith shrugged. "It can be. But it can also be about having the skills to save the people we love. Like you and I did a few weeks ago."

They had, and he'd been banished to that retreat camp because of it.

Edith would always try to save the people she loved. Joseph also knew that in some ways she needed to slow her roll and accept the realities of her age. He wondered how difficult of a fight that would be when it came down to Edith needing to slow down. So far she'd taken on tasks she was capable of doing. He wasn't letting her go in anywhere else by herself, though.

Joseph said, "If we're going to save them, are you planning on taking the fight to these guys? Because I'm only here to make sure Sarah is alive to do her job." And to not fall for her in the process. Something he was sure would be easy if he allowed it to happen.

Edith shrugged. "Once we get the two girls and turn them over to the police, we can start unpacking the issue of all these guys on ATVs. But we'll have to sidestep if the police are tugging on the same thread."

She finished the tea, then put the mug in the sink. He would have to wash it and return it to the cupboard if he didn't want Sarah to know he'd had a middle of the night visitor.

"You should take this." Edith handed him a flip phone. "I'll be in touch later. I'm all for taking these guys down. But let me know if you find the treasure. I need money for the seniors' cruise."

18

———

Sarah sat in her car after she'd turned off the engine in the parking lot for the medical examiner's office. Addie had asked her to remain inside and wait to be escorted to her office. It was still early, but Sarah's boss's car was parked a few spaces down in his marked spot. She wondered how early he'd gotten here.

Addie parked her own car, then came over to Sarah's with one hand on the holstered weapon at her hip.

She scanned around them for longer than Sarah would have. Checking to make sure no one lurked nearby waiting to take Sarah out. It had been difficult to explain given the information had come from Joseph, but Addie wasn't surprised Sarah believed she was under threat.

So far she'd managed to dodge questions about Joseph, given she wasn't prepared to lie and pretend she was still scared for his life believing he had been captured. Maybe Addie was satisfied there were things Sarah couldn't tell her, and maybe she was just biding her time. Waiting for an answer.

Then again, considering his complete rejection of her

except to stick around long enough to save her life, maybe she didn't owe Joseph anything. He wasn't prepared to take that step with her even after everything they'd been through. She didn't understand how they could have spent all that time together, leaning on each other and holding hands, and he thought walking away was the right idea. To protect his own heart.

Maybe she should be flattered that he thought she was the kind of woman he could lose his heart to. The fact he didn't even want to try to see what could be between them, and if it might be worth the risk of losing each other, just made her cry.

At least last night.

Today was a new day, and she was a professional. There was a criminal enterprise going on in Benson, and she was going to be part of taking them down before they hurt anyone else.

It wouldn't be the first time she had set her feelings aside to get on with her life. Sarah doubted it would be the last.

Addie opened her door. "Okay, let's go."

Sarah grabbed her purse from the passenger seat. At least, it was her backup purse. She had no interest in using the belongings brought back from the retreat camp. Not before she washed everything. She was going to replace the rest of it—after she explained to her boss why one of their computers had been compromised.

Addie scanned the area, her competency clear in her movements. She knew what she was doing. All Sarah could think about was the fear.

"You went through something scary." Sarah glanced over at Addie as they walked. In a lot of ways they were similar, considering they'd both been through a traumatic event in the past. "How do you deal with the fear?"

"You've been trying to push it down for so long." Addie

kept her attention on the world around them as they walked through the parking lot to the staff door. "Now you realize' that hasn't worked because the fear is still there, and in fact it never goes anywhere."

"Has your fear gone?" Sarah frowned. Maybe she should have been looking around while they walked, but she also had to climb the steps without falling on her face.

"I read this verse in the Bible recently. It said that perfect love casts out all fear. Not all trying, or our trying to make ourselves feel better with human relationships. The perfect love of God. That's the only thing more powerful than your fear."

Addie opened the door and held it.

Sarah stopped before she went inside. "Did it work?"

"It's a journey. There's a sense that every day, and some-times every moment, you have to come back to that love. To control of your thoughts and let God fill you with his love."

"But it works."

"It's the only thing that ever has," Addie said.

Sarah moved inside. Religion wasn't something she had contemplated for a long time, but if it was going to get rid of this persistent fear, then she was willing to consider trying something new rather than using the methods that never worked.

Addie said, "You're going to your office?"

"I need to talk to my boss as well, but yes. I'll be in my office basically all day."

Addie nodded. "I need to talk to security. There will also be extra police presence." She pointed out an officer in the waiting area. "One outside your office and more in the hall-ways. No one is willing to mess around with this."

Sarah was grateful to live in a place where the police took crime seriously.

She knew it wasn't completely about protecting her, but

the fact that doing so was involved in taking these people down made Sarah feel better. The same way she felt over the fact Joseph was also willing to hang around and keep her safe.

Addie stared at her for a moment.

"What is it?"

"I know you know where Joseph is."

Sarah blinked.

"You're not distraught. And I don't think it's because in the light of day you aren't that worried about him. I think it's more likely that you know he's okay." Addie lifted a brow. "If you could confirm for me that the police don't need to spend resources looking for him that would be great."

Sarah nodded. "Okay. The police don't need to look for him. He was in that ranch house you guys raided last night after the 911 call."

"Where there were two bodies?"

Sarah said nothing. Whether he had killed them, or not, it would've been in order to save his own life. Because he feared for it and had to escape. Surely no one could begrudge him defending himself.

Addie took a step back. "Have a good day."

Sarah didn't want to do anything that affected her friendship with Addie, but she might have. All kinds of things were on the line right now, the least of which was her own life as far as Sarah was concerned. Everyone else seemed intent on protecting her, but she was more worried about these criminals getting away with what they were doing.

And her losing her shot at a relationship that seemed to be the first one that could be real her whole life.

She never felt about anyone the way she thought about Joseph. Not even her former fiancé.

Even if she didn't know much about him and their time together had been full of stress, she still wanted to be with him even if it was like that. More than she wanted to be with anyone else.

She didn't get to her office before her boss stuck his head out of his and said, "Doctor Carlton, I'd like a word."

Despite the order, she couldn't help frowning. "Are you okay, Chief?" She followed him into his office where he sat behind his desk, and she faced him. "Do you feel okay this morning?"

He swiped at the sweat on his brow, dampening his hair. His face was pale. "It's probably just the stress of everything that's going on." He grabbed the handkerchief and wiped his face. "Including the serious data breach we recently had because you took one of our laptops to an unsecured place and allowed it to fall into unapproved hands."

She couldn't argue with that, considering it was exactly what'd happened. "I did try my best to keep it out of their hands, but I had no idea the entire camp was involved when I went."

"But you still willingly took your laptop with you, even though you were supposed to be on vacation."

She nodded, unable to argue with any of that. The fact she hadn't known what would happen didn't hold weight as an excuse.

He continued expounding on her failure at length while she stood there wondering at the coincidence of it all. If that was even what it was. Surely Hawthorne couldn't have known when he sent her there that it was at all related to the overdose deaths. But the fact was, someone had known all about her. Maybe even before she showed up at the camp. The attack had been personal. They'd been intent on scaring her into being ineffective as a medical examiner.

Was it possible her boss wanted her out of the way for two weeks so he could do something here at work? Or he wanted her at the camp because he knew something and had willingly played into their hands. She couldn't imagine he was part of it, but if he'd acted under duress it would make sense.

Maybe Addie needed to talk to the chief. If she asked him any questions, he would shut down and have even more of a problem with her than he already did. Right now it sounded like she wasn't far from being fired over this.

He continued, "I expect you to work twice as hard figuring this out. The police are going to find these people, but you need to connect those overdoses to their activity."

Sarah bit her lip. Did he need her to get him out of a jam? He could be feeling the squeeze of being pressured by criminals and now he was looking for her to fix the problem for him. "Any information you might be able to give me that could help, I would be very grateful. Your experience could be invaluable in helping me figure this out."

"My role as chief means that I need to spend today cleaning up this mess of yours, which means I won't have time to babysit your work as well as complete my own."

Okay, then. She figured that was an answer to her question. Just not the one she had been looking for. "I would also like to pull all the police files from the deaths and disappearances at the camp over the years. Addie Franklin, the FBI Special Agent, mentioned they might be relevant. And given my own experience at the camp years ago"—something she hadn't ever told him—"I may be able to provide additional information. My theory is that all of it is linked, going back decades."

The chief frowned. "So long as I don't have to spend an hour on the phone to tech support removing access from any more computers remotely."

Sarah had offered to do that for him, but he'd insisted considering she had been at the police station giving her statement at the time. As soon as she'd arrived there after the highway scene, one of the first things Sarah had done was contact her boss and tell him about the breach of their information.

Even though the laptop had been encrypted, it wasn't perfectly secure in the wrong hands—broken or not. She would never discount what some hackers were capable of, even with it having been smashed. There was still a chance someone could have broken the security and retrieved the information stored on it. No security system was perfect. She couldn't even take the risk they could've even accessed the medical examiner's office computer system through a remote link to the network.

"I won't let you down, Chief." Work had been her focus for years. She would fall back on that now because the alternative left her tied up in knots. For decades her focus had been work. Why change that just because of one guy?

After all, Joseph wasn't even willing to tell everyone he was okay. He thought he had to live under the radar, and he was going to skip town as soon as the threat was over. So where did that leave her?

Right here with her job still to do.

The chief lifted his coffee cup and took a sip. Sweat ran down from his temple. He took one swallow and immediately started choking. Coffee bubbled over his lips.

He gasped for breath.

"Sir, are you okay?" She moved toward him, but he shook his head. He started to lift one hand.

It was like he didn't have the strength to hold it up. The chief's face reddened. He keeled over and slammed his forehead on the desk.

Sarah ran to the door. "I need some help!"

She raced back to the desk and felt for the chief's pulse.

Nothing.

19

———

J oseph had opted to drive, because allowing Edith to do it was a recipe for disaster. She switched out cars every couple of weeks, so no one knew what she used to get around town. He figured it was more about being unable to rewrite certain learned skills. There were ways he would never put himself in danger either, even when there was no active threat.

"I'm sure she'll be fine."

He turned to Edith.

"Isn't that what I'm supposed to say?"

He wanted to roll his eyes at her comment, but that would be as ridiculous as what she'd said. "I think you're supposed to be encouraging."

"I'm encouraging you to figure out the end of this."

He knew that and was grateful for it. Instead of sitting around talking through the problem endlessly, they were currently watching Emmalee at a rest stop. From several spaces away, they could see her move between vehicles. Talking to lone women. At this hour, they weren't working the truckers driving through. It was more like recovering from a night of earning money.

"You think this is where they got the last round of test subjects from?"

Edith shrugged. "Sarah would have been able to tell if they were prostitutes."

"I don't think she ID'd them, as far as I know."

"You should call her at work and ask."

Joseph shot her a look. "She's busy."

"Too busy to talk to you?"

"That's not what this is." He'd already tried to convince her, but Edith seemed to think something was happening between him and Sarah. Regardless of how she felt about it, it seemed like she was certain. All of which was completely irrelevant, because he was only making sure she was safe and finding these guys.

He wasn't starting anything with Sarah. "My life in Benson is over. Or it will be as soon as Russ puts the paperwork through."

"You really think he's going to kick you out?"

Joseph said, "Of course he will. It's what he said he would do if I killed anyone else."

Edith wasn't going to apologize for having put him in that situation before, with Aaron Hummet. They both knew Joseph had done the right thing by taking out Edith's son. The world had one less terrorist in it—and people who would otherwise be killed got to live their lives.

"Killing Austin was extenuating circumstances. You did that to save Sarah's life."

"We tried that defense with Aaron, remember?" Joseph didn't want to get into this again, but apparently Edith had no intention of backing down. "It didn't work then, and it won't work now with Austin. Russ was clear about that. Even self-defense didn't matter."

Some people might think that wasn't fair, but since when was life fair anyway?

The police commissioner was also the point person for the Accountant's Office here in Benson. That meant he had the final say on whether Joseph could stay or if he had to leave the program.

What was the point in facing the music when Joseph knew he'd done the wrong thing. Honest folks didn't like people who took the life of another. No matter that it had been in self-defense.

It wasn't as if Joseph liked who he was, or who he'd been trained to be. Edith thought they were just a different kind of people. He should quit trying to be normal like everyone else. Still, maybe there was a part of him that would never give up the dream of being good. Being one of those honest folks who seemed to be able to live happy lives in a way someone like him couldn't.

The dream remained elusive, but it was still inside him. Flickering with hope no matter what happened.

Emmalee worked the parking lot, talked to a couple of girls and it looked like she exchanged numbers with some of them. Three, maybe four people. Young women who, if they went missing, wouldn't be missed by anyone but the others here. And they would be unlikely to call the police and report it.

What police officer would expend much energy searching for someone society didn't seem to care at all about? Especially when there were so many victims the news loved to glorify. The lost and forgotten remained that way so often for the sake of marketing and clicks.

Edith's phone buzzed. She let out a noise Joseph couldn't decipher.

"What is it?"

"Let me find out." She lifted the phone to her ear. "Yes, Russ. It's me."

Joseph stiffened in his seat. She was really calling the man who could decide if his life here was over or not right now, with him in the car?

"Who's dead?" Edith listened for a second. "Okay, because all I heard was that someone at the ME's office is dead."

Joseph's heart squeezed in his chest. He tried to keep Emmalee in view while he waited, but inside his head he screamed for more information from her. Someone at the ME's office was dead. He'd left Sarah's safety in the care of other professionals. Still, he'd chosen to safeguard his freedom by letting her be out of his sight.

That backfired and resulted in the worst happening.

"Thanks." Edith hung up the phone. "The chief medical examiner keeled over. Russ said it looks like he was poisoned."

Joseph let out a breath. "Let's get this done."

He was ready to get moving and finish this, so he pushed the door open and strode across the parking lot.

Edith could come with him if she wanted to, but Joseph didn't need her to hold his hand the entire time. Sure, they had forged an unlikely friendship. But he'd never needed a partner before and didn't plan to get to a point where he couldn't do anything without one anytime soon.

Emmalee had entered the diner a minute or so ago. Joseph pulled the door open and scanned the interior. Two truckers sat at a booth eating pancakes. One of the women Emmalee had talked to was at the counter, drinking coffee.

Emmalee sat at a table at the far end, facing the door. Her eyes widened when she spotted him. She started to get up out of the seat. Joseph shook his head.

He picked up his pace, and when he got to her booth, shoved her in farther and sat down.

Edith took the seat opposite him. "You aren't going anywhere until you answer some questions."

Emmalee's lips thinned, but Joseph hardly cared if she was unhappy. "You're smack in the middle of this," he said. "So you're going to start answering some questions."

He figured she was here recruiting, but if she was only reaching out, then they didn't have anyone yet. She was a small fish in this big pond. He needed to know who the bigger fish were. "Tell us who is in charge of the operation."

She flinched. "So I can get shanked in County lockup?" She blew out a breath. "I don't think so."

Neither Edith nor Joseph offered to protect her. The reality was that she had gotten into the situation and neglected to take any way out offered her. If she wanted to be done with these people, then she needed to give information to the police.

Across the table, Edith pulled out her phone and sent a text. She laid the phone face down and linked her fingers. "We need to know what you know, so we can end this. Unless you'd like to make a career out of working for a group who doesn't care who dies."

"I'm not going to tell you a thing." Emmalee shifted on the seat.

"So give me your phone." Joseph held out a hand. "You don't say a word, and I'll get what I need, right?"

These days people took pictures of everything. What he needed was a photo of the guy from the cabin. The one in charge. The one he saw behind his eyelids when he shut his eyes to sleep. Joseph didn't recognize it as fear, but the man had possessed the power to end his life for a while there. That left an impression on him, even if it wasn't panic.

He continued, "If we can figure out who these people

are, then the police can sweep them all up in a raid. End their operation."

Emmalee scoffed. "You think he won't just start up somewhere else?"

"I think there's FBI in this town, and a police force who aren't going to stop looking for him until he's caught."

Edith said, "Where do Brad and Karen fit into this?"

Emmalee made a face.

"So they're not at the top of the food chain?"

Emmalee snorted.

Joseph glanced at Edith. He figured that was enough of an answer to that question. "What about locations? I know there are other labs. Where do you go to meet up with Them?"

"You don't get that I'm not going to talk to you?" Emmalee shook her head. "Give me your number, I'll send you a couple of pictures and then delete the thread from my phone."

"Good idea," Joseph said. "No one will ever know where we got the information. And you'll be safe to keep doing whatever you want to do."

"As if I have a choice?"

Edith said, "There's always a choice. Unless you're being held against your will, which you obviously aren't because you're walking around like a free person."

"There are different kinds of chains."

Joseph said, "We know that more than most people. We also know what it's like to start a new life somewhere else. You just have to find the courage to try."

Emmalee stared at him a second, then pulled out her phone. He gave her Edith's number, and when the messages had come through, the older woman nodded.

Emmalee said, "You probably just want the treasure like everyone else."

"We don't care about the treasure. It's not going to solve anyone's problem to look for whatever it even is."

"You don't know what it is?" Emmalee said.

"We're interested in justice. Not a payday."

Emmalee blinked.

Joseph figured she'd never met anybody motivated by doing the right thing rather than their own greed. She needed to find new friends.

The front door of the diner opened, and a uniformed police officer stepped inside. Everything in Joseph clenched. But it took him a second to realize the officer wasn't there for him, and it was Edith's grandson. The guy had passed his detective exam a week or so ago and was waiting for his new position to open up.

Officer Hummet strode up to the table. This was who Edith had sent a message to? The guy said, "I need you to come with me."

Joseph slid from the booth and let her out.

"Great." Emmalee huffed. "I'll be dead before I say anything."

The cop shook his head. "The police department is going to do our best to make sure that doesn't happen. We don't like it when the people we're supposed to be protecting get killed, so it's in our interest to keep you alive."

Joseph figured it was an interesting tactic to make it look like the police department was only interested in saving face. But Emmalee seemed to think that was their only motive.

"You better." She faced off with Eric. "Or else."

Considering the or else was that she would be dead, he wasn't sure what she planned to do if that happened. She was being arrested. She didn't have much leverage with them.

Joseph couldn't do much to help out. Except follow the lead she had given them.

Edith said, "Have a good rest of your day, dear."

The cop shook his head. "Don't even start with me, Grams." He led the cuffed woman away.

Joseph said, "What did she send you?"

Edith turned the phone around so he could see the screen.

His brows rose. "That's the guy."

Her expression hardened, and he realized how formidable she would've been in her younger years, operating as a CIA agent.

Edith said, "Let's get this guy."

20

———

"Sarah?"

She turned at the voice to find Russ Franklin, who was Addie's uncle and the interim police commissioner, standing behind her.

"Would you come sit with me for a minute?"

She turned back to where her boss, the chief medical examiner, had been zipped into a body bag. Two paramedics wheeled him out on a stretcher.

Some people said the moment of death brought with it an absence. That the person no longer remained within the physical body. She turned and followed Russ. "What do you believe about death?"

"To be absent from the body is to be present with the Lord. If you believe He is the Savior."

She figured there was a lot to unpack there, and her tendency was to think things through when she wanted to make a decision. There was research to be done, but that didn't take care of the immediacy of the situation. Sarah had dealt with so many dead bodies in her career. She'd seen death. She'd lived the nightmare of murder.

And yet, there was still so much unknown about how it all worked. Or why.

Russ led her to a conference room and had her sit with him. "My faith is a very important part of my life."

"I think I've been so busy it was easier to ignore it, rather than face the fact I might be wrong about something."

Russ nodded. "We can get busy with life and forget about those larger questions. The issues of eternity and faith."

Sarah said, "I've heard all the Bible stories and even 'gave my heart to Jesus' at one point. But that was childhood, and as I became an adult it seemed to make sense to leave those childish things behind."

"Often the truth can be the thing that seems too good to be true. Or too simple." He shook his head. "But it's not. Or there would be nothing science couldn't explain."

There was a whole other can of worms wrapped up in this, namely the issue of what to do with her scientific study when it came head-to-head with the Bible. She had read a couple of books written by creation scientists and understood some of the ins and outs of what they said. However, choosing to go against established science was like trying to turn the tide of the ocean back on itself.

So many people would never accept the truth, even if it was plain in front of their faces.

Sarah shook her head. "Why does the mind always want to think about something else when faced with a reality it finds too harsh? Or too immediate."

"Maybe that's why I'm wondering more about Joseph than I am about this case." He scrunched up his nose. "Not that I'm ignoring the case. I have a whole police department of people who tell me they're working this as fast and as well as they can, and I believe they'll do an exemplary job. But while I have to sit on my hands and wait for them to tell me they got results all I can think about is the fact the last I heard Joseph had been kidnapped."

Sarah figured Addie had told Russ about the connection between the ranch house with two dead bodies, and Sarah no longer being worried for his safety. She also knew there was some conflict between Russ and Joseph regarding Joseph's future. If he wanted to lay low where Russ couldn't find him, she wasn't going to get in the way of that.

Russ said, "This isn't about finding him and knocking him down. It's about protecting him."

"From himself?" Sarah asked.

Russ shook his head. "He isn't a foolish man. But he also isn't like the rest of us."

She wondered if he was referring to some kind of neuro-diversity. People were all unique, and while there were huge swaths of society whose cognitive processes were similar to each other, there would always be exceptions. Varieties that were to be celebrated and not marginalized.

But she wasn't sure that was what he was talking about.

Russ said, "If he gets in too deep, there could be a point where I can't help him without compromising myself. Something I'm not prepared to do, regardless of the contract I signed to help people like Joseph."

Sarah said, "I know he respects you a lot."

"That's why I'm worried. I know he's the kind of man who won't put me in a position where I have to make a moral choice. He will take the brunt of what's going on before he lets that happen."

"Neither of us anticipated everything that happened at the camp. How could we have?" Sarah didn't know what she was supposed to say, but it seemed as though everyone expected them to have dealt differently with the situation. When the entire camp turned on them, they weren't able to do anything but run.

"You aren't in trouble."

Sarah blew out a breath. "It kind of seems as though we are. Why would I be a target now when I've been working this job for years? It makes no sense. These people apparently think I'm some kind of threat, and now they kill the chief?" Her voice broke. She blinked back tears and cleared her throat.

Russ got up, returning with two water bottles a moment later. The bustle of the hallway wasn't something she could ignore, as much as she might want to. When the chief's assistant stood out there, crying behind a tissue while she spoke with the police officer trying to get answers from her.

"Should I be worried about Joseph?"

Russ sat back down. "He's with Edith, I'm guessing."

"And you can't have someone from the police department check to make sure they're okay." After all, they hadn't found Joseph. He'd been forced to take matters into his own hands and escape that house. He could've been killed so easily, but he'd managed to fight his way out before the boss got back.

"No, and I won't waste police resources babysitting spies."

Sarah hadn't known he was a spy in his former life. But in a lot of ways that made sense. Considering the impression she got from Edith, that *definitely* made sense.

The police officer in the hall who'd been talking to the chief's assistant squeezed her shoulder and walked away.

Sarah pushed her chair back and strode over. "Rebecca, would you come here for a second please?" She figured she might end up as the chief pretty soon, so she should start acting like it. Which began with getting to the bottom of how on earth the chief was poisoned.

Better than thinking about the threat, or anything about Joseph. Or spies.

"Oh." Rebecca blinked. Sarah led her to the conference room, where Russ watched them settle in chairs. "What did you want to know? I already told the police everything I can think of."

"And what is that? Because someone put something in the chief's coffee." And Sarah figured Rebecca knew who it was.

Russ lifted his brows, silently asking a question. There was no time to tell him exactly what was going on here. Not when Rebecca was normally so…normal. Almost too normal sometimes. As though she had zero personality, or she was playing a part.

Now it seemed like the normal thing to do would be to cry behind a tissue and claim she knew nothing.

Meanwhile, alarm bells went off in Sarah's instincts. "Why don't you tell us what happened?"

Rebecca dabbed the tissue in the corners of her eyes. "Everything today happened like normal, until he keeled over and died while *you* were talking to him."

"The security cameras showed I went nowhere near him." Sarah paused. "If you are for some reason insinuating I might have murdered the chief…"

Russ held up a hand. "No one is accusing anyone. We all know the bad guys in this situation, the ones who sent someone to look through your office, Sarah." He turned to Rebecca. "Do you know who they might be?"

"How would I?" Rebecca dabbed her eyes with a tissue. "I'm just trying to work. And now he's dead. What am I going to do?"

"Continue working," Sarah said.

Rebecca needed to show up if she wanted to get paid. Whether or not the chief was dead didn't affect the woman's employment status. Unless there was a reason to let her go.

"All of us need time to grieve," Sarah said. "And then we will continue to do our jobs. The way we always do." Soldiering on was what she had done for years. In a way it was ingrained in her, that was all her mind could think of to do in response to something like this.

Press on. Keep going. Shove the fear down, and don't think about it.

A niggle of doubt in the back of her mind said she needed to realize that hadn't exactly been a foolproof plan. Maybe it didn't completely work, but what other options did she have? Aside from completely changing her belief system and jumping on a whim to another one. She had no idea if it would work better than this.

It was definitely time for some research. Then she would be able to get firsthand information about whether or not faith made it possible to completely eliminate her fear instead of just ignoring it.

Russ shifted in his chair. "Do you have any idea who might have put poison in his coffee?"

Rebecca shook her head. "No-o-o."

"But you're the one who prepared it. Is that right?" Sarah said. She didn't exactly want to interrogate the girl, but someone had to get answers.

"Yes, I…I made it." Rebecca's voice quivered.

"And when we check the video surveillance from the kitchen?"

"They made me do it," Rebecca wailed. "Threatened me until I agreed to put that stuff in his cup. It was just a tiny bit, and they said it was just to make him ill and scare him a little. I didn't know he was going to die." She dissolved into sobbing.

Sarah sat back in her chair and glanced over at Russ.

He let out a breath. "Officer?"

Sarah didn't realize there was a cop at the door, and only saw the guy when he stepped in. "Yes, Commissioner?"

"This young lady needs to be escorted to an interview room so she can explain who forced her to give the chief the substance that killed him."

The officer's eyes widened. "Yes, Commissioner."

Russ accepted handcuffs and put them on the young woman. Sarah winced at how much worse this entire situation would get. The officer took the woman away, and Russ squeezed her shoulder.

"Don't bother telling me things will be fine." Sarah already knew that wasn't true.

"You know where to find me if you want someone to talk to." He squeezed her hand, then headed for the door.

Sarah got up shortly after and went to find Addie. The FBI special agent was in her office, along with her associate Stella Davis and a couple of other agents Sarah didn't know.

"Doctor Carlton." Stella nodded.

Sarah waved a hand.

Addie came over. "What is it?"

Sarah turned. "What do you need from me to be able to find these people?"

"Is there any way you'll be able to get me names from the substance used to kill the chief medical examiner?"

Sarah blew out a long breath. "That will take time, but it is possible."

"We're working on several different leads. It's only a matter of time before we find out who they are and shut them down."

"And Brad and Karen?"

Addie said, "We have BOLOs out, but nothing has come back yet. Again, they can't hide forever."

"I need to do something."

Addie put her hand on Sarah's shoulder. "I don't know if you're going to like my suggestion."

Sarah waited.

"I want to investigate the woman who died twenty years ago. The dead woman you saw when you were little. The night you met the killer."

21

Two hours until Sarah technically got off work for the day. Whether she would stay late, Joseph wasn't sure. Either way she was supposed to call him so he could get back on duty and watch out for her outside the building where she worked.

"Not that it kept her safe."

"What was that?" Edith looked over at him, laptop on her lap. Feet up in her recliner.

He was losing his mind. If this took much longer he was going to hit the gym their building had, a perk of living here, and pound out some of this frustration. "Nothing."

"Mmm. Looks like it."

"Did you figure out who he is yet?" Then he could take out his frustration on that guy who'd insisted Joseph was at that camp for any reason other than just to work.

Edith had the photo from Emmalee's phone. She had put it into a web search engine, and a couple of sites she had access to but probably shouldn't. "The pictures were posted on Emmalee's public social media pages."

Joseph's eyes widened. "She put them on the internet?"

"Yep." Edith grinned. "And she tagged him. Though it looks like an alternate account."

"We know his name?"

"At least the one he goes by online."

"Great."

"Sure, if I could find that name listed in the phone book." Edith scrunched up her nose. "I'd ask Eric, but he'll know it's not police business and he'll ask too many questions. He's a smart man." Eric was also engaged to an FBI agent, so that might have something to do with it.

Joseph stood to pace the room.

"Let me check one more thing."

He went to the window of her living room and looked over the street below.

"Don't worry," she said, "a bomb isn't going to go off on the street down there twice in as many months."

"That doesn't make me feel better."

"Here we go."

Joseph spun back. "You found him?"

"Arnold Markowicz lives on the west of Benson. He owns both sides of a duplex according to county records."

"Any other properties?" Joseph figured he might not live in either place. Or he lived in both. Or that wasn't even the right guy.

"Not that I can find under that name."

"Write it down," he said. "I'm going to go check it out."

"And if you find this man who would've killed you?"

Joseph worked his mouth from side to side. "Call 911 and leave again?" After he tied the guy to a chair so he couldn't run, probably. He wasn't sure what would be necessary, and in the heat of the moment he might simply react on instinct.

"He threatened your life."

"You think I care about that?" Joseph said. "He gave orders to kill Sarah."

"So you cut off the head of the snake."

He had no idea if that was a suggestion or her conclusion of the best course of action. "We've both done a whole lot worse than that. But it's not supposed to be who I am now."

It was like being boxed in. Stuffed in a freezer and left to die.

Why did it take until now to realize that this situation left him feeling suffocated? There was nothing right about the way he was wired, nothing good or honorable. He couldn't be the man Sarah needed in her life.

He spun around.

"Don't," Edith said.

Joseph lowered his hand.

"You want to break a lamp because you're frustrated enough to throw one across the room." She paused. "Go to your place."

"Yes, ma'am." His apartment was a couple of doors down from Edith's.

"When you're done breaking things, come back and get the address."

He strode to her. "Give it to me now."

Edith looked far too pleased with herself. "I already sent it."

The flip phone she'd given him buzzed in his pocket. "Thank you."

"You're welcome." She precisely matched the tension in his tone. "Don't get killed." She closed the lid of the laptop and folded her arms. "I'm not going to come and identify you."

"You aren't going with me?"

"I need a nap. It's been a long couple of days."

Joseph walked to her, leaned down, and kissed her forehead. "I won't get killed."

"One day you will. Lord willing, I won't be around to see it."

He didn't know why him burying her as an alternative should be a good thing—except from her point of view. The rest of it he left alone and headed out. Down the stairs so he could use the side exit.

Joseph rarely went via the front door, which was monitored by a guard rather than just cameras. He flipped up the hood of his sweater, the one with no sleeves since it was summer. He would look like he was out for a jog—which was exactly what he did. Even if it was nearly ten miles to the address, he would be under the radar all the way there. His body was stiff and in need of exercise so he could loosen up.

Russ had his way of thinking, believing everyone should share his faith. Someone like him could never have a place as part of an institution that provided solace to good people. He was too damaged. Too broken. Too twisted up and manipulated, taught to take lives instead of honoring them. Nothing he could do for the rest of his life would make up for what he'd done.

Joseph needed to forgive himself, and he would've if it wasn't the hardest thing he'd ever do in his life.

The duplex was on the south side of a nicer neighborhood of what he figured were most likely rentals with an HOA adamant about lawn care. Or they provided the service. He headed onto the next street and found a path beside an irrigation canal. The fence between the canal path and the backyard of the duplex was vinyl. He ran to it, jumped, and grasped the top long enough to look over.

No dogs. No one in sight. Enough coverage with the bushes and trees in the yard he could get out of sight fast.

Joseph checked once more that no one watched him, then hopped the fence.

He hid behind a rose bush. When it became clear the

occupants of the house were likely at work, or at least not around the living area, he texted Edith.

Then he entered through the unlocked patio door.

Inside had that earthy tang of weed. Beer bottles lined the breakfast bar, and the sink had an odor he didn't go near. The kind that indicated no one had done dishes in a while. Maybe months. Either the fridge door was open, or someone needed to take the trash out.

He'd lived in worse places.

Hidden in some, too.

Joseph kept his phone in his hand. Not as a weapon, but just in case he needed to call for help—or take a photo of something.

No one occupied the living room. The front door was unlocked.

He crept down the hall, in case the man who'd tried to kill him—or anyone else—was asleep here. The first bedroom was empty of people, but full of boxes. Pretty much a storage unit worth of stuff all packed in there. The second had a bed, covers askew. The bathroom he could see at the far end but didn't look. There was a third room, smaller. More like an office.

Joseph pushed the door wide and stared.

Pictures lined the walls. Photos and newspaper articles. Twine had been pinned between papers stuck on the wall, connecting them. Intersecting with each other.

Pictures of the retreat camp reopening for like the third time in the '80s. Then again, in 2010. Photos of Brad and Karen, with a much younger Austin. Articles about the woman who'd gone missing thirty years ago. Letters that looked a whole lot older than that, written to "Celeste."

He found articles about Sarah being hired at the medical examiner's office, and an award she'd won. Photos of her boss and his appointment to chief. Information about the

FBI office opening, and the agents there. The articles about the agent who had died a couple of months ago made Joseph's stomach turn, seeing the handwritten slurs on the page.

The next section had everything he'd ever need to know about a lawyer, Robert Carlton. Sarah's father? Given his features he guessed he was close enough about that. She hadn't mentioned her family, but the wife didn't look like Sarah and she was a few years younger than Robert. Her dad and what looked like a stepmom, maybe, stood beside each other at a fundraiser…an auction.

Several pages had been ripped from the auction booklet, listing artifacts. The history of the item and their asking price.

Joseph tapped his cell phone against his leg.

Someone had done a whole lot of research on everyone connected to that retreat camp, intersecting with the medical examiner's office somehow. And he couldn't be sure it was about the recent deaths or perfecting a drug formula.

He flipped open the phone and sent the address to Russ. Someone smart had amassed this information. That wasn't someone they should underestimate. Whether it was Arnold Markowicz or not, this situation spread like a virus.

Joseph took a bunch of close ups of things he thought might be relevant, particularly what Sarah might want to know. He felt the tug of her again and needed to see for himself that she was all right.

Then they needed to visit her father and figure out how he factored into this.

He made his way back through the house and decided to check the garage just in case there was more information in there he could use. The heavy door took some pushing, the interior dark and stuffy. He shoved it open and heard a high-pitched whine. It was at least ninety degrees in the garage, maybe even hotter.

Joseph flipped on the light.

Two rows of four wire dog crates lined the sides of the garage. Inside each was a rail thin bully breed dog. His stomach flipped over at the sight of each one and their collective living conditions. None had any water.

Three got up and barked at him, one of which had a raw head from the low top of the cage, as if it had rubbed off the skin. The fourth lay still, its side a gaping wound.

Joseph reached out a hand and slammed his palm against the button beside the door. With a shudder, the garage door rolled up, bringing a fresh breeze from outside with the daylight. The dogs whipped into a frenzy. Two more barked with the others. The injured one didn't move.

A car pulled into the drive. Black and white. Flashing red and blue lights.

The door closed, and he realized he'd stepped back on a reflex.

He raced through the house and slid the patio door open. The second he stepped out someone crashed through the front door. "Benson PD!"

Joseph sprinted across the yard and jumped the fence.

No other cop car.

When he was winded enough that he needed to slow, he reached for his phone. Then spun around.

He'd dropped it.

Joseph's heart sank. Everything he'd gathered from the house was gone.

He had no evidence.

22

———

J oseph still wasn't answering the phone. No matter how many times Sarah called, he still hadn't picked up. She stowed the phone in her purse and headed for the parking lot, done with her day of work. The day her boss had keeled over and died.

Sarah pushed out a long breath, exhausted from all the crying interspersed with work that she'd done.

The security guard that had been assigned to her walked her to her car. He stopped at the hood. "I'll wait until you pull out. Have a good night, Doctor Carlton."

As far as Sarah knew, the police were on high alert. Someone was supposed to do regular drive-bys of her house. She wouldn't be surprised if she saw a police car behind her on the way home.

"Thank you."

She wouldn't ever again take for granted someone in her life. Not even people she saw in passing.

Life could end so easily.

She climbed in her car and gave herself a second just to

sit in the quiet with no expectations. Then she dug out her keys and turned on the engine.

"You don't need to freak out." The voice came from down low in the back seat, in the vicinity of the floor. A gentle hand touched her elbow. "And don't turn around."

"Joseph?" How on earth had he gotten in her car? With the heightened security, he should've been seen breaking into it. "What's going on?"

"I am keeping you safe on your way home. That's what's going on."

Sarah ducked her head and touched her forehead to the back of her hand holding the steering wheel.

"You're not okay." He sounded genuinely sad about that.

"Me?" Sarah blew out a breath and spoke to the steering wheel without lifting her head. "You broke into a house belonging to Anthony Markowicz today. They found a bunch of dogs that have been used in black market dogfighting rings, along with a ton of other stuff. And a man who ran from the scene and didn't respond to the police. Because that was you, right?"

"Are the dogs okay?" Joseph asked. "I mean, I have other questions. But are the dogs okay?"

"The police officers who responded got animal control there. They took all the dogs to a vet who is going to take care of them. And they are going through every inch of that house to see what all they can find."

"I can tell you what they already found if they didn't," he said. "Pictures of you. Newspaper articles. And a bunch of stuff about your father."

She nearly turned around. When she lifted her head, she realized the security guard was still waiting for her to leave the parking lot. She gave him a little wave, started her car, and pulled out of the parking lot.

"What do you mean, my father?" Sarah didn't have the greatest relationship with her dad, but it was functional at least. And a lot more loving than a lot of people had been saddled with even if things hadn't been perfect. No one's life was.

"He's got to have some kind of connection to these people." Joseph paused. "Or at least he represents as much of a threat to them as you do."

"He's a lawyer. Unless they faced him down in court, or he represented one of them, what could they possibly have to be mad about?" Even as she asked the question, she decided she was going to find out. After the day she'd had, Sarah should be headed home for a shower and some slouchy clothes. Along with the biggest plate of takeout Chinese she could get her hands on.

Instead, she flipped on her blinker and headed for her dad's house. That side of town where the houses were on two acres and his square footage was more than monthly rent in New York.

"Do you think he's in danger? I mean, I was supposed to be, but it was the chief who died today."

She felt that soft touch on her elbow, and a slight squeeze. "Are you okay?"

"He was drinking coffee. His assistant was coerced into poisoning him." Sarah blew out a breath. "He didn't look so good when I went into his office, and it was a matter of minutes. He just keeled over like Washington did, but he didn't survive." Sarah hardly wanted to talk about that.

She and Addie had been going over the case all afternoon. Looking at the possible identity of the murder victim she'd seen when she was a kid.

"We figured out that Anthony Markowicz is Karen's brother," she said. "You know, Brad's wife?"

"So there's a solid connection between that group at the

cabin making drugs, and the people who work at the retreat camp."

Sarah nodded even though she couldn't see Joseph. "Enough to get a warrant to look into their lives. Along with a search warrant for the camp." She didn't know what they would find there, but along with potentially pinning Washington's attempted murder on Joseph's, there had to be something Brad and Karen didn't want anyone else to find.

Joseph patted her elbow. "Find somewhere to pull over, like a parking lot."

She pulled into a grocery store and went to the corner of the lot, close to the dumpster.

As soon as she parked the car, the back door opened, and Joseph got in the front passenger seat.

Neither of them moved. They just looked at each other.

"You're okay?"

Sarah nodded, appreciating the softness of his expression. "You?"

He nodded as well.

The unspoken hung between them like sparks of electricity. He drew her. Until she wanted to lean close to him and touch her lips to his. But nothing he'd said invited her to do that. In fact, she was supposed to keep this wall separating them from anything that might happen between them.

Then he reached out a hand and touched her cheek.

She bit her lip, every bit of her strength taken up with not touching his hand. Holding it against her cheek, probably for longer than he wanted to. It was just a tiny gesture. Not one to invite her to something more, as much as she might want him to lean over and kiss her.

He lowered his hand back to his lap. "I think we should go talk to your dad."

"That's where I was heading."

"If you want to rest, you could tell me where he lives,

and I can go?" His offer was a sweet one, but Sarah didn't need him to baby her.

"He's not going to answer questions from someone he's never met before." Not that she thought Joseph would try some interrogation technique on her dad. But he was more likely to be receptive to her being there.

It was also in part about not splitting up. They had been in different places all day, and she wanted to spend this time with Joseph even if they were asking her dad questions.

It didn't take long to get there. She pulled the car into her usual space down the side of the house, in front of the three garage doors all in a row. The brick façade, and a wood roof tried to make it look like some kind of country barn in the middle of the suburbs.

"Is this the house where you grew up?"

Sarah shook her head. "My dad married Misty and bought this place with her after I graduated high school. I think she'd had enough of the house he lived in with my mom by then. She was always talking about buying a place that was just theirs. Not somewhere that held so many memories. But I think he kept the old place because of me."

She hadn't meant to say so much.

She continued, "I can't think how he might be involved in this."

"He certainly caught somebody's eye. He was as prominent as you on the walls in that room." Joseph reached for his door handle. "Let's go see if he can tell us why."

He waited by the door and she used her key, knocking as she entered. Her dad would already know they were here because he had a good security system with cameras that alerted him when someone pulled in the driveway. Even so, she called out, "It's me, Dad," and stepped into the kitchen.

"In the study." Misty poured a glass of wine at the

kitchen counter. She spotted Joseph, and her eyebrows rose over the glass as she sipped the generous portion of rosé.

"How are you, Misty?" Sarah tried to smile. They liked each other about as much as Sarah liked watching her boss lose his life at his desk today.

Yes, she wanted to be chief. However, she didn't want to do the job if she was going to lose her life the same way.

Her dad's wife lifted the glass in a salute. "Can't complain."

"This is my friend Joseph." Sarah motioned to him, walking behind her.

"Nice to meet you." Misty shot him a glance.

Joseph nodded to her. The two of them headed down the hallway to her dad's study. She knocked on the door so he would know it was her, then eased it open slowly just in case he was still on a call. Her dad was a criminal defense attorney and had been her whole life. Though, he had represented a couple of friends in their divorces.

She preferred her side of the court, even if that meant she had to take the stand as an expert witness. She favored the truth of science to the way court cases often ended up in a manipulation of the situation and arguments that swayed people's emotions. Testimony designed to influence the jury by preying on their feelings rather than explaining the reality of what had happened.

Her dad hung up the phone. "Honey." He came around the desk, and hugged her. "Who is this?"

"This is Joseph, a friend of mine." She motioned to him.

He stuck out his hand and they shook, sizing each other up in a way that was probably supposed to be subtle. "Nice to meet you."

Her dad's hair had been graying for as long as she could remember. He was slightly taller than her and called frequently so that she could remind him which dry cleaner it was that she preferred. Misty refused to take his things with hers, and her dad didn't like asking his assistant to act like a housekeeper.

Before her dad could ask why they were there, she said, "Can we talk to you about something? Joseph has some questions."

They sat on her dad's leather sofa set, and Sarah explained what had been going on. Leaving out the part where her life had been in danger, and they'd been forced to run through the woods.

Joseph picked up where she'd left off when she paused to figure out how to get from there to her dad being involved. "The man who seems to be in charge of this group making drugs that have killed several people already? He has a house the police discovered today. There was a lot of information in one of the rooms, including pictures of Sarah. Newspaper articles. And pictures of you."

Her dad blinked. "You think I'm somehow involved?"

"We're just trying to get more information so we can put together a better picture of what's going on."

Joseph's answer was very diplomatic, but her father needed them to be straight. "My life has been in danger more than once during this," Sarah added. "And my boss was murdered today at the office."

Her dad's eyes widened. "I heard something happened at the ME's office, but I didn't realize the chief was dead."

Sarah nodded. "If you have caught the interest of these people, you need to be careful and take the steps you need to take to be safe."

Her dad opened his mouth. Whatever he was going to say, the sound of shattered glass cut him off.

From somewhere distant in the house, Misty screamed.

23

Sarah gasped and spun around. Joseph grabbed her elbow before she could move away and tugged her gently back, past him while he moved toward the door first instead of her. No one was leaving this room unless he went first.

She rushed to the desk and pressed a button on the underside of the edge. "Panic button."

Joseph nodded.

Seconds later, the phone on the desk began to ring. Sarah picked it up, and he figured out quickly it was a dispatcher as she began to explain about the intruders.

Her dad moved toward the door. "I have to help Misty."

"Rob, hold up a second." Joseph got between him and the door. "Let me go first. I'll make sure she's okay, but not at the expense of leaving the two of you at risk."

Not that he considered Misty to be collateral damage. The two people in here had information to give the police, and both of their lives would be a risk instead of just one person if he left them to fend for themselves.

Yes, in the heat of the moment all he had was cold calculation. There was no emotion rushing through him. No surprise, or fear. Not even the rush of enjoyment that some people got when a situation became dangerous.

It was the way he'd been taught to be.

"You and Sarah need to find somewhere to hide." He glanced at her.

"Yes." She gripped the phone tightly against her cheek. "Thank you." She replaced the phone.

"Where can you guys go? Somewhere like a panic room or bathroom will do."

Rob pointed at a door on the far side. "Over there."

Sarah didn't look quite so convinced. "While you do what?"

He turned to her dad. "What about surveillance?" If he could get a look at how many people were out there, or what kind of weapons they had, he would be in a much better position. "Or a gun."

Her dad sniffed. "I have no weapons in this house."

Joseph could make a weapon out of most anything, so he didn't figure that was precisely true. Just how the man meant it.

"Joseph." Sarah clearly expected a response from him.

"Get somewhere safe. Don't come out, no matter who is at the door. Unless it's me or the police."

He moved to the door and peered out into the hallway. He could see Misty sprawled on the floor, unconscious. There was a gash on her temple, like she had received a blow to the head.

He glanced back at Sarah. "We need an ambulance."

She nodded. "There's one coming."

"I'm going to go see if I can minimize the damage. You guys hide." He didn't give them a chance to object before he slipped out and closed the door to the study.

It would be minutes before the police could get there, but that was plenty of time for whoever had broken in to do a good amount of damage.

He listened as he crept down the hall, his shoes completely silent on the floor. Misty didn't move. Her eyes were closed, her breathing shallow if the rise and fall of her torso was any indication.

He should by all rights be getting out of this house, so the cops didn't find him when they showed up. Instead, he located the first of the men who had broken into this house. In the front room sitting area, a man with a ski mask swiped objects from a bookcase onto the floor, over and over again. Making a mess.

Going for maximum damage.

Judging by the crashes from elsewhere in the house, there was more than one person here trashing things. Maybe even up to three guys.

If he left them to it, the police would probably arrest them as soon as they showed up. However, he couldn't run the risk they would split before that happened. He debated back and forth when the man in the sitting area turned again to Misty.

He eyed her in a way Joseph didn't like. Misty let out a moan and shifted as though regaining consciousness. The guy moved toward her with measured steps, determination in his stride.

So much for hanging back and letting the police do their jobs.

In the hall between him and the man there was an umbrella stand. More than one umbrella along with a walking stick had been stored there. Joseph picked up his pace, swiped the walking stick from the umbrella stand, and swung it back behind him with a two-handed grip.

He rushed at the man and swung the stick, hitting the guy on the head. Probably similar to how he'd injured Misty.

The guy dropped to the floor.

Joseph decided he liked the feel of the walking stick and held on to it as he moved through the house. Toward the closest noise indicating another intruder.

At best, he figured this was nothing but a warning to Sarah's dad that he should come to heel with whatever orders they'd given him. Putting pressure on by causing havoc in his life so that Robert Carlton had no choice but to follow their instructions.

Injuring his wife and making a mess of his home. Whether they thought he was here or not, it didn't seem to be about finding and hurting him specifically. Unless that was what they would do after they were done with this.

He found the second man in a library, pulling books off the shelf. Joseph dispatched him much the same way he had with the first man. He left the guy crumpled in a heap on the floor.

The third guy was in the main bedroom, pulling clothing from drawers and tossing it onto the floor.

"You guys aren't looking for anything in particular, then."

The guy whirled around, dark eyes blinking. That was all Joseph could see in the holes of the balaclava.

"Not even the guy who lives here?"

The intruder leveled a gun at Joseph's chest. "What are you, private security?"

"Something like that." Joseph was just glad he'd found all three of them before they discovered Sarah and her dad hiding. "The police will be here any minute, so you should probably get going if you want to stay out of jail."

The guy raced to the window.

Sarah's scream rang through the house. Joseph was

already in the hallway when a gunshot cracked through the air. He raced for the study.

They weren't inside, but the door at the far end was open.

He found an expansive bathroom there. Sarah grappled with another masked intruder clutching a gun. It looked like she was trying to keep the thing pointed away from her and her father. The older man stumbled back, face pale and eyes wide. He clutched at the counter and looked like he was about to pass out.

Joseph ran at the gunman and slammed him into the tile wall that opened to the shower around the corner.

Sarah let go and moved out of sight, hopefully to stand with her father.

Joseph grabbed the guy's wrist and slammed it against the wall.

The balaclava-covered head knocked into his.

Sparks ignited across everything he could see, dazing Joseph for a second. He shoved out with the flat of his palm. The ends of his fingers jabbed the guy in the side, right where his kidneys were.

The guy sputtered. Joseph slammed him against the wall again and smashed his wrist against the tile.

The gun clattered to the floor.

"Enough."

He didn't let up. Joseph pinned him against the wall.

"I said, enough."

The intruder was quickly losing the fight to get away. Joseph let go long enough to whip the balaclava off the guy's head.

Low level, and he was young. Not someone he recognized from the cabin or the ATVs. This kid was probably trying to gain respect within the group.

"Don't throw away your future on someone you care

nothing about." Joseph pinned the guy with his forearm against the tile.

"I don't need a guidance counselor."

"That's up for debate." Joseph angled his head to the side and called out, "Sarah! I need something to tie this guy up."

The kid fought against his hold. Joseph waited until that attempt was done, then he flipped the guy around so he was face first against the tile and pinned him again.

"Will this do?" Her voice quivered.

He glanced over and saw she held out what looked like the belt of a robe. The material wouldn't hold for long, but he could make it work. "Great. Thanks."

After their moment of closeness in the car, things were a little too connected between them. They'd had their fair share of high stress moments in the last few days. Add the attraction that didn't seem to want to relent, no matter his determination to keep her at arm's length until all of this was over, and he was fighting a losing battle.

"Is your dad okay?" He tied up the guy with the belt she'd given him, then grabbed the guy's elbow and led him out.

She nodded. "Can we go check on Misty?"

"Let me go first." He didn't want her in front of him if anything were to happen, like one of the guys he'd knocked out coming to.

"Do you need to leave before the police get here?"

The guy he was holding on to seemed to think her question was an interesting one. Joseph ignored the fact that he was listening and said, "If I can." Although, that would leave her explaining to the police how the three intruders had been subdued.

He shoved the guy down on the couch in the sitting room and dumped his unconscious friend next to him. The third one had jumped out the window, so Joseph wasn't going to worry too much about him. The one he tied up glared at him.

"How does Misty seem?" Joseph asked.

Sarah crouched beside her stepmother. "Hey, hang on. There's an ambulance coming." She looked up and locked eyes with him, giving him a tiny shrug.

Her dad filled the glass of water at the refrigerator, not even looking at his wife.

Joseph turned to him. "Want to tell me what this is?"

Sarah's dad didn't answer the question. The guy on the couch made a face.

"Somebody should start talking before the police get here." Joseph folded his arms. He glanced at Sarah's dad. "You know who these guys are?"

Her dad lowered the water glass. "Why would I?"

"Maybe because this was a targeted intrusion."

"Probably directed at you and Sarah."

Joseph didn't buy it. "These guys know who you are. That's why they're here. So what dealings do you have with Anthony Markowicz or anyone at the retreat camp?"

The skin around her dad's eyes flexed.

"You *do* know something," Sarah said, her voice breathy. "Tell me what you know."

He lowered the glass, his body language stiff. "They wanted me to represent one of their people a few months ago. They forced me to do it and launder their money through my office. Three weeks ago I told them we were done."

"Why then?" Joseph asked.

He and Sarah both waited for a response. When her dad said nothing, she commented, "I'm guessing you found out what they were doing and decided you didn't want any part of murder. Because you could argue the charges when you were under duress but knowing they're responsible for deaths makes you an accomplice if you continue to be part of their operation."

Joseph saw the flash of red and blue lights on the wall. He should run. He wanted to stay, though. To stick with Sarah through this, no matter the cost to him personally.

He just couldn't bring himself to leave her.

24

———

"Are you going to talk to me at all?"

Sarah gripped the wheel. She also ignored Joseph's question, the way she'd been ignoring him since they left her dad's house.

So far they'd driven to her house in almost complete silence. After hours spent talking to the police and giving their statements they were finally done. Her stepmother had been taken away in an ambulance. No one missed the complete lack of concern her father had shown for his wife.

He was down at the station now talking more with the FBI about his connection to Markowicz and the retreat camp.

All she could think was that Joseph had stuck around when he should've left. He'd dealt with the police alongside her, which made no sense at all given everything he'd said. All that intention he'd had of staying under the radar. Only being here to keep her safe.

"Sarah—"

"Why did you do that?" She pulled into her driveway and turned to him.

"Protected you and your dad?"

"You know that's not what I'm talking about. You should have left before the police got there. You could have. But you didn't."

Yes, it would've meant him saving himself. But there was a point where self-preservation won out over sticking around. She and her dad could have talked to the police on their own.

His presence had given them an understandable explanation of who subdued the men that were there. He'd also been able to describe the guy that had run off out the window, at least to an extent.

The cops didn't seem to know who they were. Her dad refused to answer the question, and he'd barely looked at any of them. She wasn't sure it was out of guilt or for what reason.

"I made a choice." He shifted in his seat and looked at her house. "It was mine to make."

"But you didn't want to be seen, or you would have gone to the hospital after you escaped those guys. You would've waited around for the police then."

He shook his head.

"One way or another they're going to figure out who you are." Not that she even knew at this point. There was so much about Joseph she didn't understand.

Maybe she never would.

It was probably for the best that he had drawn that line between them.

Sarah pushed open her door and headed for the house. She was about to insert her key when Joseph stopped her and took the key out of her hand. "I'm going to go inside first and make sure no one is hiding in there, waiting for you."

She beeped the locks on her car, holding her purse.

"Hang here for a second."

She was ready to wring his neck, and here he was still doing his job protecting her. The job he decided he was going to do on his own. Not because she'd asked him to do it.

It wasn't as if she wasn't grateful for what he had done protecting them at her dad's house. If he hadn't been there she'd have had to face them on her own. And now where would she be? Likely at the hospital with Misty. Any of them could be dead.

Who knew what their intention had been?

He returned to the front door and ushered her in, closing it behind her. He seemed to realize she was standing there staring at him. "What?"

Sarah let out a long sigh and dumped her purse. "I don't even know what to do with you, that's what."

It was on the tip of her tongue to tell him to go find somewhere else to stay tonight.

In the end she said, "Maybe I'll hire someone if I need protecting. You don't need to stay with me if it's not doing you any favors keeping yourself safe."

"You think I'm just going to abandon you?"

She shrugged.

"If you want someone else to protect you, then I can actually recommend someone in Benson. A company that are experts at protecting people." He folded his arms. "If that's what you want."

The hurt on his face couldn't bother her. She shouldn't let it when all that had happened as a result of them being together was that her heart was being shredded. She knew what she wanted from him, but he refused to give it to her.

Of course, she would have to say she understood the facts. He didn't want to risk going through the same pain he had suffered previously. Losing his wife and unborn son. She couldn't imagine that kind of horror, especially being the one to find them.

But why stick around? It was only making things harder.

"I'll tell you why I didn't leave." He let go of his folded arms but kept them tight by his sides. "I looked at you, and I didn't want to go."

Sarah stared at him.

He moved closer to her. She couldn't make out his gaze in the dim light of the hallway.

"Do you want me to leave?"

"Why are you even asking me that?" She didn't even know what this meant. Everything in her wanted to beg him to stay. To give her what she wanted in a relationship and the kind of connection she had always hoped to find. And yet, he was intent on staying here and denying her that.

Joseph groaned and shifted closer to her. A soft rustle of clothes, and then his lips touched hers.

She felt his fingers on her cheek, and then he ran his hand back into her hair. All she could do was hold on for dear life while everything spun around until she didn't know which way was up.

And then he was pulling back from her again. Putting distance between them.

Sarah closed her eyes and leaned back against the wall.

"I'm sorry—"

She headed down the hallway, just as confused as she'd been a minute ago. "Good. I'm glad you're sorry."

Maybe he should be feeling a little of what she was feeling right now.

She got to the kitchen, her stomach now rumbling, when someone knocked on the front door. She turned around.

"Shift out of sight and I'll answer it," Joseph said.

She wanted to give him a curt response but held her tongue. Whatever she had to say wasn't going to be helpful for either of them right now. Of course he'd given her the best kiss of her life and then apologized for it.

It was like he constantly said one thing and did something else. As if the guy didn't know his own feelings. Or maybe his heart wanted one thing, but his brain attempted to override it constantly by reminding him what was more logical.

She understood what it was like to be at war with herself. For Sarah it was that fear which crept in and overrode everything. She wanted to be strong, but instead she froze.

Except when she'd been with her father. Sarah had known Joseph was there. When the gunman came into the bathroom, she hadn't frozen. She'd actually fought him. Sarah shook her head, unable to believe she'd done that.

Joseph pulled back from the peephole in the door and ducked his head for a second. Then he opened it. "I'm guessing you're not here as the police commissioner."

"Actually," Russ said as he stepped inside. "It's a little bit of everything."

Joseph shut the door.

"I'd like to talk to both of you."

"Joseph and I never got the chance to eat, so I'm going to put something in the oven. Do you want to come into the kitchen?" Sarah motioned behind her. "I can make coffee."

Russ nodded. "That would be good."

She turned on the oven and grabbed a frozen pizza from her favorite gourmet grocery store. But the truth was, she liked any kind of pizza. It was her guilty pleasure. Right now she really wanted a shower as well, but that would have to wait until after Russ left and Joseph figured out what he was doing.

She made a pot of decaf coffee, and they sat at the table.

"Let's just say I've been briefed about what happened at your father's house. The FBI is currently interviewing him."

Sarah nodded.

Russ continued, "I called the lab and got a rush on your

tests. The substance that killed the overdose victims, which was also present in Washington Harper's blood, was veterinary fentanyl. It had been combined with several other substances, and we think it's why each victim had an abrasion on their skin. That narcotic is typically issued in a patch given to animals needing a strong pain reliever."

"I wonder if that connects the deaths to Anthony Markowicz, given he had dogs in his garage. Right?" She glanced at Joseph.

He frowned. "Maybe whoever Markowicz got to come in and take care of the dogs is the one who got him those patches."

Russ nodded. "Unfortunately, that's highly likely. A lot of people looking for narcotic pain relievers to feed their addictions these days go to vet clinics and get prescriptions that way."

Sarah wouldn't have been surprised if Markowicz had used the dogs' conditions to get the prescriptions. Until he could lean on the vet for more. He probably didn't even care at all about those dogs, given the condition Joseph had found them in.

Joseph blew out a breath and shook his head. "If the patches were altered and enhanced, that takes someone with the scientific know how to do it. And the equipment. It explains what I found in the cabin. And the fact they are working on test subjects—because they don't know exactly the right mix of everything."

Russ nodded. "We are getting all the information we can from the house and figuring out who treated them."

"Good." Joseph looked like he was about to jump up and run out the door to dish out some payback on whoever it was.

Russ said, "Are you ready for more?"

Sarah answered because he seemed to be directing the question at her. "What is it?"

"I have cadaver dogs being sent into the woods to find Austin, and anyone else who might be buried out there. Like Brad's first wife."

Joseph glanced at her. She said, "That's who went missing thirty years ago when I saw that body?"

Joseph glanced between them. "Any leads on Markowicz?"

Russ shook his head. "No one can find him or Brad and his wife. The guys we brought in from Mr. Carlton's house aren't talking. I heard a mystery writers conference was supposed to be happening, so I've got my assistant figuring that out."

"If anyone else tells me it's just a matter of time before this is over, I think I might scream." Sarah put the pizza in the preheated oven when it beeped. She could eat a whole one by herself but didn't think she wanted Joseph to know that about her.

He was supposed to think she was sophisticated and beautiful, the kind of woman who would make a fantastic chief medical examiner. He was supposed to be so enamored with her that he gave up his fear and decided to stay.

He didn't need to know that she and pizza had a clandestine relationship.

"This should be ready in about fifteen minutes if you want to stick around for a slice?" she said to Russ.

"I actually need to talk to Joseph for a moment, and then I'm going to go." He lifted his mug. "But thanks for the coffee."

She nodded. "Any time. Hopefully when there aren't a group of crazy drug dealers after me."

He gave her half a smile. "Sounds good."

Both men looked at her. She realized they wanted to talk without her in the room.

Sarah's face flamed. She couldn't believe she had been dense for a few minutes there, not realizing what they didn't spell out.

"I'm taking a shower." She breezed down the hallway before they could pity her more than anyone already had during this ordeal.

She supposed the fact someone was even bothering to look through the woods with a cadaver dog was progress. But it would have been nice to have been believed thirty years ago.

Just like it would be nice if the man she was falling for would take the risk and stay.

25

Russ gave him a pointed look. "Whatever you did there? You need to fix it."

"What's the point? I'm leaving." Joseph guessed that was why Russ wanted to talk to him—the leaving—not whatever was between him and Sarah. If it wasn't, he already had hard plans to split Benson after this case was over anyway. Sarah would no longer need him to stick around and protect her.

"You did well at her dad's house."

Joseph said nothing.

"Subdued three guys."

"One jumped out the window."

"I know." Russ nodded. "I read the file."

"They really aren't talking?"

Russ shrugged one shoulder. "It's just a matter of…" His voice trailed off. "I guess Sarah is right about that. You seem to be the one giving us all the leads. First Markowicz's house, and now Sarah's father. Anything else I should know?"

"I'm sure I'll think of something later. Or when I wake up tomorrow, I'll have it." Joseph's brain liked to have time to process things—usually while he was sleeping. He never doubted his ability to come up with something later, or the next day.

When it was longer than that, things became problematic.

"Maybe by then she'll have forgiven you for whatever has her in knots."

Joseph groaned and ran his hands down his face. "It's not that simple."

Given what happened in her entryway, Joseph wasn't likely to be forgiven anytime soon. He knew he was giving her mixed signals. He just hadn't been able to stand there and not kiss her. Not with the knowledge he would be leaving before long there in his mind. Being glad she was alive, and that they'd come through this latest risky situation. He hadn't been able to just leave it without being close to her for a moment.

Russ sat there silently.

Joseph knew the guy wanted to be a sounding board for those enrolled in the Accountant's Office. He'd just never taken advantage of it before. "Have you ever had everything you've ever wanted right in front of you, and it's the *one thing* you can't have?"

"Like bad timing?"

"More like I'm the worst option she has." Meanwhile she was the best he could imagine. She was amazing, but the last thing she needed was someone like him in her life.

Russ eyed him over his mug. "Sometimes it's worth the risk. Maybe she doesn't think about you the way you do. She sees more than who you believe you are."

"I'm not a different person here. No matter if I've got a new name, or a new job. If I give up all the old ways"—he wanted to wince, thinking about what he'd done to Austin—"and never do that again. I'm still me."

"That's why I advise faith as part of your assimilation with this community. Because I know the value in studying the Bible and seeing if Christianity is something you might want." Russ took a sip of his coffee. "Faith takes who you are and everything you bring to the table. An exchange happens. What you are is replaced with better. Like an upgrade."

So far things hadn't changed at all. What was he missing? "If I do that, I'm not me anymore."

"You get to be who you were supposed to be before sin entered the world. It's still part of our lives, and in the world around us everywhere we look. But God sees the righteousness He gives us. He sees holiness."

"Like when the pastor was talking about being a new creation?" Joseph said.

Russ nodded. "Exactly."

He remembered how it had sounded almost too good to be true, but he'd still wanted it enough to make the choice.

Like a relationship with Sarah, Joseph knew that if he took the risk he could have all of what Russ was talking about. But the chance it might fail and he would be left with nothing scared him more than leaving the program and being exposed.

"I want you to stay here in Benson."

Joseph frowned. This was more than Russ guessing his plan. "What's going on?"

"I can protect you."

"Russ."

The older man's jaw flexed. He didn't like this. Or, he knew Joseph wasn't going to like it. Russ said, "I got an alert earlier. Amadine Shammad landed in Seattle this morning."

Joseph stood so fast the chair tipped over behind him. Coffee spilled across the table and dripped onto the floor.

Russ was up, in front of him. "Easy." He touched Joseph's shoulder, his arm across Joseph's chest. Kind of like the way Joseph had pinned that guy earlier, but a whole lot less pressure. "Easy."

"He's—" There were no more words.

"The guy doesn't know you're here," Russ said. "He won't."

"What's going on?" Sarah stood in the doorway.

"Nothing." Joseph pushed away Russ's arm.

Sarah stepped into the room, a frown marring her brows.

He was about to say, *Nothing* again when Russ cut him off, saying, "The man who murdered Joseph's family had a brother. He vowed to find Joseph and get revenge. That's why he's got to live here, where he's protected."

Joseph tasted bile in the back of his throat.

"He wants to kill you?" she asked.

"And he's in Seattle." Russ turned to him. "He doesn't know where you are. He won't if you continue to follow the rules."

"All I've ever done is follow the rules. Look where it got me." Joseph fought the despair and found the well of rage inside him. "I'm *done*."

"You know I'm nothing like the people who trained you."

"Yeah?" Joseph said. "You sent me to that camp. You think I didn't figure out who it was, so you had a man on the inside to tear the whole thing wide open."

"If I did, then it worked." Russ lifted his chin.

"So you admit it."

"You signed a contract when you came on. I'm your boss, in essence," Russ said. "But have I ever acted like any of those guys who told you what to do before?"

Joseph closed his mouth.

"I'm trying to show you who you could be now. Where the intersection is between your skill set and a life of peace, where you can feel good about who you are."

"If Amadine is here, there's no peace." Joseph wanted to run out the door, down the street and keep going. Forever.

"Who you are matters to this community." Russ pinned him with all that law enforcement focus. "Otherwise I wouldn't have a job offer on my desk I think you might like."

"Why did you send me to the camp if you have a job offer for me?" Joseph moved to a chair and slumped into it.

Sarah got the pizza from the oven. She had wet hair and wore comfy clothes. It was so domestic in a way he yearned for that he had to rub a hand across his chest to relieve the ache.

Russ said, "You needed to see who you could be."

It was supposed to have been about not taking a life. Now it was something else?

Sarah turned. "Russ, did you know there was something going on at the camp before Joseph got there?"

The older man said, "We've had reports. With the task-force we have now, and all the interagency stuff with the FBI, there are no resources for additional undercover on something that only smelled fishy but had nothing concrete."

"So you sent Joseph?" When Russ nodded, she said, "Do you think my boss sent me to get rid of me, or to have me confront the case in person? Or so I'd be walking into a trap?"

"I don't know. But I'll try and find out."

Joseph glanced over. She was worried about that? He knew what it felt like to be played, and apparently so did she. Maybe that was why his actions hurt her so much. He'd yanked her chain at the same time she faced being given the run around by her boss. The guy was dead now, so she had no way to get information about it even if Russ thought he could.

Maybe she would never know.

She set a plate with three pizza slices in front of him. He stared at it.

Russ shifted. "I should go, but there's still something I want to say."

Joseph glanced over.

"How many times have you saved someone's life recently?" Russ waited. "I think you save Edith a little every day, because she knows she isn't alone." He took a breath. "You get to decide what you want now. Not because someone else tells you what's right, or what to do. Yes, I sent you to the camp to see if you could solve this problem. Now you're handing over leads left and right, so fast the police department can barely keep up. I was hoping you'd see what *could* be. So I could show you the job offer from Vanguard."

He'd heard of the private investigation group in Benson. "They know who I am?"

Russ said, "They have friends, and they asked about you. Now they know enough."

He blew out a breath.

"You could've said no anytime. But you didn't, because you let your guilt lead you to believe you deserved to be exiled at that camp. You don't think you have the right to be happy or lead a normal life." Russ headed for the front door. "I'll tell you now. Normal is overrated."

The front door shut.

Sarah didn't move. Joseph didn't speak.

She broke the stalemate, came over and leaned down. She pressed a kiss against his cheek. "Eat up, or it'll get cold."

She sat across from him, making appreciative noises over the pizza.

Sarah was anything but normal. He knew that because he knew she was one of a kind. The woman was amazing. From the way she put things together, to her devotion to her job. She had a mission to fight any way she could and not let fear swallow her.

He'd given in long ago. And when he could no longer handle the threat leveled against him from his enemies, he'd disappeared. Cut and run. Opted to be protected by the Accountant's Office. Not because he'd earned it, or somehow deserved it because he was a hero.

Joseph had always been the villain.

The life Russ said he could have in Benson wasn't something he could even begin to figure out how to piece together.

"Are you okay?" she asked.

Joseph shrugged one shoulder. "I have no idea."

Sarah's lips curled up just a tiny bit. "I know exactly what you mean." She shook her head. "I can't believe they might find the body I saw when I was a kid."

"I hope they do."

She frowned. "And you have to stay here, while that guy who wants to kill you is so close." She reached over and laid a hand on his arm. "You don't think he came here because it's where you are?"

"No way he knows I'm here. Russ makes sure I stay out of the media, off social media, and his friends don't let my new identity get leaked." Joseph shrugged.

"It really is like witness protection."

He nodded.

"I'm sorry you're not happy here." *With me*. She didn't say that last part out loud, but he heard it anyway.

Joseph got up and held out his hand. She took it and stood. Joseph pulled her close for a hug. "You're the best part of being here." He rubbed a hand up and down her back and she let out a sigh, releasing some of the tension. "I want to protect you."

She lifted her face. "Thank you."

Joseph felt that unfamiliar tug of a smile. "You're welcome."

He didn't kiss her, even though it crossed his mind. They weren't at that place now. Even if both of them wanted to be, life would always get in the way.

She started to pull back. Her phone rang, tucked in her sweater pocket.

Joseph started on his first slice while she answered it. He had to figure himself out or he'd be spinning his wheels the rest of his life. Maybe Russ was on to something about faith. *Is he right, God?*

She gasped. "Yes, I'll be there as soon as I can." She hung up. "I—we, I guess—have to go. There's been another overdose. I have to go to the scene."

26

———

Joseph parked the car. Sarah laid a hand on his arm. She wanted to ask him so many things, but instead what came out was, "Thank you for driving me."

Even if there was conflict between them and she couldn't get rid of the frustration she still cared about him. He obviously wanted a relationship with her and yet wouldn't allow himself to do it. She believed he cared about her. Maybe they wouldn't end up in a relationship, but that didn't mean they couldn't be friends.

Until he left town and she never saw him again.

The alternative was that he stayed, and she saw him frequently. It might hurt but she would still deal with it. Because she had to unless she was the one who left.

"Everything okay?"

She shrugged and wondered if there was an open spot for a chief medical examiner someplace else. She could use a fresh start to get her life back on track—or finally where she wanted it to be.

"It seems strange to say it," she started. "But I'm sorry there's someone trying to kill you."

He did the same shrug thing she'd just done. She didn't get the impression he was brushing off her apology.

"It's normal for you to have someone hunting you?"

"I just don't want it to become normal for you." He paused for a second. "That guy wanting vengeance has been part of my life for years. Ever since Genevieve and my son were killed, he's been on my radar and I've been on his."

She knew it was because he'd killed the man that murdered his wife. An eye for an eye had set off a chain reaction that left him hiding out here, needing to be protected.

It wasn't as though she blamed him for ending the life of a monster. How could she, just because she found herself consumed by fear far too much? That wasn't higher moral ground. Or some kind of holier than thou attitude that led her to being all judgy about the choices he'd made as a result of a difficult life. That wasn't how people should get along with each other. Throwing stones just to make themselves feel better because they took the stance that there was always someone worse.

"There's nothing you need to worry about," he said. "I'm here to protect you, and the threat against me isn't going to affect that. I can do my job here."

Sarah picked at a piece of lint on the knee of her pants. She was just a job to him?

"I should go inside." She pushed open the door and took a look at the building.

An old abandoned warehouse where a security guard had found a single dead woman. It was almost two in the morning. The chill in the air had her tugging the sweater closer around her as she got her case from the back seat of her car.

Joseph got out, doing that thing he did where he scanned all around him, as though he felt the need to keep his head on a swivel all the time. Because it was how they were going to stay alive.

That was the job he was here to do—and he seemed determined to do it regardless of how she felt. Sarah needed to do her own job and not worry about him. After all, she was basically the chief now because there was no way her coworker was getting the job.

She needed to act like it.

Sarah strode first to the cop at the door and was ushered through the barricade.

The officer said, "Is this guy with you?"

It was on the tip of her tongue to tell him he should call the police commissioner if he wanted to know whether the guy was authorized to be here or not, but she held it. "Yes, he's private security. Given everything going on, I thought it was best to take some of the burden off the police department."

They didn't need to think that she believed they couldn't protect her.

"Oh." The guy nodded. "Sounds good."

She headed inside, Joseph right behind her. Addie and Stella, both FBI agents, stood over a single female victim.

"Hey." Sarah dropped her satchel and pulled out a pair of gloves. "How was court?"

Stella shrugged. "This is better."

Addie's lips curled up in a slight smile, short lived considering where they were. "The security guard found her about an hour ago. He was doing his second sweep, so we know she wasn't here at midnight."

Sarah took a look at the victim's nose and mouth. She had a standard process for checking off everything she needed to ascertain at a scene. But with this death she was also immediately looking for correlations between the victim and the overdoses she had already seen.

The victim wore a short denim skirt and tank top, necklace, and earrings. A ring on her right pinky finger. A toe ring on her left foot. No shoes.

Sarah moved around the body. "She didn't walk in here." The victim's feet were clean on the bottom and had the marks from straps on her shoes. "She was wearing shoes earlier when she was standing around." She took a temperature from the victim's liver and noted everything on her tablet. "It's not an exact science, but I'd estimate she died between four and six hours ago."

"And then they waited, and brought her here?" Stella wasn't asking her to figure out the answer to that question. Sarah had no clue *why* people did the things that they did—only the particulars of this woman's death. The facts in front of her. The rest of the answers to questions was the jurisdiction of the police and FBI.

Addie shifted and glanced at her colleague. "We know it's not the first time they've lost someone, but this one could have been a surprise with the new group. Maybe the others didn't die, and they only lost her. Assuming they currently have more than one test subject."

Sarah looked at the left arm, where the patch had been on the previous victims. "They gave her the same thing in the same place. New formula?" She looked at the victim's eyes and the skin around where the patch had been. She sat back on her heels.

Addie said, "What is it?"

"I need to run some tests. But I think she had an allergic reaction, maybe to something they put in the formula this time." She glanced up at Stella and Addie, standing over her.

Stella said, "But you'll need to get her back to the morgue so you can be sure."

Apparently, Sarah said that a lot. But it was true there was a limited amount of information she could ascertain from the field. She would do a full autopsy of this woman. The way she did with all the others, whenever necessary.

Giving a voice to those who no longer had one.

In a way, she felt like there was at least some correlation between her and Joseph. They both did jobs most people couldn't find the stomach to do. Not because they were somehow more skilled, but because some jobs took a certain kind of person. Not everyone could cut a dead body open and use science to figure out how they died. But with Sarah, she had to do it. There was nothing else that made sense. Her job was a mission.

Two staff members from the medical examiner's office showed up to escort the body back to the office.

Sarah pulled off her gloves and stood. "Do you need me to get started tonight?"

Addie shook her head. "First thing tomorrow is good. We all need sleep."

Stella squeezed the back of her neck with both hands, fingers linked together. "What we need is a lead on Markowicz. Or a way to find Brad and Karen. That's the only way we can get to the bottom of this."

"What about the vet?" Sarah asked.

Addie nodded. "The police department is taking the lead on finding out who treated those dogs."

Sarah figured there was a connection between the two. "We're looking for someone with the scientific knowledge and skill to modify narcotics made for pets. That means breaking down the base compounds of that patch and reconfiguring it for sale."

Stella said, "I figured they were just cutting and up, or attaching it to something else—putting something on it like a cream, and then it's good to go. Which was why it resulted in so many deaths."

"I think it might be more complicated than that. They'd

need a lab." Sarah let her mind process what she was thinking. "This has to be done by someone who knows what they're doing, not just some backwoods guy in a trailer."

"That's usually how the meth lab ends up blowing up." Addie shrugged. "This does seem a lot more sophisticated, or just established. They've got a procedure down for picking up victims that Emmalee told us all about, but she doesn't know how many girls they've got now. Losing the first batch of four to overdoses brought attention they didn't need. Now they're underground and trying to do this without getting caught."

"What about my dad?" Sarah didn't want to ask, but she had to. "Anything in his financials or business dealings that can lead you to them?"

Addie said, "We're hoping the judge will give us that warrant in the morning." She squeezed Sarah's shoulder, as though aware she was struggling with the fact her father was involved.

"And no one has seen Brad or Karen, or Markowicz, since the highway?" Sarah asked.

Stella shook her head. "Everyone is looking for them. They're probably holed up somewhere." She glanced over at where Joseph stood, keeping an eye on Sarah.

Now that she knew there was an active threat against him, Sarah wondered who was going to keep him safe. Sure, whatever he had going with Russ meant he believed he was protected. But what if someone found him?

Stella said, "He's kind of scary, right?"

Sarah glanced over at Joseph, trying to see what they saw. "He's a good man." But still, there was something dark, maybe edgy, about him.

He was a risk. Not just to her heart, but to everything else.

Maybe she needed a more secure footing. A foundation

she could rely on before she took a leap like him. That way she could fall back on something on the times she felt like she was out of her depth.

Since she'd felt that way since she was eight, it seemed strange to think she could suddenly have peace and safety in her life.

Stella said, "Oh, I know he's a good man. I'm just saying, he's also kind of scary. In a good way, like you'd know you never have to worry because he could take on the whole world."

The body was loaded onto a stretcher, and zipped up in the bag.

Sarah glanced over at Joseph, thinking about what Stella had said.

Addie squeezed her shoulder. "Let me know if you can get an ID on our victim."

Sarah nodded and followed the stretcher and her two colleagues out the door. Joseph went with her, and she hoped he didn't ask her what they'd been talking about. She wasn't sure how to explain the way Stella and Addie thought about him.

Maybe he didn't want the darkness in him.

She knew she didn't want the nightmares in her but had no idea how to get them out of her head. Pushing it down and pretending the fear wasn't there hadn't worked.

She needed to be completely changed from the inside out and made totally new. The way Addie had once told her God did for her after she surrendered to Him.

Sarah felt Joseph shift beside her.

A fraction of a second *before* the gunshots rang out across the parking lot, he was already moving. Almost at the same time, he slammed into her and tackled her to the ground.

One of her colleagues jerked and fell as well.

27

Joseph waited one breath, then pushed up enough for Sarah to be able to see his face. "Stay here until the police tell you it's safe to get up."

He pushed off the ground and ran along the outside of the building, headed in the direction the shot had come from. Given only one had gone off, and as he ran he wasn't shot by the gunman, he figured the guy was running.

Joseph picked up his pace. The neighboring building was the logical place to set up shop and take out Sarah—or attempt to.

It was a gamble as to whether this person knew what they were doing or not. From the distance over which they'd fired, wind resistance or poor training had meant they'd had a better shot to take out one of Sarah's coworkers instead of her. But even that guy wasn't dead—just winged. A graze. He would live.

Joseph had done his job keeping her safe, and now he would catch this guy.

He ran around the west side of the building. At the back corner he spotted a door open halfway down. The door slammed against the exterior wall and a man raced away from Joseph, carrying a rifle in one hand.

Aware his footfalls would echo off the side of the building, Joseph picked up his pace yet again. He closed in as the guy turned around.

Joseph figured there were cops right behind him. He shoved an arm out to push away the rifle before it could be aimed and tackled the guy to the ground.

He heard the man's skull crack on the concrete. Not something that was ever fun to experience.

Joseph held him down. "Don't move."

Brad Deverly stared up at him, fiery anger in his eyes. "You need to die."

The words were slurred, his expression glassy.

"She doesn't die." Joseph shook his head. "That's not how this ends."

Joseph hung on while the police ran to them, and one officer kicked away the weapon. They secured Brad just as Addie ran over.

Joseph shifted his weight and stood up. "He needs an ambulance. He hit his head pretty hard."

The officer grabbed his radio and requested a bus.

Stella clapped him on the shoulder. "You're pretty fast. You ever think about signing on as one of the good guys?"

Addie said, "I heard Vanguard wants to chat with him about a job."

"I need to get back to Sarah. Make sure she's okay." After all, if the three of them were over here behind the neighboring building, then who was with her?

Addie winced. "She's helping her colleague."

Joseph headed to her, hardly knowing what to think. If an FBI agent thought he had what it took to be one of the good guys, then maybe it was possible. Could he really have a life here, working for a private agency? What they wanted him to do, he had no idea. It depended on how much they knew about who he was.

Who he used to be.

If he stuck around, took a job, and lived in Benson, it would probably save his life. The man hunting him would never find him if things went according to plan. There was no guarantee, but much like with WITSEC, if he followed the rules, the outcome should be safety.

There was no reason to believe it wouldn't work when the Accountant's Office clearly knew what they were doing.

He walked around the building and spotted Sarah with two cops and her colleague. Using her skills to do good, despite her past.

He wanted to ask her if she would go to church with him. Talk about those things Russ had said, and what they meant. Everyone around him seemed to believe. While he had made that initial decision, it would take a whole heart change to continue to walk that path. And how did he do that?

Sarah glanced over.

Joseph stopped. They stared at each other for a moment while he tried to figure out if he could risk it all and take the leap.

He still hadn't figured it out the next morning when he dropped her off by the door of the medical examiner's office. Just before eight in the morning, so she could get in a full day's work on the autopsy of last night's victim.

They'd talked a little over breakfast, but since she had to be at work it wasn't as though they could linger and chat. And with him still trying to figure out what he was going to do, he wasn't sure what he was supposed to say. Apart from them talking over their surprise that Brad had shot at her and hit one of her colleagues. Thankfully, the guy was going to be fine.

"What are you planning on doing today?"

Joseph had already called Edith. "I am going to go check on those dogs I found. Make sure they're okay."

Her expression softened, losing some of the guardedness that had been there recently. "That's sweet."

He didn't know what to say to that. "Have a good day?"

He barely wanted to leave her here, but everyone knew the score. She would be protected at work.

"Very domestic." A glint flashed in her eyes. "Like this." She leaned over and kissed his cheek. "Have a good day, yourself."

She pulled back, but not far enough she was out of reach. Joseph leaned in and kissed her next, savoring the moment of connection between them as he explored the hope he'd found in what could be. What might be.

When he leaned back, she said, "Thank you for saving my life yesterday."

And then she was gone.

He watched her walk in the door, taking everything he wanted with her.

Joseph drove to the apartment building where he lived, a place he hadn't been back to in days except to grab more changes of clothes.

Edith walked out of the lobby as soon as he pulled up at the curb. She slid into the seat Sarah had occupied a moment ago. "What's with that look on your face?"

Joseph shook his head and pulled out. He drove to the vet's office because he'd told Sarah the truth about where they were going. He just hadn't mentioned the fact Edith was coming as well, and he intended to question the vet about other vets in the area who might be involved with Markowicz.

"Want to hear what Eric told me about Brad?" Edith asked.

Joseph glanced over. "He's talking?" She nodded, and he glanced back at the street in front of him.

"Markowicz is in charge," she said. "He's rolling over on the guy, telling everyone he was coerced into working for him because Markowicz is related to his wife."

"As if." Joseph shook his head. "And the suspicious disappearance of his first wife?"

Edith scoffed. "Exactly. Like we all don't know that's who Sarah saw in the woods? Now we just need the police K-9s to find the body."

"Do we think Brad killed her?" Joseph asked. "Maybe it was Markowicz."

"Or both of them. Maybe it was an agreement and Brad couldn't get out of it."

"I'm not convinced Markowicz is at the top of the food chain." He'd been thinking about this during the night. "I think he's up high, but someone else is either his partner or his boss in this."

And he wanted to know who the vet was because that would tell them more.

Joseph pulled into the neighborhood vet's office, and they called the number on the door. He asked to see the dogs that were brought in the other day.

The vet's office was already offering some of them for adoption—as long as it was to the right home. Animals used in a fighting ring couldn't go to just anyone's house. Especially ones where children lived. But he knew they were already trying to find them forever families.

"Hundred bucks says you've adopted one of these dogs by the end of the month." Edith grinned at him.

"Why would I take that bet when I'll probably lose?"

She chuckled as the vet's assistant opened the front door.

They stepped inside, and the assistant asked them to wait a moment, then wandered away.

Edith said, "A woman. A home here. A job with Vanguard. The dog would round out everything nicely, don't you think?"

"How do you know about the job with Vanguard?" Joseph didn't even know what it entailed.

Edith blanked her expression. "Maybe I'm confused. That could be about someone else."

"Russ already told me they're interested. What they want me to do, I have no idea." For all he knew they could be looking for someone to take up the same missions he used to go on. Maybe they had enemies, and they were looking for someone to take those enemies out.

Edith squeezed his arm. "They protect people. Kind of like the way you're doing with Sarah. They also investigate cases the police haven't been able to solve, and they're starting a cold case unit within the company. They also take on clients who can't afford a private investigator. They get pro bono help."

That actually sounded pretty good in terms of a job. The idea he had marketable skills was baffling, considering everything he'd done in his life. If he chose to take a job offered to him by these people, it would go a long way in helping him feel good about himself.

Sometimes he had to stop and look around, take a moment, and wonder how he got to where he was.

The vet wandered out wearing blue scrubs. He had long dark hair pulled back into a ponytail and was likely not thirty yet. "You're here to see the dogs that were brought in?"

Joseph nodded. "I'm the one who found them in that house."

The vet shook his head. "It's unbelievable the way they were treated. And yet, at the same time it's not so unbelievable at all. Which makes me despair about people."

Edith said, "You're preaching to the choir."

Joseph didn't disagree with them. But somehow here in Benson it felt as though things weren't as bad. Not that it was some kind of sinless utopia. Just that the outside world seemed a little farther away.

Living and working here, maybe even having a family, was an idea that made him want to quit running. Risk his heart. Give Sarah everything he could. Go to church and figure out what he hadn't grasped yet. Help take care of Edith. All of it.

"You want to see them?"

Joseph nodded and followed the vet through to a back room, where several dogs were in oversized pens.

The one who had been injured lay on a dog bed in the corner of the room but didn't get up. The animal blinked at him as Joseph knelt beside her.

He scratched the dog under the chin, thinking she looked a little loopy. Maybe drugged still from whatever procedure they had to perform.

"Huh."

Joseph didn't glance back to get a read on the vet's tone.

Edith said, "What is it?"

"Just that no one has been able to get that close to her without her snapping since she woke up from the anesthesia."

Joseph kept scratching her chin. "Are all of them going to get adopted?"

The vet blew out a breath.

Joseph stood, glancing around.

"Depends on how they do," the vet said. "We have a dog trainer coming in later to work with some of them, trying to see how bad the damage is. At least two will never be able to live with another dog in close proximity. It would be far too dangerous for the dog, or anyone caught between."

"But there are people who can fix that stuff, right?"

"If the dog is willing to make a change." The vet shifted his weight.

"Did you see any signs that they were treated by another vet while in captivity?"

The vet nodded. "The one there on the bed seemed to have had a broken leg at one point, and it was clear it had been set."

"Any idea who locally might have done that? Another vet you're aware of, with fewer scruples than you." Edith pinned him with a stare.

The vet said, "The police asked me all of this."

"Sometimes we remember things afterward that we forgot to say in the moment." Joseph didn't want him to think they were accusing him, but there could be more.

The vet blew out a breath. "Fine, there was a guy who used to work in town. He retired. And that was a good thing."

Edith said, "Give us the guy's name."

28

Soft classical music played through the speakers in the morgue. Sarah had a police officer in the hallway who occasionally stepped in to check she was all right. The fact it was Edith's grandson Eric, who started his new position as a detective in a week, made her feel better. But it also made her want to ask him some questions.

She needed to push aside the Joseph thing now that Brad was in custody, and she was back at work doing the autopsy so they could get some answers. There was no professionalism in being distracted by a relationship when she was supposed to be working. Especially if people's lives were on the line. Along with the course of justice.

She looked through the microscope. "Huh."

Sarah wheeled her chair over to the computer she had set up and pulled up the files for the four overdoses, wanting the ease of access her laptop would've brought her. Karen had smashed the thing, and her new one wasn't set up yet.

When she found what she was looking for, Sarah picked up the phone and dialed Addie directly.

"Special Agent Franklin."

"It's Doctor Carlton."

Addie said, "You want me to come down there?"

"I can email you the report with my findings, but I figured you would want to know ASAP."

"What did you find?"

"The victim we found last night had dust on her, but not from the warehouse where we found her. It was on her back. Under her shirt. Prior to her death, she lay on the ground and the dust stuck to her skin. She was probably sweating. After that, the shirt was replaced."

Addie made a *huh* sound. "Is there significance to this dust?"

"The particles are identical to the ones found in the head wound that one of the overdose victims suffered," Sarah said. That young woman seemed to have hit her head before her death. Most likely when she'd been thrashing around in the throes of the overdose. She'd managed to bang her head on something made of stone. "The results came back from the overdose victims."

"Right," Addie said. "That's how we know it was a trans-dermal patch they're using to deliver the drugs."

Sarah wouldn't be surprised if it was supposed to end up as some kind of temporary tattoo. It would likely sell extremely well to the clientele they were trying to attract. "The particulates that I'm looking at now are a match to the substance found on the victim with the head wound."

"Any idea what it is?"

"High-end quartz. The kind used to make kitchen coun-ters. And given the amount of dust on her, it's not just a house. More like the shop that sells the material to contrac-tors. Or wherever they cut it to size. Because these particu-lates are all over her."

"The kitchen counter store." Addie sounded excited. "I had something about that somewhere here..." Papers rustled. "Got it. Thanks!" The phone line went dead.

The FBI was on the case, off to try to track down the place where these tests subjects were being given the drug.

The door opened. Eric, her police guard for the day, wandered in. "Everything going okay?"

She nodded. "I found something that could be helpful to Addie. I'm guessing she's running out the door right now checking kitchen counter warehouses."

Sarah didn't like the idea of being in any more harrowing situations, so she was perfectly happy to stay down here. In the chill and the dim light. Doing her job and not running away from gunfire or the target of people who wanted to get away with their crimes.

"Would you mind showing me?" Eric motioned to the computer. "I figure it might come in handy for me as a detective to see a little more of what you do."

She explained about the head wound on the previous victim, and then showed him the dust she'd collected from the most recent victim's skin. "I was able to determine they're a match. The lab will have to confirm the precise makeup of the substance, just so it holds up in court more than my visual comparison. However, it's enough for Addie to get a warrant for wherever she believes the victim was."

"Wow. That's quite impressive."

Sarah finished up the last of the autopsy, for the most part cleaning up so she could return this young woman to a drawer that would preserve her until her family could claim the body.

As she was covering the young woman with a sheet, the computer behind her chimed a notification. Sarah glanced over her shoulder. "Looks like the fingerprints came back."

Eric stood at the computer beside her as she opened the file. He read the name. "The victim's name is Francesca Sanchez." He leaned forward and clicked the mouse. "And that's quite a rap sheet. Picked up three times for solicitation. Two counts of petty theft before that, and it looks like she's had some run-ins with substance abuse."

Sarah sent the results of the fingerprint ID to the FBI agents and police who were working this case, by way of a general update. One of them would contact the next of kin and informed them that Francesca was now deceased. The family would be able to lay her to rest.

All around them life would continue on.

She poured herself and Eric a cup of coffee. "Is Brad being interviewed?"

She wanted to know what was happening, but even just thinking about that guy made her shiver. He could have killed someone so easily. In reality he'd only winged her colleague. The way Joseph had been a day or so ago—and yet he seemed to be fine for the most part.

Did that make sense?

She'd forgotten completely about him getting shot.

Eric sat on one of the chairs in the morgue office.

Whichever medical examiner was doing an autopsy used this office, so there was nothing personal in here. But she still sat behind the desk.

"Overnight there was a lot of wailing about how he's being strong-armed into all of this by his wife and brother-in-law." Eric sipped his coffee. "He also says he didn't murder his first wife. But no one really believes that. He's just trying to talk his way out of suspicion. However, given he shot at you and the others, it's not like you'll be free anytime soon."

Sarah nodded.

"You have firsthand experience with his first wife and her death, isn't that right?"

She knew he was probing for information. Considering he was becoming a working police detective soon she didn't mind being an interviewee for him. It might be nice to have someone believe her for once. "When I was eight years old I wandered away from camp. I must've got lost because I ran into someone wearing a monster mask. When I ran from him I fell into a hole. She was there at the bottom. I must have passed out at some point because I woke up in my bed. Everyone passed it off as a nightmare."

"Except that it likely wasn't." Eric's phone chimed. He looked at the screen and frowned.

"Everything okay?"

"Just keeping an eye on Grams and what she's up to."

"Is she with Joseph?" He hadn't mentioned that to her over breakfast, but she knew they were close. "He was going to visit the dogs."

Eric made a face. "People like my Grams don't just visit. She wouldn't have gone to the vet without good reason, and it's probably not so that Joseph can make sure they're okay. No disrespect to the dogs. They probably need nice people to visit them."

"So what do you think she's doing there?"

Eric shrugged. "My guess would be asking the vet if he knows who treated them when they were with Markowicz." A vet with the know how to alter transdermal patches. Turning them into illegal drugs for humans to get high with.

Sarah leaned back in her chair. "I bet Joseph is all on board with that."

"They just left the vet's office. They're driving across town."

Sarah frowned. "You're tracking them?"

"Both of them have not-so-smart phones." Eric lifted his brows. "I put an air tag in her shoe."

"You put GPS on your grandmother."

He grinned. "Trust me. It's for the best."

"Like she's some kind of menace?"

He shrugged.

There was a lot of similarity between Edith and Joseph. Enough for Sarah to say, "How do you deal with it?"

"Because they aren't like us?"

Sarah didn't know that was completely true. "They just have…skills we don't have. Joseph thinks about things in ways I never would, and vice versa. There's also the guilt he carries around with him. I'm the same way, with fear that I've held on to for so long. I'd like to help him, but I'm not sure how to do that."

"Simple answer?" Eric said. "The truth is what sets people free."

She was about to argue when he continued.

"I'm talking about the truth of the gospel, and the way God can change everything in an instant. Take all that old garbage and replace it with hope and His love. That's the only way Joseph, or someone like Grams, can find peace."

"What about someone like me?"

Eric nodded. "It's for all of us. No matter what we've done, or what we've been forced to endure. We're all the same on the inside. People looking for acceptance and love, that we won't truly find anywhere else but at the cross."

Sarah thought over those church meetings she'd been to when she was little. The way it seemed like she just drifted away when life got busy. As though she'd graduated from those childish things when she left high school and went to college.

Eric said, "Stella goes to a class at church that's for new

believers and people who want to know more. If you'd like to go, or you just want more information…"

Sarah nodded. "I'd like that."

His phone buzzed again. He looked at the screen, his eyes widening. "A bomb threat just came through, targeting the stadium across town."

"Is there a baseball game on today?"

"Yes." Eric frowned. "The whole place will be packed."

"I'm fine, if you want to go help out." She couldn't imagine wanting to go and do the right thing, but instead having to sit around here with her where nothing was happening.

"I can leave this place locked down, so no one comes in or out." He stood. "If you're sure you'll be fine here."

"I'm not going anywhere. So if no one can get in, then I'll just get my work done."

"I won't leave the building until I know they for sure need my help." He headed for the door. "I'll go across the way and check in with my sergeant. See if they need me, and if they don't then I'll come back over. Hopefully I'll only be gone a few minutes, and then we'll know for sure."

She figured that was a good enough trade-off, and meant he wasn't abandoning her for long. Not that she considered it that. He had a job, and she didn't want to be the reason why he couldn't do it.

She heard the click of the door as he stepped out to the hallway. Sarah fired up the PC on the desk and opened the files she needed to type up her full report.

She was just getting into the third sentence when the door out in the morgue clicked again. "Is that you, Eric?"

No one replied.

Sarah sat back in her chair. She couldn't hear any foot-steps in the morgue, and no one darkened her doorway. She reached for the phone on the desk just in case she needed to call someone for help.

A figure dressed in all black wearing that monster mask stepped into the room. A woman, given the body shape. But that was not what had Sarah's attention.

It was the gun in the woman's hand.

The voice from behind the mask was distorted. "You aren't going to ruin this for us."

29

The office had a For Sale sign out front tacked across the sign for the veterinary office run by Carlos Alvarez. The vet currently treating the dogs Joseph had found in the garage had pointed them to this man. Carlos had been recently disgraced for some medical infraction Joseph hadn't needed the vet to explain.

All he needed to know was that Alvarez's veterinary business was over. The vet had told them that the guy's wife and family had left him as soon as the news came out about whatever he'd done. Apparently, this guy was the kind of person who could lay aside any scruples he might have for the right price.

Edith walked beside him from the car, but her attention was on her phone. "The cops are prepping to raid the counter store where they think the latest victim was before she died. The business is connected to Markowicz somehow."

The vet's office had a single light on in the rear of the building, once a house but now rezoned for business.

Edith stowed the phone. "Eric is checking in with his

sergeant, and then he's headed back down to watch out for Sarah."

Joseph nodded. "Good. What's the plan here?"

"You take the back door. I'll break in the front," Edith said. Probably because that meant he was more likely to meet the guy inside first and she would provide backup. Which was fine by him, considering his partner was in her eighties.

"Did you bring a gun?" He needed to know what kind of firepower she had.

Edith patted her jacket pocket. "Stun gun. Much easier to explain to the police."

Considering her family connection, it was probably a good idea that she didn't get caught breaking and entering with an illegal weapon.

"You?"

Joseph said, "Don't worry about me."

"Except that worry is part of this deal." Edith pinned him with a stare. "You're family now, and that means I'm going to worry about you."

She really considered him like one of her grandsons?

He wondered if he'd be in the column with the good one who was a cop, or the deceased ones who had been criminals. Then he had to let that thought go, because it was going to stay there in his mind and make him worry what she thought. Or what contingencies she had in place, when he inevitably did what she worried he would do.

Was she sure he would ultimately fail?

"I have a baton," Joseph said. "But I'm only planning on using it if necessary." Mostly it was for protection, but he also didn't need to get caught with any kind of weapon on him.

"So we're going to capture him and turn him over to the police?" Edith seemed kind of perturbed about that. Maybe she missed her old life of interrogations.

Joseph didn't need those particular skills right now. "Confirm he's connected. Detain. If we can hand him over with evidence, all the better." Russ might be the police commissioner, but that didn't mean he needed to break the law protecting Joseph.

"Copy that."

"Let's get inside." The quicker he could get this done and get back to Sarah, the better as far as he was concerned. All his protective instincts fired. But the need to finish this case and get all these guys to the police remained in the forefront of his mind.

After the arrests had been made and he knew Sarah was no longer under threat, then they could sit down—preferably over dinner—and have a conversation. Either they would agree to never see each other again or start something that would hopefully last as long as their lives did.

And there was the rub, he decided as he headed down the side of the house. Past a couple of trash cans. To the back gate, which he climbed over. Joseph crouched on the opposite side of the gate and waited a moment, making sure he wasn't going to be seen or attacked.

Even if he and Sarah decided to continue with a relationship, one of them would die first eventually. The other one would have to live without them. The way he had lived without Genevieve. He wasn't sure he could take any more heartbreak, even if it didn't happen for thirty years.

He moved to the back door and picked the lock. Inside he could hear someone moving around, frantically opening and closing drawers. Packing up so he could make a run for it?

He crept down the hall, past a bathroom far beyond when it should have been cleaned. He found Carlos Alvarez in what was probably his office at one point. Scooping papers from a file cabinet and tossing them into the fireplace, where flames roared.

"That's quite enough destroying of evidence."

Carlos swung around. He dove for the gun on his desk, but Joseph got there first. He ejected the clip and the bullet that had been chambered. Then he set the gun back on the desk.

He heard movement behind him and quickly checked. Edith stood by the door.

Carlos's gaze moved between them. "You aren't cops."

"Maybe not, but that's where you're headed." Joseph wasn't going to mince any words.

Carlos was older and had a dark edge to him. This wasn't someone Joseph would trust to take care of a beloved animal.

Joseph went to the fire and pulled out a paper that hadn't burned yet. The heat from the flames was enough to cause his face to flush.

The document was a receipt from a pharmaceutical company for narcotics. He waved the paper at Alvarez. "Fentanyl patches, maybe?"

"Doesn't matter." Alvarez lifted his chin. "The business is done, so what's the point keeping any paperwork? I need to get ready and sell this place."

"Because Markowicz cut you out now that the formula is complete?" Joseph said. "You've got nothing, so you're scrambling to figure out what to do next."

Alvarez's eyes flared. "How do you know the formula is done?"

It had been mostly a guess, but now he knew he was right. "You're going to tell us everything. And we're going to take you to the police."

The draw to do the right thing, and then go talk to Vanguard about their job offer was strong.

Strong enough to keep him in line, which he figured had

been Russ's plan all along. Combined with getting Joseph to figure out what was happening at the retreat camp. He would be mad that Russ hadn't said anything if he was accustomed to being told everything about a mission before he embarked on it. Maybe there had been a moment of irritation. But the truth was, Russ's decision made sense.

The corner of Alvarez's mouth curled up. "Just like that? I don't even know you guys, so I'm not telling you squat."

Joseph moved to him, grabbed the guy by the shirt collar, and sat him in the chair. "How long have you been working with Markowicz?"

Alvarez smirked. "Long enough to get myself a nice little nest egg, thank you very much."

"Nice for you." Joseph folded his arms. "How expansive is his operation?"

"You think you'll take everyone down?" Alvarez scoffed. "Markowicz will be long gone by then."

"You don't care that he had you do all the work, then split?"

"Oh, you think Markowicz cut me out?"

Joseph put a couple of things together. "He paid you, but you have to clean up. So you didn't leave town yet. Which is a shame, considering you're not going anywhere now."

Alvarez had come back here to destroy the paper trail that would lead anyone to him. He should've just left town and made a run for it, opting to put miles between him and the police rather than come here. Even if he wasn't planning on being long gone.

"How is the formula complete?" Joseph asked. "The last batch killed a woman."

"Because she had an allergic reaction. Markowicz is taking it to production."

And yet Alvarez wasn't involved.

Joseph said, "Where?"

Alvarez shook his head. "He'll know it was me that talked. I'll be dead man, not just one being hunted by the police."

He didn't seem too scared about that. Probably because Markowicz had set him up handsomely with a nest egg. That had to be what'd happened.

"Don't worry about that now." Joseph shrugged one shoulder. "In fact, the police will probably cut you a deal for giving them Markowicz. Maybe you can get a sweet set up in witness protection."

It was a long shot, and Joseph had zero ability to promise anything to this guy. But if it got him talking then it didn't matter. The other option he had was to interrogate Alvarez. He certainly knew how to use enhanced techniques, as he'd been fully trained like Edith. However, there was too much in him that didn't want to go back to the old way of doing things. He was supposed to be a new guy. Living a new life.

"You think I'm going to narc on him?" Alvarez laughed. "You have no idea who this guy is."

"That's why we're here," Joseph said. "So you can tell us where to find him, then we can go and get to know him ourselves."

"Good luck with that."

"It's over, Alvarez. You may as well just tell us where he is."

"Markowicz is crazy. I'm never going to cross him."

Joseph figured they'd never convince Alvarez they were a bigger threat than his former boss represented. And neither would the police.

"What is he planning?" Edith stepped farther into the room.

"You are going to the police," Joseph said. "What happens after that is entirely up to you. But we're talking about saving lives, something you might not have considered.

Whatever part you had in Markowicz's operation is over now. You don't get to escape. You've done some things you aren't proud of, and you knew it wouldn't last. Part of you knew that even if he set you up, you'd never get away from him."

Alvarez's eyes flared.

"This is your shot at a new life, the only one you're going to get. It's your chance to be the kind of person you respect instead of someone the police will hunt for the rest of your life."

"You think appealing to my sense of decency is going to work?"

That was when Joseph realized he wasn't anything like this guy.

He'd considered himself a bad guy for years. However, he was never going to act like this man. Alvarez didn't care a single bit about human life. Just what he could get out of it.

Joseph stared at him.

Alvarez lifted his chin.

Joseph glanced over his shoulder at Edith. "Call Addie. Tell her—"

A shockwave shook the building.

He ran to the front door and looked out, seeing smoke pouring up into the sky to the west of Benson. There had been an explosion, a bombing. Thankfully not in the direction of the medical examiner's office.

Joseph moved back to Alvarez, where the man now stood at the door. Edith held out her stun gun.

The guy didn't seem to be deterred, so she fired the thing at him. His body jerked and he hit the floor.

Edith said, "Find me something to secure him with. We can drop him off at the precinct."

He figured that was a good idea, considering all the on duty first responders would be heading to the scene of whatever explosion had just happened. No one needed to be pulled away from helping. Joseph intended on going there to help as soon as he could.

"Let's—"

Edith's phone rang. "It's Eric." She answered it, listened for a few seconds. "What do you mean, she's gone?"

30

S arah rolled over. Her hands had been bound in front of her. She tried to break the ties by slamming the inside of her wrists down on her knee, but it didn't work. Her hands were tied too tightly together when she needed an inch of space between them.

Karen had piled her into an SUV, forcing her at gunpoint to get in the back. *Karen.* Sarah had hardly been able to believe she was the one now behind the mask.

The trunk area was separated from the seats by a wire partition, the kind that kept dogs from getting in the front. Right now, Sarah was the one in the cage.

The vehicle swerved around a corner, and she rolled right into that mask. The one Karen had ripped off after she scared the daylights out of Sarah. Coming face-to-face with her nightmare while in that office, a place she was supposed to be protected, still made her want to quiver with fear.

Sarah grasped the mask with her bound hands and tossed it over by the wire partition before she scrambled to the back window.

Sarah lay on her back and brought her legs up. She bent

her knees in and with both feet kicked at the back windshield. Over and over again.

Up in the driver's seat, Karen screamed. Sarah ignored it, unable to believe Karen was the one who had killed Brad's wife all those years ago. She was old enough she might have been a young adult, or an older teen, at the time. As a child, Sarah hadn't been able to ascertain any details about who the person was. She had just seen that mask—the one that taunted her in her nightmares.

Karen might not have been the exact person there that night, but she clearly knew all about it. Which meant she likely knew who the killer was.

Sarah kept kicking the back windshield. She looked at the windows on the sides. *Hmm.* The smaller ones might be easier to smash, but she might be fighting a losing battle either way. She didn't care. She just kept kicking it with both feet.

Karen swerved again. Sarah rolled all the way to the side and hit the interior wall. One of her fingers bent the wrong way. Sarah screamed out her frustration, the way Karen had done.

If she could get the woman to crash, then they would never get where they were going.

Or someone else around them could see how erratically she was driving and call the police. After all, it wasn't late evening yet. Maybe she could get someone's attention.

Sarah clambered up onto her knees and looked out the back window.

An SUV followed them, and she could just about make out the driver. Sarah slammed her hands on the window as best she could. She knocked at the glass and tried to get the guy's attention. "Help!" she screamed. "Help me. I've been kidnapped!"

Even though she had no idea if he could hear her, she

had to do something. Otherwise, she wasn't giving herself any chance of getting free.

She slammed her hands on the glass, even though it made her finger fire with pain.

In the front seat, Karen screamed again. The SUV swerved in its lane. They turned a corner, bumping off the curb as they headed for the library. That probably wasn't where Karen was going, it was just the next milestone up ahead.

Now she could see the smoke column rising above buildings. The boom had rocked the SUV just a few moments ago. Sarah had no watch on. She couldn't think enough to figure out how long it had been since Karen surprised her in the morgue and forced her out at gunpoint. The woman had even put a bullet in the artwork that hung behind the desk, just to prove her point that she knew how to use the weapon.

Karen screamed again. If she was supposed to be some deadly killer, Sarah figured it wasn't about cold calculation. It was more about vengeance against people she considered to be her enemies. The woman probably murdered whoever she felt like killing when she was so full of anger that she couldn't help herself. Rage killings seemed like something Karen was a fan of.

But even that theory didn't help her calm. In fact, it made it worse.

The SUV swerved so sharply Sarah was thrown against the other side. Her head slammed against the plastic of the interior. She cried out as she face-planted, her nose pressed against the carpet. She tried to breathe through the throbbing pain in her head, and the way the ties pinched her hands together.

Karen was going to take her somewhere and rage kill her.

The woman was completely out of control, as though she

had suffered some kind of psychotic break. Then again, maybe this was her "normal."

Sarah lay in the back of the SUV, trying to figure out what she could try next. Alone with the person she had faced in the woods—or at least the manifestation of that nightmare. The eight-year-old in her memories didn't know the difference between that night and this day. All she felt was the same terror. The fact she was alone again with the fear.

Her scientific knowledge and reason didn't give her a way out of this. Not when she lacked the physical strength to break a car window.

How else was she supposed to get out of here? They were driving, so the back hatch wouldn't open.

As soon as Karen opened the door, Sarah would have to try and make a run for it then. Karen would probably shoot her in the back. And where were they going, anyway?

Tears gathered in the corners of her eyes and spilled down her cheeks.

Everyone said she needed to go back to that time in her life when faith in God had seemed so simple.

Sarah whispered, "Are You there, Lord?"

He had been Lord to her at one time in her life. Maybe all she had right now was whatever He could do to save her. After all, it wasn't like she could save herself.

More tears spilled out. She'd managed to make a career and a life, even if it was a lonely one all by herself. She'd done it all with her own brain power and independence. Her determination to succeed at the things she put her mind to.

But in the heat of the moment when she needed to figure a way out of danger, what did all that amount to?

"I need Your help, God."

The truth was, she wanted God to send Joseph to rescue her. It wasn't like she discounted the job the police did. They were probably busy dealing with whatever that explosion had been in the smoke rising from a building across town. Maybe Joseph was free, and they were all occupied.

Maybe the truth was that she didn't want people who knew her from work to see her like this. All that striving had given her a need to be seen as capable and strong, as a doctor who could figure anything out. The pride she had used to keep her heart protected, and to present everyone with the wall she had erected around her fears and insecurities didn't help her at all right now.

"I need You."

Immediately, a feeling washed over her. Sarah felt secure in a way she never had. Not for a very long time. It was as though she was being held by something. Or someone.

And in that moment, it was exactly what she needed.

No matter what happened, she wasn't alone.

After Karen took another sharp corner, Sarah rolled and braced her hands against the side, determined not to let this woman win.

They bumped up something, and Karen hit the brakes.

Sarah looked out the side window and saw familiar brickwork. All the energy she had slipped away, and she lay there wondering if she should simply refuse to cooperate. Maybe it would be for the best if Karen couldn't get her out of the back of the SUV. Whatever plan Karen had Sarah needed to stall it long enough for help to arrive. Or destroy it completely...somehow.

The driver's side door slammed shut.

When the back opened, Sarah braced. In a way she expected to be shot right here.

Instead, Karen leveled the gun at her. "Let's go. Your dad's waiting."

Sarah frowned. This was her father's house. "Why are we here?"

"Just get out, or I'll shoot you in the car. I lose nothing."

Sarah wasn't sure that was entirely true. She sat up slowly. Her limbs didn't seem to want to cooperate.

"Come on." Karen huffed. "Move it."

"Is my father inside?" Fear caused her stomach to flip over. "Is Markowicz in there?"

"So the police know he's involved, huh?"

Sarah scooted to the edge. "They think he's in charge. They have no idea you're the one with all the smarts."

"Flattering me isn't going to get you anywhere. You still die, so don't bother trying to talk me out of it." Karen grabbed her arm. She walked Sarah in front of her, pointing the gun at her back.

Sarah winced and nearly stumbled.

"Open the door."

Before she could reach for the handle, the door opened. Her father stood there with a haggard expression on his face.

"Dad, she—"

Her father turned away, leaving the door open.

"—has a gun."

Karen shoved her after her father. Sarah stumbled down the hallway. Surely he would trip the security alarm, the way she'd done when those men broke in last time.

Her dad went to the living room and poured himself a drink. Karen stood at the entry arch, holding Sarah in a firm grip. As they watched, her dad slumped onto the couch.

Karen shoved her over to him. "Sit."

"So you're here to kill both of us?"

"Murder-suicide is a whole lot easier to explain than one random death."

Sarah said, "It sounds like you have experience."

Karen rolled her eyes. "How do you think I've kept going all these years?"

"And the police never even realized that you're the one in charge?"

Karen smirked.

Sarah bit the inside of her lip. Karen might want her to believe that, but Sarah wasn't sure it was true. "Why do you need to kill me and my father?"

Karen shifted the gun to point at her dad. "Maybe I won't, if he gives me what I want."

"The more lives you take, the more evidence you leave behind for the police. It doesn't matter how much you stage the scene. Someone will eventually figure it out. Are you willing to take that risk?"

"Don't bother trying to argue with me. If your dad gives me what I want, then I'll leave. It doesn't matter about the scene." Karen made a face. "I'll be long gone."

Sarah glanced at her father. "What is she talking about? What do you have to give her?"

She figured this was about money. Why else would Karen make a stop before she left town?

Her dad's face had paled, sweat dripping from his hairline. Her stepmom was still in the hospital. But given how he'd treated Misty, Sarah doubted the woman would come back to this house after she was released.

Right now she was staring down the barrel of a gun. Not the time to worry about the future of her dad's marriage.

"Dad." She needed him to tell her what was going on.

"Yes, tell her." Karen smirked. "Tell her all about how you've been the broker for every piece of treasure we pulled out of that shaft."

31

Joseph had drawn the line at stealing a police officer's uniform. Edith had some interesting ideas sometimes. But that meant he was currently hiding in a closet with the door cracked, waiting for two cops to pass by before he headed on.

Yes, he was sneaking into a police station, but nothing was going to stop him getting the information he needed to save Sarah.

Someone had kidnapped her from the morgue. Meanwhile, across town the raid on the counter store had gone horribly wrong.

He had no idea what happened as a result of the explosion that went off. There had been too much traffic to get anywhere near it, even if they'd wanted to. It wasn't where Sarah was. It was where almost every first responder in the city had gone, and that meant they had plenty of help to figure out the damage.

Joseph took a second and prayed for anyone that had been inside the counter store when it exploded. Right now, he had no idea if there were casualties.

He was determined to make sure Sarah wasn't one that went unnoticed.

"That's what I'm saying, honey." Edith's voice trickled toward him.

She was cut off. "Grams, I don't need you in the middle of this. I'm already coordinating several things. Why can't you wait around to hear like everyone else?"

To his credit, he sounded suspicious. Maybe Eric knew what was going on. If it was Joseph's grandma, he wouldn't trust her. Not given her history. Eric was too smart to take what she said at face value.

"I just want to make sure Stella and the others are okay."

"I have no idea who is hurt and who is all right." Eric blew out a breath. "The info I'm getting is spotty at best. I want to go over there and help out, but I can't. Someone has to stay behind at the precinct and hold down the fort."

"But we all know it was Markowicz, right?"

Eric winced. "What do you think you know about this guy?"

"Just that he's probably the one behind it," Edith said. "It seems like everyone involved in this is cutting and running."

"Where's Joseph?"

"Busy."

"And the fact Sarah was taken from the morgue?"

Edith said, "I'm surprised you aren't out there trying to find her."

"I have techs looking at the surveillance footage. All I can tell you is from the build, it was likely a woman."

Edith huffed. "Karen."

"So why don't you run along and inform Joseph of that piece of intel. If he can get to Sarah quicker than we can—which I wouldn't discount—then good for him. And he can call if he needs backup."

Joseph would do that. Maybe.

Eric wandered off. After a few seconds of nothing, Edith pulled the door open. "Let's go."

"You think he knows we're here to talk to Brad?"

Edith shrugged, heading for the stairs at the end of the hallway. "Maybe he figures you're more likely to get information out of him than any of the cops here."

"Good." Joseph didn't know the procedure of interviewing someone in holding, but he just hoped he'd be able to do it. "I don't need any of them getting in my way."

He knew he was pushing it. Russ would likely give him problems after all this was done, but right now everyone was far too busy saving lives. Hopefully when it all blew over, they would know he'd done the right thing and didn't get in the way of any first responder trying to do their job.

The door to holding was propped open, which he figured was to let in the draft. The temperature down in the basement was considerably warmer than upstairs.

Edith headed in first, talking to the sergeant as though she was lost on a tour of the precinct. She had the guy walk her over to the elevators.

While she was around the corner, Joseph slipped down the hall and searched each cell for Brad.

He found the guy at the end of the row in an oversized cell with four guys in it. One was asleep, his head against the wall. Two chatted with each other, one of them not looking so good. Probably because of a hangover given the pallor of his skin.

Joseph went to the side of the bars where Brad leaned against the wall sitting on a bench. "I need to talk to you."

Brad moved only his gaze to Joseph. That was all the effort he put into acknowledging Joseph's presence in the hall. "You think I want to talk to you?"

"Maybe when you find out Karen kidnapped Sarah because she's going to make a run for it."

Brad made a *pfft* sound with his lips. "Setting up shop somewhere else isn't making a run for it. As if she could get all of the..." His eyes narrowed. But he closed his mouth, and said nothing else.

Joseph held on to the bars, squeezing them with a tight grip. It was good the door stood between them. If he had his bare hands on Brad's neck, it might get him answers to his questions, but it wasn't going to go well for the guy.

With Sarah who knew where, possibly in danger. Maybe dead? Joseph hung on to the tether of his control like a man about to snap. No one wanted to know what happened if she was hurt, or killed, because of these people.

Joseph didn't like being back at that place where everything he wanted was destroyed in front of him and he was left with nothing. Caring about someone again would always be a risk, but to have the woman he loved taken from him a second time would be completely unfair.

Then again, there was no guarantee in life that things would be fair.

He dipped his head, bending slightly as he looked at the floor. He blew out a few breaths and sucked in long clean ones.

Don't make me go through this again.

He shouldn't be bargaining with God. But what else was he supposed to do when he needed to make a deal. He needed a promise—no, a guarantee—that she would be all right.

Joseph lifted his head. "Tell me where Karen would've taken Sarah before she left town?"

Brett said, "I knew you weren't a chef."

"I never said I was a chef. But I am a cook, and I thought

that was why I was at the retreat camp." Joseph shrugged. "If anyone was lying about their reason for being there, it would be you and your wife. And everyone else who worked there except for me."

"Oh good, we're going with the 'high and mighty' defense." Brad blew out a breath. "What do I care about telling you where she is?"

"Doesn't matter if you care or not. You're still going to tell me."

"I'm in here, and she's out there. If she's leaving, then she's already cut me out. She's going to start over with her brother somewhere else, and I'm done. Which I already knew."

Joseph said, "Where is she starting over?"

"She never told me." Brad glanced to the side.

"What would she retrieve before she left?" He wanted to ask why Karen would take Sarah, but he had no idea if that was even the right question.

"Whatever is left."

"Why does she need Sarah?" The question came out before he even thought it through. Maybe that wasn't what was going on. Was she leverage? Sarah could be just the tying up of another loose end.

There was a reckoning coming between Joseph and Markowicz. Whether the guy had left town or not Joseph figured sooner or later they would face one another.

"My guess?" Brad said. "To force the old man to give her what's left."

"What's left of what?"

"The treasure, obviously."

The rest of the holding cell perked up. One of them got up. "Treasure?"

"I figured that was just a myth," Joseph said.

Brad made a face. "I wish it had been, but we found a bunch of stuff in the tunnels under the camp. They were built before we ever got there, and whoever owned the place hid their artifacts down there. By the time we found them everything was vintage. Valuable stuff, like silver plates and candlestick holders. Not a ton of money, but enough to keep us going while we built the business."

"Who has the rest?" He asked the question even though in his mind synapses fired and he was already figuring out the answer.

"Rob Carlton. The lawyer."

Sarah's dad. "How does he fit into this?" Joseph couldn't work that part out.

"He has connections at art auctions. He would sell pieces a couple of times a year, not so many that anyone would ask questions about where they came from."

"What about laundering money through his firm?"

Brad shrugged. "He did all kinds of things for us. Until he decided he was done, which Markowicz didn't like at all."

"Where do I find him?"

"You don't." Brad shook his head.

Joseph pushed off the bars of the holding cell and turned to the hall. Eric stood at the far end, along with the duty sergeant and Edith. To her credit, she looked a little apologetic.

Eric said, "Are you done?"

"I know where Sarah is."

Eric glanced at the sergeant, who nodded. Then he said, "I'll go with you. Grams can wait in the car."

Joseph was going to drive himself, because he wasn't waiting for whatever protective gear Eric would want to grab on his way out. He raced up two flights of stairs, across the building to the front door of the precinct.

He jumped in his car and drove all the way to Sarah's

dad's house, praying the entire time that he wouldn't get there too late.

The niggling idea that God wanted his trust regardless of the outcome wasn't something he could accept at first.

It started as a flicker of an idea, a nascent thought passing through his mind.

The God he had understood as a boy never wanted a personal relationship with people. He only wanted to lord it over their lives while they lived in strict obedience to him. The heavenly Father who seemed ready to come near to him now was much different. The reality that He might be asking for Joseph's broken heart was scarier than blind obedience. It meant he would have to change everything about himself and put Sarah's life in His hands rather than Joseph doing everything he could to save her life.

Then again, he hadn't been successful in that before. He'd lost Genevieve and his son.

A stray tear rolled down Joseph's cheek, and he swiped it away.

Even though he didn't want to admit it to himself, God had been there in those moments after she died. Joseph should have looked to Him then. Maybe he wouldn't have become what he was now if he had. But the past was in the past, and there was no way to change it.

All he could do was change his behavior going forward.

"Help me through this." Joseph took a breath and swallowed. "No matter the outcome." God would be with him now, the same way He seemed to have always been there before. In a way that was unavoidable.

Joseph parked down the street from Sarah's dad's house. A man stood in the drive, carrying a gun. Maybe the guy who had slipped out the window. Or was it Markowicz?

Regardless, he intended to get inside and get her back.

Police sirens in the distance made him wince, then picked

up his pace. The guy turned. Joseph slammed into him and tackled the guy to the ground. He knocked him out and stole his weapon. Just as he straightened, a gunshot shattered the front window.

From inside the house, Sarah's dad cried out, "No!"

32

Karen waved the gun around wildly. Sarah lowered her hands from her ears and looked at her dad. She'd been sure they were about to be killed, but Karen seemed content to terrorize them until she got what she wanted.

"Do you have what she's after?"

Her dad looked between her and Karen, his eyes slightly glassy. Disoriented, or in shock. He'd seemed almost disgruntled when those men had broken in last time. What was it about Karen that left him off-kilter?

"Dad." She reached out with her bound hands and touched his arm.

He drew it away. "Don't." The drink he'd poured sloshed over the side.

"Just give her what she wants. It's not worth our lives." Surely he wasn't going to dig his heels in when Karen had a gun.

"Yeah, just give me what I want." Karen stalked across the room to level the gun at Sarah's head. "Or I kill your precious daughter. Her dead brains all over your couch."

Sarah squeezed her eyes shut, expecting the shot at any time. Karen would do it. She would take a life to get what she wanted. But why? "You don't need to do this."

"No?" Karen's expression hardened. "Your dad can just give me what I want. Then I *won't* be doing this. I'll be out of here. No muss. No fuss." She touched the muzzle of the gun to Sarah's temple.

Sarah gasped. The metal was hot—since it had just been fired. She cried out.

"Give me what I want!" Karen yelled. "Now!"

"Dad, just do it." She braced for the shot that would surely come at any moment. "Give her what she wants!"

Something crashed outside. Karen rushed to the window and tugged back the drape.

Sarah twisted around to her dad and laid her hands on his arm again. "Can you just give her what she wants?"

"And let her win?" His jaw flexed. He seemed so determined, and at the same time so beat down.

"You'll be saving our lives," Sarah hissed. "She'll leave."

"She'll kill us whether she gets what she wants, or not."

Karen stared out the window and muttered to herself, apparently not concerned with their whispered conversation.

Sarah said, "Did you hit the panic button somewhere, so the police are coming?"

He opened his mouth, then pressed his lips together.

She figured that was a no. Though, she had no idea why he hadn't taken any chance he was given to get help.

She wondered about the explosion she'd seen from the car. What had happened, and how many people were hurt? There had been a bombing at a nightclub a few weeks ago. Eighteen people had died that night, more had lost the fight later. Even more suffered injuries—or were forever altered by their grief. Had something like that happened again?

She wanted to know what was happening out there. But right now Karen had that gun pointed at them again.

The police were all busy, probably. Was anyone coming to help? Maybe she needed to drag this whole situation out until someone realized she'd been taken, found her and mounted some kind of rescue.

Could she do that for long enough when it was possible no one knew? Eric had gone to find out what was happening about a stadium bomb threat. But that wasn't where the explosion had come from.

"You should just go, Karen." Sarah shifted in the seat and sat straighter. "You aren't going to get what you want here. And if you kill us, you can guarantee the police are going to hunt you until they catch you, and then you'll be in jail forever."

She expected the fear to overwhelm her, but it didn't. Sarah's deep dark places, where the nightmare resided, didn't swell to encompass everything. So often the fear eclipsed her rational thinking and she was left almost incapacitated. It had happened many times.

But not today.

It wasn't that she didn't see Karen as a serious threat. More than those deep places seemed to be full of calm. That peace she'd never felt before like this. *God, are You doing that?* She wanted to lean into it, as though she could draw it around her like a blanket on a cold day.

She'd never even known that was possible. But then, she'd always trusted her own strength and intelligence to fight the darkness. As if that ever worked. She didn't have enough to combat this, and now God seemed to have swooped in to surround her with His peace it seemed that old way of doing things was so futile. She could still die, along with her father. She might not make it out of this in one piece. God's help didn't guarantee everything would be fine—just that she would be held through it all.

Karen stalked back to them. "You think the police care if I kill this piece of trash?" She pointed the gun at Sarah's father. "No one will when they find out what he's done!"

Sarah flinched. "Dad." She didn't like the tone of her voice, but it was strange to worry about that right now. "What is she talking about?"

"Yeah, tell her all about it." Karen sneered.

Her dad swallowed. "They bring me artifacts a couple of times a year. I forge papers and sell them at auction."

"Karen already said that. I know this isn't about money laundering." Except that in a way, it was since it converted an illegally obtained asset into legitimate money. A cash payout Karen could use to fund her lifestyle. Or whatever plan she had next.

"I had no choice." He took a sip, as though he needed that liquid courage.

Sarah already knew that plan was as futile as trying to find strength inside herself, where the fear resided. "What do you know about Markowicz and what they've been doing?"

Maybe he had no clue about the overdoses and how it all linked to the formula they were creating out of transdermal patches.

"They're killing people, Dad. And you're helping them do it." Tears spilled from her eyes. Sarah swiped them away, so much grief in her for the destruction these people had caused.

He sat back on the couch and said nothing. He didn't even look at her.

Sarah had to figure out how else she could drag this out.

Karen rounded the armchair and waved the gun at her dad. "Tell me where you keep the artifacts, Rob!"

A flash at the window caught Sarah's attention. Through the drapes she could see someone…Joseph. He was outside? Relief washed over her at the sight of him. But she couldn't let Karen know someone was there, so she kept her reaction to herself—or tried to.

Joseph started to mouth something. Karen spun around. He disappeared so fast she didn't even have time to blink.

Karen didn't need to get freaked out and start shooting.

Sarah had to distract her. Give Joseph enough time to come in here. "Was it you I saw that night at camp when I was eight?"

Karen flinched. "What are you talking about?" She whirled around and pointed the gun at Sarah.

"In the mask. Was that you?" She bit her lip.

"You're that sniveling kid?"

"You killed Brad's first wife." The memories tried to threaten her composure. Sarah drew on the well of peace, and they were beaten back. Like the tide swallowing up the beach, the peace moved as though it was relentless in a way that brought hydration to her parched soul.

"That was Brad." Karen scoffed. "She was going to run off with the treasure."

"He killed his wife?"

"I'm his wife," Karen yelled. "We were high school sweethearts. She was *nothing!*"

"So he got rid of her, or you did? And you guys ran that camp out of the goodness of your hearts?"

"I was there to take her place." Karen scoffed. "Is that what you wanna hear? Cause you already think I'm a skank, Ms. High and Mighty Doctor of Whatever. We're the pillars of the community, not you."

Sarah didn't even know where to start with that. "You should just go, Karen."

"When I get my money and whatever artifacts he's got, I will." Karen dragged Sarah out of the chair and held on to her arm while she pressed that gun against the side of Sarah's neck. "Tell me where it is, Rob. Or do you care about her the way you care about your *wife*?" She spat the last word.

"Can you just give her what you have, Dad?"

He blinked. "I already did. I gave them everything."

"She's going to kill me!" Sarah expected the shot at any moment. "I need you to *do something*." More tears rolled down her cheeks.

Joseph was here, but he couldn't move faster than a bullet that would exit the gun and immediately kill her.

"Get me that stuff, Rob. Or she's dead."

Her dad levered himself off the couch like he was a hundred years old. "Okay. Okay. Don't kill her."

Karen dragged Sarah along, following him to the study. She stopped them at the doorway. "Where is it, Rob?"

Sarah couldn't hear anything over the rush in her ears.

Her dad lifted the painting from the wall beside the bathroom. Behind it was a safe Sarah hadn't known about. He typed in the code and the thing clunked as it opened automatically. He tugged the little door open. "Everything I have is in here."

He stumbled back and slumped onto the arm of his study couch.

Karen moved to the safe. "You got another one of these, Rob? A second safe no one knows about?" She levered the gun at him, still holding on to Sarah's arm with a punishing grip.

Sarah wanted to shove Karen away and run for the bathroom. Maybe she would get there before Karen could shoot her in the back. She would lock the door and escape out the window.

"You tell me where that is, and I'm gone, Rob."

Sarah winced. "Dad." She wasn't sure what she was asking him to do, but if he didn't do something Karen would probably kill both of them. *Joseph, where are you?*

She wanted him here with her. She wanted a family, with love and children of her own. She'd found peace with God. Could she have the rest with Joseph? He could have back what he lost. Not exactly, but something new that might help to heal the part of him that had been broken when something unimaginable happened.

Karen yelled, "Rob!" and swung out with the gun. She clipped his head with it, and he immediately fell sideways.

He slumped to the ground, caught himself with both hands and lay there panting.

Sarah rushed to her father, but Karen grabbed her arm and shoved Sarah toward the safe. "Get everything out."

Sarah looked at her dad, then did what Karen said. She wanted to be out of arm's reach so she wasn't grabbed anymore. Her bound hands made things awkward, but she got it done.

She spotted movement in the bathroom out the corner of her eye. Just the shift of a shadow, the barest flash. Sarah pulled the files and a silver plate out of the safe.

She spun around and threw it all at Karen.

Papers fanned everywhere. Karen squealed and flung her arms up.

Joseph slammed into her, so fast Sarah hadn't even seen him before he was already past her. The two of them went down. He got the gun out of her hand and flipped her on her face while Karen screeched. "It's over. I took care of the guy outside."

He would need something to tie her up.

Sarah said, "Dad—"

He clutched his chest, gasping. Face red. Trying to breathe. Fighting for his life.

"Dad?" She knelt beside her father.

He was having a heart attack.

Joseph said, "Sarah?"

"We need an ambulance!"

33

The FBI showed up just as Sarah's dad was loaded into the ambulance.

Joseph watched the flush come over her cheeks, along with a look of relief.

Sarah waved her over. "Addie!"

Special Agent Franklin and Special Agent Davis strode to them, and both gave Sarah a hug.

"I'm going with my dad."

"Good," Addie said. "We need to talk with Joseph." Thankfully it didn't seem like he was in trouble. The first officers who arrived took the man who'd been outside and Karen into custody just as the ambulance arrived.

Sarah glanced at him, then at the ambulance that was waiting for her. She had seconds but took the time to rush over and touch her lips to his. In front of people. She held his gaze in a way he didn't ever want to move away. "Thank you."

He nodded. "I'll be there soon."

Sarah nodded back and ran to the ambulance, ready to take her father to the hospital. Thankfully she'd been able to treat him—and grab his heart medication. He'd been stable by the time he was loaded onto the gurney.

"Got a minute?"

He turned to Addie. She really did need him for something, and that wasn't just a line she'd fed Sarah to make him look more impressive. Of course not. Addie wasn't that kind of person.

Joseph blew out a breath. "Yes."

Stella shifted closer so three of them stood in a huddle. "What's going on?" He started to shake his head and she cut him off with a lifted hand. "Don't brush it off. Tell us."

"I thought you were in court."

"When all this is happening?" Stella waved a hand around. "I hit the lights and sirens and drove back." She folded her arms. "Now spill."

"I was just thinking of you guys, but in terms of people I used to know and how they were."

Stella's gaze softened. "Takes a while to believe in it, right? When you're used to people being one way. Or doing things one way."

"Yeah, it does."

"I had to learn how to trust that the people I cared about wouldn't leave."

Addie said, "I had to learn how to share myself with the people I love. Not just be closed off all the time but open up."

Joseph said, "But you do it now, right?"

"It's a journey." Stella shrugged. "Some days I'm better at believing than others. I'm in this for the long haul, though. So no matter if I fail sometimes, I'm still determined to head in one direction."

Addie picked up as soon as she left off. "It's not a switch that's flipped and suddenly you're different. It's about making the choice every day to be who you want to be."

He seemed to be making giant strides in the right direction, but sometimes it felt like slow progress. Still, he'd rather be talking about this with Sarah than two FBI agents. "What happened with the counter store, which I'm guessing—but I have no idea—has something to do with an explosion across town?"

Addie said, "Thankfully no one was killed, though there's an officer with a concussion and a few with bruises and scrapes. Markowicz must have been cleaning up because the counter store and warehouse behind it were all decimated. Right before we were about to go inside."

"Sounds like a close call."

Stella shook her head. "It was basically a miracle by the sound of it."

Joseph said, "Did you find Markowicz?"

"No. And we've been interviewing bystanders and running down leads for hours while the fire dept put out the blaze caused by whatever exploded in the counter store." Addie pointed at Karen, who was sitting in the back of a police car. "That's why we're here."

Stella strode over to the officer, and they had Karen get out of the car.

Joseph explained everything he'd heard between Karen, Sarah, and Sarah's father inside the house, so she was up to speed with what had gone on. Addie's eyebrows raised when he mentioned the treasure he'd overheard Karen talking about. But mostly he figured calling it that might be overstating things.

The real crimes here involved death and drugs, along with conspiracy and money laundering with Mr. Carlton's law firm. Those were the charges that the DA would probably bring against them. Treasure hunters would show up looking for what was left. Rumors would abound about what had been found, and who still knew where the rest could be —or if there was even anything to find.

Joseph had a life here to build. He wasn't about to go chasing something that could easily amount to nothing. He needed to find peace in his soul, and then he could be the man Sarah needed in her life.

Addie and Joseph moved their huddle to the spot with Stella.

Karen eyed him, but Joseph didn't care. She said, "So you *are* a cop."

He shook his head. "Nope. Never have been, doubt I ever will be." And that wasn't a slight. It just wasn't the life he'd ever lived.

Karen gaped at him. "Then who are you?"

Stella chuckled. "Girl, get in line for an answer to that question."

Addie glanced over at Joseph, a knowing smile on her face. As Russ's niece and someone who had been read in on a certain amount of the detail of the Accountant's Office and its clients, she knew enough. Nowhere near everything, though.

Addie said, "I'm not going to beat around the bush, Karen. And I won't be recommending any deals until I know for sure that Mr. Carlton is going to make it. As far as I'm concerned you should be working on a defense for murder charges with your lawyer as soon as they can show up to officially take your case."

Karen started to sputter.

"In the meantime, the more help you give me the better it will look for you."

Karen's expression shifted to something belligerent.

"Woman, you have no leverage." Joseph was so done with her drama and demands. He could still see her in his mind, waving that gun around. Threatening to blow Sarah's head off. If he was supposed to forgive her, that was going to be one of those things that would be a journey with ups and downs as well as wins and failures. A choice he made every day.

Joseph was more interested in Sarah, her kisses, and the fact all he wanted to do was choose to be there for her—and love her—every day.

The rest of the world wasn't something he cared to bother with.

Not a lot of people would understand his need to be solitary. Living at the retreat camp had been refreshing for his soul, even with how it ended. He needed a small life. One that wasn't influenced too much by people around him, beyond those he trusted to be part of it. What the rest of the world did was up to them.

He was going to live the life he'd been given to the best of his ability, the way he believed he was supposed to.

Stella said, "Well?"

It snapped Joseph out of his thought train, but the question wasn't for him. Karen made a face, but she said, "You already have Brad. Isn't he telling you everything?"

"He told me where to find you." Joseph folded her arms. "Now you can tell us where to find Markowicz so people stop dying, and all this mayhem can be over."

"Yeah," Karen's tone sounded hollow. "Tell you where the big boss is."

Stella frowned.

Joseph and Addie stood quietly.

Karen rattled off an address, cross streets, and the name of a park. "That's where we're supposed to meet. At midnight tonight."

"How do we know it's not a trick like the counter store?" Addie said. "Could be another ploy to take out the police."

Karen rolled her eyes. "I don't know anything about that.

I was just supposed to get what Rob Carlton had and meet my brother so we can make a run for it."

"So where is he right now?" Joseph wasn't interested in waiting all the way until midnight. He wanted this thing over before he headed to the hospital to find out if Sarah's dad was all right.

Karen's expression shifted. She likely tried to disguise it but didn't manage to as much as she thought she was.

The woman shouldn't ever sign up to be a spy. She'd make for a terrible one.

Karen said, "How should I know where he's at now?"

"The entire police department and the FBI here in Benson are all looking for him." Stella folded her arms. "It's only a matter of time. And the longer it takes, the worse it will be for him."

Karen pressed her lips together. A few seconds later she gave them an address.

Joseph turned for his car. He had the driver's door open when Addie grabbed the handle for the passenger side. He'd been so single minded he hadn't noticed her behind him. "You're not riding with Stella?"

"I'm not letting you go alone." Addie slid in. "Call it insurance."

Joseph headed to the address she put in her GPS. "You really think this is where he is?"

Addie shrugged, barely a shift of her mouth, but it said enough about her feelings on the subject. "She might be content to take everyone with her if she's going down for this. Or she's playing some other game. But it didn't seem like she thought she had a choice."

Ten minutes later Joseph pulled up in front of the house.

"Oh, and you're staying in the car." Addie shoved the door open and got out.

He turned the engine off. The two female FBI agents

headed up the front walk. He stuck by the car but wasn't going to stay inside while they did their jobs with no idea what was happening.

He figured at the least he could watch the street in case Markowicz decided to rabbit and make a run for it.

The guy had tortured him with that trough of water. Tried to get Joseph to talk. They had a score to settle, and that meant he wanted to see the guy behind bars alongside Brad.

And everyone they worked with that was left free.

Addie went in the front. Stella took the back door. Fifteen seconds later Markowicz climbed out what was probably a bathroom window onto the driveway and raced for the front. Joseph crouched behind his back bumper out of sight until Markowicz reached the sidewalk. No visible weapon.

Joseph launched up and tackled him to the ground, landing awkwardly on his wrist in a way that didn't feel good. They rolled. He punched Markowicz in the kidney. "That's for nearly drowning me."

The guy didn't hear or didn't care. He tried to strangle Joseph, but he had little hand to hand experience beyond bar fights. That was painfully clear.

Joseph pinched a nerve in his neck and felt Markowicz twitch as blood was cut off to his brain. He slammed both palms against the guy's ears. While he was stunned from the disorientation, Joseph flipped him to his front and pulled his arms behind his back.

"Good." Addie produced cuffs from the back of her belt. "Works for me."

"A citizen's arrest?"

"Maybe you'll get a commendation."

Joseph huffed. Did he want one of those? Right now he just wanted to see Sarah. Make sure she was okay, and her dad, too. Tell her this was over now. Everyone was in cuffs and she wouldn't be a target again.

Addie pulled Markowicz to his feet and read him his rights. "Let's go."

"Wait. I'll talk." He struggled. "I'll tell you what I know. All of it."

Stella followed them. "Sure, you can do it in an interrogation room."

"This won't be over." He shook his head, desperate now. "It never will be."

"It is now you're in custody," Addie said.

"You think I'm the one in charge?" Markowicz fought against the restraints. "I'm not the one who calls the shots. I work for him."

Addie said, "Don't bother trying to convince us that Brad is the boss."

"Brad?" Markowicz glanced around. "You mean you haven't figured it out yet?"

Joseph remembered him being on the phone more than once. Receiving orders. "Who tells you what to do?"

Markowicz swallowed. "Washington Harper."

The groundskeeper? "You tried to have him killed days ago."

Markowicz shook his head. "He did that to throw off Sarah, so she'd let her guard down thinking he's a victim. He's the one in charge."

And he was at the hospital now.

Where Sarah was.

34

Sarah let herself into her dad's hospital room. An officer down the hall had told her there was an explosion when they went to raid the place where they thought Markowicz was testing the formula. Thankfully no one had been killed.

There were so many cops down at the other end of the floor, waiting for word about their concussed fellow officer. She knew all their faces. She'd chatted for a bit with Captain McCauley after the doctor put cream on her wrists and bandaged them. Then he'd gotten a phone call, and all the cops had gone on alert. She had no idea why.

All she wanted to do was sit with her dad and wait for him to wake up.

The room was dimly lit and given the rhythmic rise and fall of his chest he was still resting. He'd had a myocardial infarction, and she'd persuaded the doctor to let her look at her dad's chart so she knew what was going on with him. He really should've told her that he was still having heart problems even after being put on the medication, and that they were most likely related to stress.

She settled into the chair with a sigh.

He really knew about the treasure. He'd been pressured into working for Markowicz. She shook her head. For all her dad's shortcomings, she never would've thought he'd get wrapped up in criminal activity.

Her thoughts inevitably drifted to Joseph. He'd suffered for years under duress. Made decisions that felt like the only ones he *could* make. In a way, it seemed not too dissimilar to her choice to spend her life studying the dead to find answers. It might come across as morbid to some. Or overly clinical to others—given all she was interested in was finding answers from science. But that had been her safety net when her feelings betrayed her.

It had been a safe place to be. Where the truth was empirical, and her emotions didn't factor.

Now that she had asked God to help her, things were a lot closer to the surface. She'd cried more in the last day or two than she had in years. It wasn't an entirely comfortable place to be, but it was the choice she'd made. The one that would hopefully help her lead a fuller life now.

Sarah knew what she wanted.

Isn't it Your job to make that happen, Lord?

He'd been that to her once. In her childish way, as a kid, she'd felt Him take her fear. He could do that again. He had, and she didn't doubt he would again now if she let Him.

Her father stirred in the bed and smacked his lips together. "Hey, honey."

"Need a drink?" She imagined his mouth was dry. When he nodded, she poured water into the cup beside the bed and had him use a straw. "Take small sips for now."

He let his head fall back to the pillow.

"Feel better?"

"Yeah, honey."

Sarah replaced the cup but remained beside the bed. "You haven't called me that for years."

In fact, their relationship had been a lot like her decision to work in a clinical field. They'd kept each other at arm's length. Their interactions had been stilted. She'd been scared she would be rejected, still stinging from how no one had believed her—not even the father she'd practically worshiped. After that it had been about making him proud of her.

All the while he had been getting involved with criminals.

"I can't believe you let yourself get sucked into all that stuff with Brad and Karen, and her brother." She didn't want to sound judgmental, but he'd been so idealistic about her working for the medical examiner's office and not some hospital only in it for the money. Jaded enough to believe in her when she chose public service.

Sarah let out a breath and decided to change the subject.

Before she could, he said, "I made a lot of wrong choices."

She wondered if he would apologize for anything. But wishing for that hadn't ever made it happen before.

He continued, "At first I just represented them, and some associates. Then they told me they were tight on money, and I could help them get what they owed me plus more. I knew it was money laundering at best. Why not take a little off the top for me? Things were tight. The economy was in the toilet." He shrugged one shoulder. "It worked…for a while."

"And the treasure?" She could hardly believe that rumor was even real. Let alone that her dad was their middleman.

"I have connections in art sales, and the auction world."

That part wasn't a surprise since her mom had been an artist in Chicago when they met. He'd whisked her away from that world not knowing she would never be happy in the Pacific Northwest. She'd gone back to her old life.

Sarah remembered a slender woman, and the smell of perfume. But she didn't remember being held.

He added, "They brought me a piece or two regularly, and I got them sold."

"So you lied about the provenance?"

He paused. "I did what they said, and they stayed out of my way the rest of the time. I expect they'd have asked me to represent them if that were necessary, but it won't be happening now. They can find another lawyer."

Sarah figured the police might be speaking with the DA about charges against her father soon enough. He might need representation of his own. "Do you have one?"

"Because I'm going to prison?"

"No one has told me anything, but who knows what the police will decide?"

"So they brought in all of them?" he said. "I'll be charged with conspiracy, or as an accessory to all their crimes, and everyone will start pointing fingers at everyone else."

That was usually how it worked with cases where everyone involved was charged separately and not as a group —which was a different kind of case entirely.

Sarah nodded. "Brad and Karen are behind bars. I'm not sure about Markowicz, but I'd guess that's what they're doing now. Trying to find him, or bringing him in."

"And what about the boss?"

She frowned. "Markowicz is who I was just talking about." The guy had terrorized her, and nearly killed Joseph. She wouldn't mind finding him herself—except that wasn't a good idea any way she looked at it.

Her dad shook his head. "He's not in charge. He works for Harper."

Sarah started to speak but caught herself. What was he— "As in, Washington Harper?"

"The police don't know that?"

"But…he keeled over in front of me." She couldn't believe it. "They tried to kill him to get rid of him."

Her dad said, "My guess is he knew he'd be implicated at some point. He put himself in the hospital so the police would think he was a victim. Not the one in charge of everything."

He shrugged one shoulder.

Sarah just gaped. "I helped that man. I tried to save him, while the rest of them…" Of course. That was why they all just stood there. She'd thought it was because they didn't care one bit about him.

What if they'd *known* what he was trying to do? They wouldn't have tried to save him if they wanted him to die for real, on the off chance their boss would die and they could get out from under his thumb. And then if he didn't, they wouldn't want to help him so that he recovered before he could be taken to hospital.

Sarah turned from her dad's bed and paced across the tiny room. "Washington Harper," she whispered, her voice breathy. She couldn't believe this.

"He's lived at that retreat camp for as long as it's been open," her dad said. "Decades. Maybe fifty years. The guy is in his eighties but tough as an ox still."

Sarah's stomach clenched. "He's been there since Celeste Garland killed herself?"

"I was wondering when someone would put that together." The voice came from behind her, low and graveled.

Her dad's eyes widened. Sarah spun around to see Washington Harper, fully dressed like he'd been released from the hospital, holding a pouch.

At least it wasn't a gun, or a knife.

He blocked the door. Before now she'd have said she could overpower him, but Washington seemed massive now. She didn't think she could get past him out the door.

Sarah sucked in a breath. "Help—"

She couldn't even get the whole word out before Washington cuffed her across the face with the back of his hand. She hadn't even seen him move, concentrating on screaming for all she was worth.

Sarah touched the side of her face. "Ouch."

"Shut your mouth, girl." Washington shoved her to the chair.

She stumbled and fell into it, jarring her hip on the thin wood armrest. What was he—

Washington unzipped the pouch, standing over her father's bed. Sarah pushed up from the chair and ran for the door. A hand grabbed her hair in an unrelenting grip. She cried out.

He pulled hard and her legs collapsed. Sarah fell to the floor. "You're not making this easy." He huffed. "Should be painless and quick, so stay put."

Tears leaked from her eyes. "You're not going to kill my father. I won't let you."

"He made his choice." Washington prepped a syringe.

"No." She shook her head, pain everywhere. Her face. The back of her hair. "Don't."

"Funny." Washington pushed the plunger. A little liquid squirted from the end. "Celeste said the same thing, crying and carrying on. Don't worry, though. Your death won't be nearly as violent as hers."

Sarah blinked. Celeste hadn't jumped. Joseph was the one who hadn't believed she killed herself, but that she'd been murdered.

"You killed her." Sarah's voice was barely a whisper.

"Got some fool idea in her head we were going to run off together. So she took all her family heirlooms to sell and 'start our new life.'" He huffed, probably a laugh. "Had it all planned out. But I was never gonna leave. I did need those artifacts, though. Very handy."

He moved toward her.

"Don't—"

The door opened. Cop after cop poured in the door, McCauley in the front. "Put it down!"

"Don't do it!"

All of them had guns trained on Washington.

The big man stepped back, and the syringe dropped to the floor. McCauley said, "Someone cuff this piece of garbage."

Sarah slid across the floor to the wall so they had enough room to get in and out. She couldn't think. All she could do was touch her cheeks and try to breathe.

She heard, "Can you guys let me in there?" Then a shuffle.

Then Joseph knelt in front of her. He tugged her hands from her face. "Hey." He winced. "Hey, you okay?"

She started to nod, but realized she definitely was *not* okay. "Joseph?"

"Yeah, it's me."

Sarah started to cry.

The doctor and a couple of nurses came in to see to her father. One said, "Do we need to look at her as well?"

Sarah didn't take her attention from Joseph. She shook her head.

"Let's give them some room." He tugged her to standing and led her into the hall where she saw the cops leading Washington away. "Come on." He kept going, away from them.

Sarah didn't want to move. She spun around in his hold and buried her face in Joseph's neck. Shaking. Tears rolled down her face, but she didn't care.

He held her, whispering nothing words that made her

feel better even if they didn't make sense. Then he leaned down, his lips brushing her ear. "I love you."

Sarah held on tighter. *I love you, too.*

She couldn't get the words out, but the feeling was there.

Still crying, Sarah poured everything she felt into her touch, tugging his face down so she could kiss him.

35

―――――

J oseph closed the door and stepped out into the hallway.

Russ got up from a seat where he'd been waiting. "She okay?"

He nodded. "The doctor gave her something to help her sleep." And then in a couple of days she would be released. She would go home, and they wouldn't be spending all this time together.

"I need to tell you something."

Joseph waited.

"Amadine Shammad is dead. He was killed in a bar fight in Seattle a couple of days ago. Nice place, but still a bar. They found him in the back alley the next morning."

Joseph held himself very still.

Russ said, "I don't think it was you. Or that you ordered it."

"Good, because I didn't." Joseph might not be a normal guy—a good guy—but he'd been here protecting Sarah. Now the threat was definitely over he could rest. But he didn't plan on letting his guard down where she was concerned.

"You don't need to worry about him anymore." There was a glint in Russ's eye that almost made Joseph wonder if *he* had a hand in the guy's death. However, considering he was a former US Marshal and currently the police commissioner that was an out there thought. No way would Russ do something like that.

"I'm glad." Joseph walked to the chairs where Russ had been waiting and sank into one. It surprised him the relief he felt knowing he didn't have to worry about Shammad anymore. There had been a low-grade fear that eventually he would have to face the man whose brother had ended the lives of Joseph's family.

Their eye for an eye just ended up with more destruction in a never-ending cycle until he'd been forced to accept the Accountant's Office's offer to start over where Shammad would never find him.

"Feel a little lighter, huh?" Russ patted his shoulder, then leaned his head back against the wall. His security detail of police officers were down the hall. There was another cop on the door of Sarah's room, and her father's.

"What happens now?" Joseph asked.

"Depends on if you're ready to talk to Vanguard about that job offer," Russ replied.

"What is it? Do you know?" Joseph had never met any of them, but knew it was mostly women who worked there, plus Stella's father was setting up a cold case investigation department. What else did they do?

And what did they want him to do?

Now that he knew Edith had told them what they needed to know about him made him worry even more what skills he had they thought they could utilize.

If he was going to live this new life, walking as the man God wanted him to be, it couldn't involve those old ways of doing things.

He had to accept that God had made him a new creation…and then go out and live like it.

"Sounds to me like they're looking for a few roles to be filled. They didn't know what exactly you wanted, but the low-key ones based in Benson involve consulting on security systems for businesses and high-end residences. Some bodyguard work here in town if you want that." Russ shrugged.

That meant they did work all over. And if he did that, it was more likely he'd be seen by the wrong person.

"I need to stay here." He didn't want to do anything but look out for Sarah, but eventually they'd both need to work. So beyond the next few days that wasn't practical. "I don't want to travel outside Benson for whatever job I do."

"Good. I agree, even if he's dead and the threat is arguably over, that's still a good idea. Don't let it stop you from going on vacation but stick it out here in Benson for the most part." Russ nodded. "And what's the plan with that girl? Because the Accountant's Office isn't going to provide housing if you're living in sin."

Joseph burst out laughing even though it wasn't funny. "Sorry." He cleared his throat.

Most people might call Russ's ideas old-fashioned, but Joseph knew he was on to something. Following them would make his life a whole lot easier to live happy and find peace. But just doing the right thing wasn't a guarantee.

"I'm going to ask Sarah if she'll go to church with me on Sunday."

"Really?" Russ grinned. "That's great."

Joseph nodded. He'd told her he loved her, and she hadn't said it back. But she'd been distraught, and she'd kissed him. Maybe that was her way of saying it back. He wanted to sit down and have a conversation with her when she was feeling better.

They had time.

Joseph said, "I think there will always be part of me that's in a constant state of blind fear that I'll lose everything sooner or later. But I'm going to try and let go enough to trust that God will lead me in the right direction. That I'll get to spend years with Sarah. And maybe we can build a family together that I'll get to see grow up."

Russ grinned. "Jacob and Addie are getting married in a couple of weeks. I never would've thought they could make it work. She was in DC. Their relationship ended years ago when she left town. Now they're together and looking to God for what's coming in their marriage. Who knows what the future will bring?"

Joseph knew Jacob because the guy owned the building where the Accountant's Office clients lived.

Russ continued, "Then there was Lyric and Isaac. He lives down the hall from you. It was a risk, putting them together. But I felt that tug from God, and I obeyed. He did the rest, and now Isaac and Lyric are eloping in a few weeks. Getting married on a private beach somewhere with their friends. Eric and Stella are engaged and planning a Christmas ceremony so they can have snow outside and twinkly lights everywhere."

"Sounds like some serious matchmaking."

"God knows we aren't good alone."

Joseph said, "Doesn't that mean everyone should be in a relationship?" Russ hadn't been with anyone as far as he'd seen since he arrived.

"For some of us, it's our job to just walk in obedience in whatever He puts in front of us." Russ shrugged. "It's not always easy, but we get to pray for the families around us. Support people we care about. I live a life that means I can go anywhere without having to check with someone or take a job with long hours doing important work because no one is waiting on me." He grinned. "I like my freedom."

Joseph said, "Enjoy it."

Russ chuckled, moving away down the hall. "Oh, I do." He called back over his shoulder. "Now I've gotta go see a man about buying a camp for kids."

Whatever that meant, his laughter was contagious. Joseph had no idea who would want to send their kids to a place where so much mayhem had happened, but what did he know?

He looked at the chair where Russ had been sitting and saw a business card.

Clare Juarez. Vanguard Investigations.

Joseph figured he had a call to make. But first, he wanted to talk to Sarah about the future.

Their future.

36

S arah awoke instantly aware there was someone in her hospital room. She figured it was likely Joseph, since Addie and Stella had come by to visit at breakfast. Then Sarah had fallen asleep again. It was probably afternoon now, and she was hungry.

In all that time she hadn't seen him. Not since last night, which made her wonder what he had been doing this morning.

She rolled over, but it wasn't Joseph in the chair beside the window. "Edith."

The older woman laid aside the magazine she'd been leafing through. "You're awake. That's good."

After everything she'd been through recently, it was hard to convince her mind and body to relax. "How are you?"

"Better than you, dear." Edith patted her hand. "But you'll heal. Life will move on."

Since Joseph had told her he loved her she hoped it moved on to good things. Now that she'd let God's love come in and wash away the fear she had a place to go when the old doubts crept in and she tried to combat it on her own. It was time to figure out this new way of doing things.

And she hoped Joseph wanted to seek the Lord with her. That they would be able to wrestle with these things and learn together.

Edith got up and came over. She laid a hand on Sarah's arm. "I'll admit, I didn't think it would be you. But you're good for him."

She wondered what Joseph had told her.

"Mothers know."

Sarah frowned. "Are you—"

"Goodness, no." Edith chuckled. "We're not blood. But he and I are the same. And that means if you have him, then you also have me. No matter what."

"Thank you." She couldn't help thinking this was a bargain she might not want to accept. And yet, with her father having an uncertain future and no mother in her life, why not? Edith wanted to be there for her.

"And when you're bringing babies in, I hope I can be considered for the grandma role. If there's a need for one."

She shifted her hand and covered Edith's. "Thank you, Edith."

The older woman squeezed her hand. "You're welcome, honey. But I should be the one thanking you. Because you brought him back to life."

Sarah wasn't sure she was the only one who'd had a hand in that. "I'm just happy he feels a little freer than he did before."

Edith smiled. "Keep taking it one day at a time. Years from now you'll look back and realize how far you've come just from taking those tiny steps every day." The older woman leaned down and kissed Sarah's forehead. "I'm glad you're all right."

She straightened and they both turned to see Joseph in

the door. Somehow just knowing it was no longer the two of them.

"What's this?" He looked almost mad.

"Don't worry, I'm just leaving." Edith patted Joseph's chest as she passed him at the door. "You're welcome."

Sarah noticed he wore a polo shirt that said Vanguard Investigations.

Looking down, he touched the logo, then crossed the room. "I had a job interview this morning."

"It must've gone well if you're wearing the shirt." She held out her hand, and he slipped his bigger, calloused one into it. "What did they hire you for?"

He sighed. "I was worried about that. But I heard them out, and I accepted a position consulting on security systems. When a client reaches out to them asking for a system to be put in, I go there and see what they need. I make a recommendation based on that, and I oversee the contractor who puts it in. Locally, in Benson. All the time. Starting Monday."

Had he been worried she thought he was leaving?

Sarah squeezed his hand. "As long as that's what you want to do, I'm happy for you."

He nodded. "I think it'll be good."

"They're lucky to have you. Whoever they are."

Joseph chuckled. "I'll take you in. Introduce you to them. It's mostly women, ex-cops. Ex-military. Even an ex-spy, but she didn't admit that. It's just a look. I can tell who they are." He paused. "There are guys in their tech division, and Stella's dad was there. The company is bigger than I ever thought it was. They do some good stuff. Like helping out people who can't afford a private investigator."

He sounded so excited about it she let go of some of her worry. Sarah would likely always battle how she felt like people saw her. But if she had Joseph, she wasn't going to worry as much.

"I love you," she said.

His eyes flared. "I love you, too."

"I know, you told me." She grinned. "But I didn't get to say it back." She shook her head, thinking what a state she'd been in. And he'd seen her like that? Held her, even. The fact he hadn't run screaming from her ugly crying boded pretty well.

He stilled, like he was nervous. "Will you go to church with me on Sunday?"

"I'd love to. I want to join that new believers' class Stella is in."

"Okay, good." He nodded. "Me, too."

"Are you going to kiss me?"

He leaned close. "Are you going to ask nicely, or just be demanding?"

"Depends." She spoke like she had any bravado at all lying in a hospital bed.

"What does it depend on?" He sounded serious, but the corners of his mouth curled up.

She could stare at that smile for years. "Is this going somewhere, or will I get my heart broken?"

"Depends."

She chuckled. "On what?"

"How you feel about extremely short engagements."

"I think we should probably have a first date." After that, it was up for discussion as far as she was concerned.

"That's your only qualifier?"

She shrugged one shoulder. "Kiss me and find out."

Joseph pressed his lips together, and she could feel his smile touch hers. He kissed her, and she felt all the promise of the future wrapped up in it. "Thank you."

"It should be me saying that."

He kissed her again.

Sarah would be forever grateful.

Thank You.

EDITH HUMMET SHUFFLED up the front steps of Lyric's cabin. The girl had volunteered to host the mystery writers' camp at the last minute. Of course they needed a good story—writers always did.

Isaac held the door for her. Edith smiled to herself and patted his cheek. "You're a good boy."

He chuckled. "Wanna tell me why you're here?"

She shook her head.

All the writers were gathered in the living area, passing around plates of tiny sandwiches and sipping drinks.

Edith took a seat in the corner of the room. "Who wants to hear the story of how I solved the murder of Celeste Garland?"

Across the room, Isaac laughed.

But all around Edith, mystery writers took their seats and leaned close.

Ready to hear the tale.

Turn the page to read a special message to you, my reader, about what's coming next!

AUTHOR'S NOTE

Thank you so much for venturing to the end of another series with me. I hope you've enjoyed the journey as much as I have.

Every series is a little surprising in the way it comes out. This one more so than most. I knew I wanted plenty of secrets from the past, and intrigue. The urban setting was a surprise, but I hope that brought a sense of community for you. I'm working on developing the spiritual threads in my romantic suspense books and I hope that was reflected in Downrange.

I think I will stay in Benson with a future series, focusing on first responders and including plenty of Vanguard shenanigans. I'm not planning their own series (Vanguard), unless there's a loud cry for that. (Feel free to email me, or FB messenger on my author page if you've got an opinion!) I will include all the Vanguard people in the Benson First Responders series.

In terms of what's "Coming Next" I recently got the rights back to an LIS book, and I've revamped that, adding a couple of scenes. Easy Prey will get retitled as HUNTED and will be out this summer.

At the end of August, I'm releasing book 1 in what will be a long running series with one main character throughout and a slower building romance. **Brand of Justice** are all thrillers, and if you keep turning pages you can see the amazing cover and get a sneak peek of the first chapter! Since I know not everyone will enjoy a grittier thriller, I'm still going to publish plenty of romantic suspense books. And of course, the Last Chance County Sunrise season is coming in 2023!

I'm going to alternate releases of the Brand of Justice thrillers with romantic suspense titles set in Benson. So I have not one but TWO new series' starting this fall: Brand of Justice and Benson First Responders. And then next year you'll be able to read another Love Inspired Suspense K-9 Search and Rescue story, as well as the Last Chance County Fire and Rescue books from my amazing Sunrise Publishing authors!

Keep reading for your sneak peek of COLD DEAD NIGHT, Brand of Justice book 1…

COLD DEAD NIGHT

BRAND OF JUSTICE - BOOK 1

COLD DEAD NIGHT

BRAND OF JUSTICE BOOK 1

LISA PHILLIPS

eBook ISBN: 979-8-88552-135-2

Paperback ISBN: 979-8-88552-136-9

Large print hardback ISBN: 979-8-88552-139-0

Published by: Two Dogs Publishing, LLC. Idaho, USA.

Cover design by: Sasha Almazan and Gene Mollica, GS Cover Design Studio, LLC

Edited by Jen Weiber

1

Friday, 10:37 pm.
Salt Lake City, Utah.

I f Kenna didn't run fast enough, a child would die
tonight.

Each breath puffed a visible cloud from her mouth and
into the cold air as she raced down the alley past shoveled
mounds of crusty gray snow that had fallen a week ago. On
the street at the end, lanes of Friday night traffic buzzed in
both directions. People blew through the city with the
oppressive force of a blizzard.

She sprinted for the lone door that split the exterior wall.

Until a patrol car pulled into the alley.

Kenna slammed her shoulder into the brick and
crouched beside a pile of pallets and soggy cardboard boxes.

The car eased by her.

She squeezed her eyes shut and stilled as if frozen solid.
Encased in ice.

He couldn't know she was here. Not yet.

The second it passed her, she headed for the door. A minute thirty to pick the padlock and she was in.

The building was an abandoned theater where the rubber soles of her boots pounded the floor with a dense reverberation. Kenna continued her race through the lobby. The air of her movement curled up old show posters as she flew past torn velvet chairs to a door marked STAIRS. She twisted the handle, breathing hard, and flew inside the stairwell. Her clothing made no sound as she sprinted down the concrete steps.

All the way down.

Down.

She stopped on the basement landing. The schematics she'd found online showed a boiler room and laundry room just beyond the door. Storage rooms. Basically a labyrinth of hallways and chambers. Plenty of space for a killer to do his work without being disturbed.

She knew that all too well.

Everything within her investigation of the killer—and the kidnapping and murder of two little girls—pointed her to this place. Tonight, the killer had a third victim in his grasp, and Kenna wasn't going to let this life be extinguished the way the others had.

She couldn't. This was what she'd been born to do.

And yet, Kenna didn't move. Everything in her just… stopped. She'd faced down a killer before and it had all but destroyed her. Each time she confronted those heinous memories and fears, she wanted to be as far from it as possible.

She stood in that basement stairwell and the ice crept over her again. It always came over her the same way. First, the memories. Then, she'd become almost paralyzed. Not able to move or even breathe. After, the most frigid chill would swallow her whole until the hope of ever getting warm again seemed futile. One day, tomorrow or years from now, she would be found frozen to death somewhere. Whether that foreknowledge portended a peaceful end, or a horrific one, she didn't yet know.

Either way, the outcome would be the same. Time was going to run out, and Kenna would have to give an account for her life. What would they say about her? She'd faced her fears and done her best, or she'd let a sick man take everything away? Again.

In the distance, a child let out a short cry. Ellayna Feathers. Nine years old. The latest prey of the Seventh Day Killer.

Kenna pushed through to the hall. Beyond the heavy door was cold as a morgue. She had to ease it closed so it didn't slam, but nonetheless, air whistled down the corridor. A rush of wind that would alert anyone hiding down here.

Kenna flicked her baton and extended it to its full length. Sweat rolled down her temple. Cold moisture tracked like frozen fingers down her cheek. She didn't bother to swipe it away, just kept walking.

One foot. Then the other. The alternative of not continuing with each step wasn't something she wanted to see behind her eyelids when she tried to sleep tonight. There were enough lifeless gazes there. Kenna didn't want one more, least of all that of a child. Ellayna Feathers wasn't a body she wanted to find in the mountains the way she had with his other victims. Used and discarded. Tossed out like trash. No. This girl was going to live no matter what it took.

She headed for the source of the cry—a room at the end of the hall labeled within the building schematics as STOR-AGE. The whole place had been unoccupied, in disrepair and abandoned, since the theater company collapsed a few months back.

The killer needed to be in custody. Kenna would have to involve the cops in order to hand over this guy. They would be forced to acknowledge her presence in their world, whether they liked it or not.

But Kenna's priority here was Ellayna. Not just because of the tears in the mother's eyes the day she'd hired Kenna, as she'd told the story of her daughter's disappearance six days ago. But because she knew how it felt to be taken. Violated.

The FBI hadn't been able to find Ellayna. Neither had the police. The mother had turned to Kenna, a private investigator *and* her last hope. Someone who'd lived in both worlds —as cop and victim—and now walked in neither. She wasn't an FBI agent anymore. And she certainly wasn't a victim.

She was a PI.

It was on the seventh day that this killer struck his final blow, giving him the moniker, "The Seventh Day Killer" in the news and online. But his name was Gerald Rickshire, and Kenna didn't care what everyone else thought or said about him. Or her, for that matter. Only that Ellayna made it home, and he never did this to anyone ever again.

Then she would go back to her solitary life, and the next case.

The storage room was bare except for a bloody, stained mattress in the middle. Ellayna Feathers huddled in the corner, her head turned away from the mattress. Kenna wouldn't have wanted to look at it either.

She took one glance at the hall—both directions. They needed to get out of here.

Then she stepped inside the room. Trapped with the girl. *No.* She couldn't allow her thoughts to coalesce like that. She wasn't a victim anymore.

Kenna moved left immediately so she could hug the wall.

She had to do this in such a way the little girl didn't make a noise. Would she scream, or comply?

The little girl stiffened at the disturbance, her eyes squeezed shut.

Kenna crouched. She didn't want to appear big and intimidating like the man must've. She had to be far less imposing. She whispered, "Laynie." That was what her mother called her.

"Mama," the little girl whispered back.

Kenna nearly moaned. She choked back the lump in her throat. *This happened to me, too.* The trickle down her cheek was sweat, just like before. She didn't cry anymore. Why waste tears when the past remained unchanged?

Kenna heard no sound in the hall, so she dropped the whisper. "Ellayna, everything is going to be okay."

The little girl's eyes flew open.

Kenna tried a smile. "Hey." How did she tell the girl she knew exactly how she felt when they didn't have any moment to spare? How did she forge the bond they shared to find solidarity together? "I'm here to bring you back to your Mommy. She asked me to come get you."

Ellayna Feathers whispered, "I'm not supposed to go with strangers."

Kenna steadied herself and stood to slowly approach the little girl wearing the dirty dress. "Mommy said to tell you that Bubby loves you."

Ellayna's mother was currently seven months pregnant and confined to bed rest. It was a boy—something they hadn't told anyone else yet. A baby brother Ellayna called, "Bubby."

The little girl's eyes flickered. Kenna held out her hand. It would be cold to the touch, her fingers like ice. The way Ellayna's would be—until she recovered.

"I'm going to take you home, and we'll call your mom so you can talk to her, okay?"

Her eye flickered again, past Kenna's shoulder. The flicker turned to wide eyes. Terror.

Kenna heard nothing. But she knew instantly he was there.

She gripped the baton, now in her left hand, and spun. His hand was already coming down, and whatever he had clenched in his fist headed for her temple. She ducked her head to the side and swiped out to clip him across the legs.

He cried out and stumbled but didn't go down. A digital camera clattered across the floor.

Kenna launched up, knocked him off balance with a shove and rammed her heel into his stomach. His body bent as he tripped back two steps. Too quickly he shook it off. She switched her baton to the other hand and braced.

He ran at her, screaming a foul name.

Ellayna shrieked.

Kenna ducked. He connected with her shoulder in a jarring thud. Breath escaped his lungs as they grappled together. His fist hammered into her stomach. She coughed out the air and slammed the baton down on his thigh. An elbow clipped her forehead. Kenna gritted her teeth, dropped the baton, and reached for the holster on her leg.

She brought the stun gun up, her finger already on the button.

A crackle sounded. His body jerked. While he shuddered against her, she wondered if she would ever get that odor out of her nose. The second he dropped to the floor, Kenna spun him to his face, put a knee on his lower back, and reached into her side pocket. She secured his hands and feet behind him using the double cuffs, then stood. For good measure, she pulled out a third set and secured his hands to his feet.

Just in case.

The phone was tucked in her right back pocket. She dialed 911 and waited for them to pick up. The second they did, she rattled off the FBI case number and the man's name.

"And your name?"

Kenna hung up and stowed the phone away. Gerald Rickshire glared at her from the floor. She turned to Ellayna. "You wanna go now, Laynie?"

The little girl just stared.

Kenna scooped her up, walked down the hall, and ascended the stairs. Two uniformed officers met her in the lobby, one younger and female and the other probably fifty. He wore the lines of years on the job—the training officer. Pierce and Meacham respectively, according to their name plates. They looked tired. Long shift, at the end of a long week.

"He's tied up downstairs." Kenna told them how to get to the storage room, then took a step back out of their space to put the cold air of the lobby between them and her—and Ellayna.

Meacham lifted one hand. "You're not leaving."

Pierce reached for her radio. "I'll call for an ambulance."

"The guy downstairs?" She hugged Ellayna closer, the girl now worryingly still. "It's the Seventh Day Killer."

Both cops flinched.

Pierce said, "How—"

Meacham cut her off. "Let's go." Their footsteps pounded the floor, belts squeaking and jingling as they headed for the stairs, calling back, "Don't leave!"

Kenna watched them race away. Before, she'd have been right there as well, doing the job of special agent for the FBI. At the same moment she thought that she realized she'd taken a step toward them. She turned on her heel and strode to the entrance instead, then out into the desolate alley where she belonged.

Her car was parked a street away, so she bypassed the black and white patrol car and headed in that direction. Blue and red lights flashed against the brick of the building, too bright of a contrast with the dark stage lights long since switched off.

The night sky hung thick with an inversion that obscured the stars over Salt Lake City. Mountains stood tall over this pocket of civilization, where business and religion were often one and the same. Great peaks arched above the lives below, as though standing guard. Or hemming them in.

She needed to leave. The pilgrimage home to pick up her mail—and find Ellayna—was done now. It was time to get back on the road.

Kenna climbed in the front seat of her Acura and held Ellayna on her lap as she drove slowly around the corner, back to the front entrance where the cop vehicle was parked. Those flashing lights lit up the interior of her car as she watched the officers walk out with Gerald Rickshire in cuffs.

She tightened her hold on Ellayna and managed to choke out a sentiment. "It will be okay." Was that even true?

Maybe for Ellayna it would be. She had a mother. She had friends and extended family. Caregivers. Support.

Kenna had none of those things, so what did she know?

The cops shut Gerald Rickshire in the back seat. An ambulance pulled in from the street. Kenna got out and carried Ellayna to the EMTs, handing the little girl off. "She's really quiet."

The EMT nodded, compassion softening her gaze as she turned to assess the girl. Ellayna didn't lie down. And she didn't take her gaze from Kenna, who lifted her phone to her ear and listened to it ring.

"Hello?" Ellayna's mother's voice shook, consumed with

a motherly fear Kenna would never understand. But she knew what it felt like to lose someone—to know in her soul that she would always be alone.

"Ms. Feathers, it's Makenna Banbury."

The woman groaned, as though already in labor. Pregnant both with fear for her child *and* the baby she was about to have.

"Ellayna is safe. She'll be on her way to the hospital in a moment."

"Laynie…" Her daughter's name was a cry.

"She's right here." Kenna handed over the phone and made sure the little girl had a good grip on it.

Ellayna's hands trembled as she lifted it to her ear. "Mama?"

Kenna waited through the conversation while life buzzed around her. EMTs. The cops.

"You saved her."

The words came from her left. She glanced over at Officer Pierce. Words caught in her throat.

As soon as she had her phone back, Kenna walked away. The job was complete. There was certainly nothing else to stick around for.

Pierce called out to her. She waved the officer off, hardly able to even voice words when the adrenaline shuddered through her and the ice in her veins fought back. She strode to her car and slid in the front seat where she gripped the cold steering wheel and sucked in a handful of breaths. Life receded and the frost crept back in. Her body stilled; as good as dead once again.

A fist rapped on the window.

She jerked around, dropping one of her gloves before she could tug it on. Kenna rolled down the window.

Meacham held out a phone. "It's for you."

Her stomach lurched. Answering it meant connecting her

life here. She reached with shaky fingers and took hold of the phone. "Banbury."

Silence greeted her. Then his voice, deep and strong. "Makenna?"

A sharp pain jabbed through her chest. Probably just where the Seventh Day Killer's elbow had impacted.

"It's true then. Two years, and you're back?"

"I'm *not* back." She had to choke out the words.

Two hours, and she'd be gone again. Away from this frozen wasteland of memories. Where all the good she tried to do amounted to nothing. On the road, it was just her. She didn't have to deal with anyone else. Their emotions. Their expectations. What they thought she should think or feel.

She needed the silence.

Ryson spoke again. "And yet you're here."

He'd been her friend, once upon a time. Maybe even her best friend. Now he just sounded irritated and familiar in a way that made her chest ache, as though a part of her actually wanted to see him again.

She had to get out of the city. "Sarge—"

"It's Lieutenant Ryson now."

Kenna touched her fingers to her neck and let the cold seep into her skin. "What do you want?" She held the phone between her chin and shoulder and pulled both gloves on.

"More than you want to give." He was silent for a second. "But for starters, you can tell me why I'm looking at a dead body with your business card on him."

Find out more about *Cold Dead Night* and the *Brand of Justice* series at my website:
https://authorlisaphillips.com/brand-of-justice

ALSO BY LISA PHILLIPS

The whole Last Chance Downrange series:

Point of Impact

Hard Target

Hollow Point

Terminal Velocity

Find more stories based in Last Chance County at:

www.lastchancecounty.com

Other series by Lisa:

Chevalier Protection Specialists

Last Chance County

Northwest Counter-Terrorism Taskforce

Double Down

WITSEC Town (Sanctuary)

Numerous other titles including several Love Inspired Suspense, find the complete list here: https://authorlisaphillips.com/full-book-list

ABOUT THE AUTHOR

Find out more about Lisa Phillips, and other books she has written, by visiting her website: https://authorlisaphillips.com

Would you also share about the book on Social Media, leave a review on Lisa's page and share about your experience? Your review will help others find great clean fiction and decide what to read next!

Visit https://authorlisaphillips.com/subscribe where you can sign up for my NEWSLETTER and get free books!